THE BLACK ROSE

DETECTIVE CARLA MCBRIDE CHRONICLES
BOOK 2

NICK LEWIS

ROUGH
EDGES
PRESS

The Black Rose
Paperback Edition
Copyright © 2023 (As Revised) Nick Lewis

Rough Edges Press
An Imprint of Wolfpack Publishing
9850 S. Maryland Parkway, Suite A-5 #323
Las Vegas, Nevada 89183

roughedgespress.com

Paperback ISBN 978-1-68549-209-0
eBook ISBN 978-1-68549-208-3

*For my wife, Bonnie, who has supported me with
undeniable and unequivocal love from the day we said
our vows on our wedding day. Through all our ups and
downs, her love and faith never wavered no matter where
my career took us. I will always love her "till death do us
part."*

THE BLACK ROSE

PROLOGUE

Although it was winter by meteorological standards in Kentucky's Bluegrass Region, the weather in Oakmont was anything but winter-like. The pleasant temperatures made it ideal for an evening run around Lake Catalpa. The beautiful park provided a walking and jogging path challenging enough for anyone. Following the topography of the lake, the jogging path bordered by thick brush gave way to a rocky shoreline.

During the day, joggers enjoyed an assortment of flora and fauna indigenous to the area. However, those preferring an evening jog experienced a moonlit lake with twinkling stars gracing the dark sky above.

On this enjoyable evening, a lady in hot-pink form-fitting spandex began her regular stretching and breathing regimen to warm up, juice up, for an evening run under the stars. As she completed her final stretching and breathing exercises, several individuals crossed the finish line.

Ready to set a new personal best for three miles, she

pushed the start button on her digital watch. Starting slow, she quickened her pace as her watch tracked her time. Her hot-pink spandex accentuated her well-toned sensual curves as she moved around the lake. Always wearing a baseball cap from her alma mater, her ponytail bounced randomly with each stride she took.

After completing her first five-hundred-yards, two other joggers had just finished stretching and began their run around the lake. Focused on her pace, she was oblivious to the individuals trailing her. Glancing at her digital timer, a smile crossed her face. As she continued around the lake, she enjoyed the sounds of classical music through her earbuds while oblivious to her surroundings.

Entering the home stretch, as she called it, her digital watch indicated she was ten seconds under her best time. Knowing a full out sprint would ensure a new personal best, she used every bit of energy and stamina she could muster. As she crossed the imaginary finish line, her arms extended upward, reaching for the stars, as she celebrated her triumph.

Remembering those days from college, she screamed, breaking the serenity of the pristine evening. Her voice echoed throughout the trees and hills. As she gazed through an opening in the thick brush, the beautiful, mesmerizing moonlit lake seemed to celebrate with her.

Grabbing her knees to catch her breath, she enjoyed the shimmering ripples as her imaginary audience applauded her. After a few cleansing breaths, she stood up, enjoying her achievement all over again. Arms fully extended toward the twinkling sky; her voice echoed one last time. As the shimmering waters turned to a glassy-like mirror, her encore was over.

Enjoying the serenity and peacefulness of the

moment, a bone-crushing jolt to her backside interrupted her final cleansing breath. Hitting the cold hard ground, the weight of her attacker violently squeezed the life out of her lungs.

Gasping and heaving for precious air, her silent screams withered in the thick brush. Facedown toward the shoreline, with her arms pinned underneath her body, the pain in her chest was unbearable. Paralyzed and helpless, she prayed as the moonlit lake began turning a murky black.

Feeling something around her neck, the assailant turned a ligature tighter and tighter, squashing her feeble pleas for help. As she began losing consciousness, a bright, soft halo appeared in front of her. Out of the corona, she recognized the diamond ring on the outstretched hand, reaching for her.

As the halo dissipated, her hand latched on to it, and her physical body succumbed to the cold darkness of death. Before her soul passed into eternity, it hovered above her lifeless body. Her spirit observed her attacker turning her over and pulling down her hot-pink spandex past her knees, displaying her most sacred possession.

Pausing for a moment, the attacker moistened his lips, observing her delicate and untarnished treasure. Inside his zippered vest, he pulled out an artificial black rose. While smelling its synthetic fragrance, its petals caressed his lips. Staring at his prize one last time, he gently placed the black rose across her pure innocence.

CHAPTER 1

Taking the day off from her stressful job at the county health department, Michele Cook was extremely excited about spending the day with her daughter, Chloe. Suffering from Juvenile Lupus since she was six, this bubbly eight-year-old girl didn't let her disease keep her from enjoying life to the fullest. As Christmas break arrived, excitement ran through her veins. She had looked forward to this day with her mom since the Thanksgiving holiday break.

Being a special day, it meant having breakfast at her favorite place, McDonald's. After a hearty breakfast of pancakes, sausage, and chocolate milk, big-city shopping awaited them. Spending the entire morning in Lexington was a big deal to her. However, having lunch with her dad at the Avondale Country Club made this day extra special for her.

After lunch, the Oakmont Mall was the final destination of their holiday shopping adventure. Arriving in the food court, Christmas wishes on Santa's lap was at the top of every child's list. Bustling with activity, many of

Chloe's classmates waited in line to feel the spirit of Christmas. Even though Chloe believed she was too old to sit on Santa's lap, her mother insisted. While waiting in line, Michele said, "Sweetie, what are you going to ask Santa to bring you for Christmas?"

Tugging on her mother's arm, she smiled. "Mommy! That's a secret between Santa and me; you know that."

A quick hug and a kiss on her forehead, Michele seemed more excited than her daughter. While waiting patiently in line, a serious expression grew stronger on Chloe's face as she watched Taylor, one of her classmates, jumped down off Santa's lap, running to his mother's waiting embrace.

Chloe's big moment had arrived, aided by a gentle push by her mom, she scurried over to Santa, climbing onto his lap. As she gazed at his face, Santa winked with a sparkle in his eye. With a big beaming smile, she tugged on his long white beard. After a big hearty laugh, he placed his arm around her shoulder, bellowing out, "Ho, Ho, Ho, Merry Christmas." Smiling at her innocent face, he continued, "What's your name, little one?"

"Chloe."

"That's such a pretty name sweetheart, who gave you that name?" Pointing towards her mother, Michele was beaming with pride and joy at her precious daughter. "Did you know Chloe means 'young blooming one'?" She quickly shook her head back-and-forth. "Well, it does. What can Santa bring you this Christmas?"

"Santa, I don't want any toys or anything else this Christmas." His happy grin morphed into a puzzling expression. She paused as a single tear dripped from her eye. "Uh, I want you to bring, umm, my girlfriend back."

"Oh my, where did she go?"

"My mommy says she's in Heaven with her mommy."

Touching his heartstrings, he sighed. "Umm, what's her name?"

One tear turned into several; sniffling, she wiped them away. "Zoe, I miss her so much, umm could you bring her back?"

"Uh, that might be hard to do, but Santa will do his best."

With a quick nod, she peered into his glistening eyes. Smiling at him, she replied, "I will put milk and cookies out for you like always. I love you, Santa."

"That's so sweet of you, little one, umm, Santa loves every little girl and boy." As she jumped down, Santa's festive bellowing cracked as his heartstrings cried.

Running back to the waiting arms of her mother, Chloe's tears of sadness were invisible to her mom. After a loving hug and a kiss on her head, they left the food court hand-in-hand to finish their grand shopping adventure. As time flew by, and with more presents to buy, Michele called her husband informing him they would eat at the mall before coming home.

After visiting about every store, and Chloe seeing most of her friends, the food court was upon them once more. Exhausted and hungry, Chloe's favorite dinner destination was right in front of her. After receiving their orders from McDonald's, they chose a table near Santa, who was finishing up hearing Christmas wishes for the day. Dying to know what her daughter said to Santa, Michele asked, "Sweetie, what did you ask Santa to bring you for Christmas, you can tell me, he won't be mad at you?"

"Yes, he will, mommy!"

"No, he won't, I promise you."

"Okay, mommy, if you really must know." As tears streamed down her cheeks, she wiped them away. "I asked Santa to bring my girlfriend back, you know, Zoe."

While beaming with pride, Michele's heartstrings welled-up. "Oh, honey, that's so sweet and thoughtful of you, but she's in Heaven with her mother, where there is no pain and suffering. They are happy there like we are and…"

While sniffling, tears streamed down her cheeks, wiping them away, she replied, "Mommy! I still miss her, and I told Santa that. I thought I saw a tear run down his cheek just before I got off his lap."

"Well, honey, it probably surprised him and touched his heart. Most kids ask for the most popular toys and never think about the real meaning of Christmas. I love you so much."

At their table, joyful tears of sadness morphed into loving smiles between a mother and her daughter. Santa's chair had grown lonely and dark. Tomorrow, Christmas wishes would come alive again when Santa's deep bellowing and sparkling eyes would excite the minds of little girls and boys. With cheeseburgers and fries consumed, Michele cleared off the table, and their shopping adventure was finally over.

As they left the mall entrance, Michele and Chloe laughed and giggled in the frosty air. Upon reaching their car, Michele scanned the surroundings, and nothing concerned her. While unlocking the trunk and all the doors, Chloe hopped in the back seat and buckled up while her mother put the packages in the trunk.

After closing it, a man in a hoodie facing her took her breath away. The man's dimly lit face sent her pulse soaring as fear invaded her soul. As brighter shades of light illuminated his face, her fears eased somewhat. Knowing the individual, the angry butterflies in her gut subsided. "Jake, you surprised me. I haven't seen you in a long time. How are you?"

"Mrs. Cook, I'm not doing very well these days, you know, uh, how about you?"

"Jake, I'm sorry to hear that, and I certainly understand why. I'm doing just fine, spent the day shopping with my daughter. You remember Chloe, don't you?"

"Yeah, I remember her. You know, times have been hard on me, umm, I took a job as Santa, it was the only job I could get. I remember her very well, she just sat on my lap asking me to bring her little girlfriend back, you remember, my little, Zoe."

As Michele peered into Jake's glistening eyes, anxiety and fear roared louder in her crying heart. As far as she knew, Jake had never been a violent person; however, a real concern for their safety crept into her soul.

"Ah Jake, you know kids say the craziest things, you understand that, don't you? She didn't know it was you as Santa. She's just a young, innocent child letting her emotions control her thoughts. She still misses your daughter; we all do."

"Yeah, I get it. But nothing, um, matters to me anymore, if you know what I mean." Pausing for just a moment, Jake scanned the area as his broken heart exploded. Quickly glancing around the parking lot, Michele saw no one near. Returning her gaze to Jake, a gun close to her chest, sucker-punched her soul. "Mrs. Cook get in and drive. Uh, don't do anything stupid like screaming, or I will kill you right now. I have nothing to lose."

Heart racing, respiration shallow, fear ravaged her soul. "Uh, Jake, please don't do this. It won't bring your daughter back."

"Yeah, I know that, but nothing matters anymore. Just follow my instructions, or I'll kill you both right now, finally ending the pain I've been suffering for the last two years."

Frantic and teary-eyed, she looked for help. Her surroundings, cold and lonely, crashed down upon her limiting her options to escape unharmed. "Jake, what do you want?"

"Give me your key fob, purse, and phone. Just get in the car and drive, I'll tell you where to go. I'll be in the back seat with Chloe. Anything stupid like honking the horn, weaving erratically, or anything out of the ordinary, she dies first, got it?" Michele nodded frantically, handing him her purse, which contained her key fob and phone. "Good, I wouldn't want you to hear your daughter die just before I shoot you."

Hearing Chloe's sniffles cry out in the back seat, she had no choice but to follow Jake's demands if they were to have any chance to survive the night. Pulling out of the mall parking lot, she prayed for a Christmas miracle. With a gun pointed at her daughter, Jake whispered, "Don't worry, I won't hurt you as long as your mommy does what I tell her. Right, Mrs. Cook?"

Whimpering frantically, Michele nodded and traveled north out of the city, driving cautiously to an unknown destination with an uncertain future.

CHAPTER 2

The evening news had been interrupted by breaking news that John Dickerson, a powerful U.S. Senator from Florida, had been taken into custody by the FBI. Detective Carla McBride and Walt Blevins, publisher of the Daily Reporter, were instrumental in helping them create an airtight case against him. So close to breaking the case wide open on their own, Chief Brock Evans decided to hand over the Gold Fedora case to the feds. Carla was still upset at him for his gutless decision.

With the Christmas holiday upon her, a festive celebration with friends was just what she needed to forget the disappointment of losing her most significant case ever. Walt had proposed to Laura Watson, Carla's best friend. She was happy that fate brought them together. On the other hand, Carla was waiting for her knight in shining armor to capture her heart. Real love did not come easy for her. Laura's brother, Chris Abbott, was madly in love with her; however, she didn't feel the same about him. She loved him, but in a brotherly kind of way.

He always knew how to cheer her up, be there for her when she needed him, and tonight was one of those times.

Together, they laughed and talked about old times. Celebrating with him eased her frustrations, while Jameson on the rocks was warming her soul. As Chris refreshed her drink, her phone vibrated. While staring at the caller ID, a pissed-off scowled crossed her face. Answering the call, she listened intently. Chris arrived with her Jameson and overheard her as she spoke.

"Dammit Chief, your timing sucks. I'm off duty and having a great time with my friends, what's so important you had to call and ruin my evening?" While listening, Jameson felt good against her lips. "Yeah, I get it, I'm on my way." The call ended, and Jameson burned as it went down.

Carla's festive night was over. As she left, the uncertainty of the night greeted her with a cold, ugly embrace. In silent pursuit, she made it to the station in record time. Walking down the hallway to Chief Evans' office, the sounds of a distraught husband and father began to concern her the closer she got to his office. Larry Cook, a city commissioner, was visibly shaken and in tears as she entered the chief's office.

"Larry, this is Detective Carla McBride, one of the best detectives on the force. She will be the lead investigator on this matter."

Commissioner Cook nodded, and Carla took over immediately. "Commissioner Cook, please tell me everything you can about where your wife and daughter had been today. I'm sure you've already told the chief everything, but I need to hear it from you firsthand."

"Well, they left early this morning, uh, I believe

around Eight AM, heading for Lexington to shop there first. Michele called me around noon, telling me they would be back around One PM and wanted to know if I would join them for lunch. After lunch at Avondale Country Club, I left around Two PM for a work session at the city hall. I'm not sure what time they left the club; however, she called me around Six PM that they still had a lot of shopping to do, said they would grab something to eat at the mall before coming home. That's the last time I heard from them. I tried Michele's cell, but it goes straight to voicemail. Please tell me, um, that they're going, uh, to be okay."

"You need to stay calm and slow down. I know this is tough, but we are going to find your wife and daughter."

"Okay, okay! Give me, uh, a minute or two to calm down, will you?"

"Sure, would you like some water?"

"Yeah, please, maybe it will, uh, help me calm down."

Leaving to get him a bottle of water, Carla wanted to check whether something had come in on Michele's car. Returning to the chief's office, Commissioner Cook was sitting down, rubbing his temples. Handing him the water, he took a long sip and a deep breath. Noticing a sour expression on Carla's face, his anxiety exploded.

"What the hell's wrong, detective? I read faces pretty well, uh, and yours tells me something is wrong."

"Okay, you're right. We found your wife's car abandoned five miles north of town. It was in the parking lot at Hatcher's Nursery. Your wife's cell phone, along with the key fob, was on the passenger seat with her purse—no sign of them. We'll tow the car in, once it's here, we'll check it for fingerprints and DNA. It appears robbery was not the motive for the abduction. All the presents they bought are still in the trunk."

With uncontrollable anger building inside Commissioner Cook, he stood up, clenching his fist. "What now, you've got nothing to go on, do you? Chief, I'm going to hold you and Detective McBride accountable if anything happens to my family, you got that?"

"Larry, calm down, we are doing everything we can. We'll bring them back to you safe and sound. As cruel as it may sound, maybe you should go home and settle down. I will have Officer Wiesmann take you home and stay with you in case someone tries to contact you. Do you think you can do that and let us do our job?"

"Okay, okay, but remember, um, I'm holding you both accountable, and I will, you can count on that."

Remaining calm, Chief Evans replied, "Larry, I don't take threats kindly. We've got every available officer on the case, now go home and calm down, we'll be in touch when we have something."

CHAPTER 3

After Commissioner Cook left with Officer Wiesmann, Carla remained in Chief Evans' office to assess the situation. Silence filled the room as they searched for answers.

"Chief, I don't like Commissioner Cook's tone of voice, something else is going on, not sure what it is. A city commissioner is a part-time job, so what else is he doing when he's not trying to screw over the citizens?"

"Watch your mouth, Carla; he controls my destiny. He is the coordinator of the Arkoma Pharmaceutical and Research Institute located in the Oakmont Industrial Park. Not sure what he does, but I understand it has something to do with experimental drugs used in clinical trial programs. I understand he is an outstanding city commissioner as well."

"How about his wife?"

"She is the director of county social services, not an easy job either."

"What about his daughter, where does she go to school?"

"Oakmont Charter School on the university campus, but I doubt it has anything to do with the school or her."

"Well, that probably leaves us with the Commish, wouldn't you say? Must have something to do with either his job or the city commission. Anything big going on in city government warranting an incident of this nature?"

"I don't know; I'll call the mayor and find out."

"Okay, I'll go pay Commissioner Cook a visit and see what I can find out about any enemies he may have either at work or any citizens that may have a beef with him."

The commissioner lived in an old established subdivision appropriately named Covington Oaks because of the large oak trees throughout the development. His house was a modest two-story brick with a well-manicured lawn. Officer Wiesmann was standing outside the front door and greeted her.

"How's he holding up? Has he received any calls?"

"Pacing the floor back-and-forth, but with what he is going through right now, you'd expect that. As far as I know, he hasn't received or made any calls. And making matters much worse, he's on at least his second bourbon."

"That's not going to help things."

Officer Wiesmann nodded and remained outside, keeping an eye out for anyone or anything suspicious while she entered to question him. Pacing the floor, his bourbon on the rocks shook nervously in his hands. Glancing at the half-empty bourbon bottle on the counter, she could see Woodford Reserve was his bourbon of choice. Noticing Carla in the foyer, he downed the rest of his bourbon and approached her. The bourbon was already taking effect as a red-faced emotional voice greeted her.

"Have you got, um, anything new?"

"Nothing at all. Chief Evans is talking with the mayor about anything in the city government that would cause someone to do something like this. I want to talk with you about any work-related situations, past or present. Why don't we sit on the couch, and you can tell me everything about your job, okay?"

Nodding and feeling the effects of two stiff drinks, he stumbled before taking a seat across from her. He explained that he was the coordinator of Experimental Pharmaceutical Services at Arkoma Pharmaceuticals and Research Institute. His prime responsibility was screening patients for clinical trials using experimental drugs for rare and aggressive diseases with no known cure. Recommendations for the clinical trials usually were made through the health department or the local medical community. As he finished, he was breathing heavily, beads of sweat erupted on his brow. Wiping the sweat away, he rose and walked toward the bar for another Woodford Reserve.

"Mr. Cook, please sit back down and take a deep breath. You need to stay calm so you can help us find your wife and daughter."

Taking several deep breaths, he sat back down. Although his glass contained nothing but melting ice, he swallowed the bourbon-infused ice and water. His respiration had slowed somewhat as he continued.

"Just because a person has a specific disease, it doesn't mean they are a candidate for treatment. We have a five-person review committee that I direct, but ultimately, I'm the one making the final decision. Decisions of this nature are always tough. With millions of dollars at stake, we must make sure the candidate meets every bit of criteria and will have a high chance of a positive outcome from the clinical trials."

"I see. Whatever caused this person to abduct your wife and daughter might not have occurred recently, it might have happened months or even years ago. So, you need to think really hard and reflect on every case where it's been a gut-wrenching decision for you to make. Someone has a grudge against you and probably wants you to suffer the same way they did. It could be something simple, so think hard. I will step outside and give you a few minutes by yourself."

"Okay, um, I need another drink anyway, may I get you one?"

"I'm on duty, so the answer is no. Maybe you should stick to water, don't you think?"

Anger and disgust smeared across his face, his respiration quickened, he mumbled something under his breath before exploding. "Listen, detective, I'll drink whatever the hell I feel like, it's not your loved ones that are missing. So, don't tell me what to do, you got that?"

Shaking her head back-and-forth, Carla walked toward the door. In her mind, she knew a man high on booze might not think clearly; however, it was clear to her that he would have another Woodford Reserve regardless of her request. Stepping outside, she called Chief Evans to see if he had talked with the mayor yet. After their brief conversation, she was more confident than ever that the abduction was related to his job.

CHAPTER 4

Re-entering the house, Commissioner Cook was still pacing the floor with an empty glass in his hand. He again showed signs of anxiety, anger, and frustration to anyone in his path. He walked over to the bar and poured himself another Woodford Reserve, the bottle was more than half empty now. At least drink number four was hindering his thought process, Carla knew she had to get answers soon, or he would be in no shape to help.

"Well, Commish, how about taking a seat so we can continue. Time is running out." Taking a sip of his bourbon, he nodded and sat back down, facing her. "Thank you. Has anything popped-up in that brain of yours?"

"First of all, detective, um, please don't call me Commish." Carla nodded, and he continued, "It's just not that simple. I've had many cases over the years that were difficult. With what I do, and the decisions I have to make, no case is easy. Some people accused me of playing God because of the decisions I've had to make. Although those decisions had life or death consequences,

I also had to keep the company's financial goals in perspective."

"I understand, but there has to be one case that sticks out. One that still haunts you, making you second guess your decision."

Silence surrounded them for a few minutes as he rubbed his hands through his hair. After another sip, he made eye contact. The look in his eyes was encouraging. An eerie silence painted the room.

"Ah, shit, please, not Jake Chrisman."

"Who's Jake?"

Although Woodford Reserve was in full effect and he had been slurring his words, the realization that Jake could have done this rocked his soul, and he became more focused and coherent. He told Carla the story. Jake's daughter, Zoe, who had a rare blood disease with no cure, was a candidate for clinical trials of an experimental drug to slow down the progression of the disease. Michele Cook's recommendation that Zoe be accepted for the clinical trials made the decision that much tougher for Larry Cook. Also, Zoe and Chloe were good friends making his decision all the more difficult.

After careful and painstaking discussions, Zoe entered the clinical trial program. When she started, the outlook was not that promising, and the odds were not high for a positive outcome. However, Jake and his wife, Sally, understood the risks and agreed to the program. Several months went by, and although Zoe was a normal child on the outside, her disease continued to ravage her body. With clinical trials very expensive, it became apparent that even though the drug had positive results in other patients, Zoe was not responding enough, and her participation ended.

Two months later, Zoe passed away at the young age of eight-years-old, leaving her parents devastated. Finished with the story, Commissioner Cook wore his emotions on his sleeves. Rising from the sofa, he approached the bar, and Woodford Reserve swirled in the bottom of his whiskey glass. He dropped one clear ice cube in, and the bourbon burned as it went down. Returning to the sofa, he sat in silence.

"So, there you have it. The decision to end the trial was gut-wrenching, and after Zoe died, Jake blamed me for her death."

"When did this occur?"

As he rubbed his stubbled face, he replied, "Two years ago, before Christmas. We went to her funeral because our daughters were such good friends, and we wanted to pay our respects. Even though I was not responsible for her death, Jake still blamed me, and it was their only child. As I mentioned, none of my decisions are easy. If it is him, why let two years go by before getting revenge?"

"Sometimes, it may take years before a person reaches the breaking point or something emotional pushes them over the edge. What's their life been like since she died?"

"From what I can recall, Jake and Sally sought counseling after she died, it helped them for a while. However, the treatment provided by their health insurance ran out. Unable to handle the stress, Jake drank heavily. One night at a checkpoint, he failed a sobriety test and was arrested for DUI. That's not good when you work for UPS, and he lost his job. Although Sally was a part-time waitress at the Apollo Café, minimum wage with no benefits wasn't enough to pay the bills, and they went on public assistance for the first time in their lives. On the anniversary of Zoe's death, the pain and emptiness were too much for Sally to bear, she took her own life. I'm sure Jake's life has been a living hell since that awful tragedy."

"How tragic that must have been. When did that happen?"

"Uh, I believe it was last year on Christmas Eve."

"Shit, that's got to be it, he has to be our man. Where does he live?"

"Not sure, uh, somewhere in the county, uh, I believe."

"Stay put; Officer Wiesmann will continue to stay here with you, and please stay off the booze. You need to have a clear head if we need any further information from you. I will notify you when we get your wife and daughter back safe and sound. We will, I promise you."

Acknowledging her, he still headed to the bar to refresh his drink. Shaking her head back-and-forth, she walked outside and had a brief conversation with Officer Wiesmann. Arriving back at the police station, she informed Chief Evans what she'd found out. He remembered that tragic event, and that the Daily Reporter did a series of stories about it. Then followed it up when Sally Chrisman took her own life.

"Wow, good work, Carla. I guess, in the end, it was too much for Jake to handle. Do you have any idea what drove him over the edge?"

"Who knows what drives people over the edge and do stupid things, we may never know unless we can find him and resolve the situation. Do you know where he lives?"

"I'm not sure, but I know someone that probably does."

"We have little time to waste, get them on the phone!"

Chief Evans put the phone on speaker and dialed a number. After several rings, a man answered. Chief Evans replied, "Father Tim, Chief Evans here. We need your help. Do you remember Jake Chrisman?"

"How could I ever forget him. I counseled him for several months after his daughter died and then again after Sally took her own life. Counseled him again, but he could never understand why God would do that to him. That likely drove him away from the church. How may I help?"

"Father Tim, this is Detective Carla McBride. We believe he abducted Michele and Chloe Cook, probably holding them at his home. Where does he live?"

"Oh my, he lives on Blue Tick Road just outside the city limits. I've been there many times when I counseled him. It's a one-story shack nestled back in the woods across from Hatcher's Nursery. It's hard to see from the road."

"Okay, get your garb on, we'll pick you up in five minutes. We need you to work your magic."

"Not sure what magic you are referring to Detective McBride, but I'll be waiting and will help in any way I can."

The call ended. After picking up Father Tim, a police convoy made their way to Jake Chrisman's house north of Oakmont. Turning left on a dirt road just past the nursery, they approached his home in silent mode. A single light inside the house softened the otherwise dark atmosphere outside the house. Father Tim gave Carla

Jake's phone number; she put her phone on speaker and dialed the number. Immediately, someone answered; however, only silence buzzed on the speaker.

"Mr. Chrisman, this is Detective Carla McBride, we know you have Michele and Chloe. Are they okay?"

"Umm, for now."

"Good. To prove that, put Michele on the phone, or we won't be able to help you."

"No, you will just have to trust me."

"Okay, Jake. You don't want to hurt them. Your wife and daughter wouldn't want that, would they? Now, put Michele on the phone, so I know they both are okay."

"You don't know what my wife and daughter would want. You didn't even know them. Zoe was my little angel, and Mr. Cook couldn't save her. Umm, Father Tim couldn't save her, either. God couldn't even save her as well. Now, umm, everyone must pay for that."

"Jake, you don't want to do that, we can help you if you just give us a chance. Now, put Michele on the phone, or we will…" As the call ended, nothing but dark silence filled the chilly night.

CHAPTER 5

The crushing sound of silence smacked everyone in the face. Total darkness and despair filled the night. Hope was running out, and time was running out for everyone.

Father Tim said, "Call him back and let me talk with him. I've had many sessions with him. He would always get upset at first, but I seemed to have a calming effect on him, eventually."

Chief Evans replied, "Okay, Father, work your magic; someone's life depends on it."

Jake heard his phone ring again and let it continue ringing until it stopped. With the speaker on, Chief Evans tried it once more. This time Jake answered; however, as before, nothing but silence reverberated from his phone. Father Tim made the sign of the cross before speaking.

"Jake, this is Father Tim. Are you there?"

In a broken, agitated voice, he replied, "Father, um, please forgive me, uh, for what I'm, I'm about to do. I must, must stop the pain, uh, and the suffering once and for all."

"Jake, don't do this, I can help you get through this as I have in the past."

"Father, I have no future anymore. The only way I can end my pain, um, it's time to end it now. Forgive me, father, uh, and say a prayer for me, for my wife, for my sweet little angel. I can't get my, uh, little girl back, so, uh, I must take Chloe, uh, with me now."

"Jake, please don't do that; please don't…"

Deathly silence took everyone's breath away. A moment passed, then a child's scream shattered the eerie silence of the night. A few seconds later, one-shot blasted the night's tranquility. As two patrolmen crashed through the door with weapons drawn, a second shot echoed throughout the house. Carla and Chief Evans followed with their guns ready, expecting the worst.

Weeping and shaking uncontrollably, Michele held her daughter in her arms while still clinching her gun in her right hand. Carla walked over and removed it while Chief Evans kicked Jake's gun away from his body and checked for a pulse. He shook his head back-and-forth.

Chief Evans promptly called Commissioner Cook, telling him the ordeal was over, and his wife and daughter were safe. He spoke to Officer Wiesmann, giving him directions to the house. After a couple of minutes, Father Tim entered the home taking Chloe in his arms, consoling her and carried her outside, and away from death's aftermath.

Inside the house, Carla comforted Michele; however, she still had to interview her while everything is still fresh in her mind. "I know you have been through hell these last couple of hours, but tell me what happened in here."

"I had to do it. I never used my gun before, but I had no choice. I killed Jake to save my daughter and me."

"Okay, calm down. Will you tell me how we got here?"

"Jake abducted us after we left the mall and got to my car. He took a seasonal job as Santa. When it was Chloe's turn, she jumped on his lap, and I noticed he winked at her. Not sure why he was winking, but she ate it up. Later as we were eating in the food court, I asked her what she asked him to bring her. She told me she asked him to bring her friend back for Christmas. That friend was Jake's daughter, Zoe. It's been two years since she died, I guess Chloe sitting on his lap sent him over the edge. I don't think he thought about harming us or planned it this way, you know, I guess you never know when small things push people off the deep end."

"Yeah, but what prompted you to use your gun?"

"I have a permit to carry. I keep my gun in my pocket instead of my purse because it's easier to get to if I would ever have to use it. When Jake put the gun against Chloe's temple, she screamed so loud, and my instinct took over. I had to take a chance if I was going to save us. Jake's focus was solely on her. I quickly pulled out my gun and fired one shot. He didn't go down right away, so I fired another one. His gun fell out of his hand as he put his hands to his chest. He took one step and finally crumbled to the floor. Blood began soaking his shirt; seconds later, his twitching stopped. Chloe ran to me, crying, and I held her tight."

"Okay, you've been through hell. That's all I have, for now. I may have some follow-up questions, but they can wait until tomorrow. I believe your husband is waiting outside with your daughter. Go home and hug your daughter real tight."

Escorting Michele out of the house, Carla continued to console her. Seeing her husband holding Chloe, Michele ran to them as Carla watched from the porch. Chloe was quiet now; however, her parents were sharing tears of joy that their daughter was alive and, in their arms.

Carla re-entered the house where Chief Evans was holding Jake's gun and shaking his head back-and-forth. His bewildered eyes greeted her. "Carla, his gun wasn't loaded. He had no intention of killing anyone tonight, not even himself. I don't get it."

"Chief, maybe he wanted to die, but couldn't do it himself. Let's get out of here and get Father Tim back to the church and call it a night."

On the way back to the church, silence filled her car as if the world had ended. No one in the car would have ever thought it would end as it did. Her reverent side took center stage, "Father, God must have been watching over us tonight."

Father Tim, in a very soft angelic tone, replied, "My child, God watches over of us every night, sometimes we don't know it, don't feel it, or don't believe it, but he does. I see we are here now. How about I say a little prayer before you leave?"

"Thank you, Father, I think we all need that, wouldn't you say, Carla?"

Nodding, Carla and Chief Evans bowed their heads as Father Tim began his prayer. After amen bounced off the windows, he said, "Detective McBride, I'll see you at Sunday Mass, won't I?"

She hadn't been to Mass in some time, but nodded

anyway, he got out of her car and entered the sanctuary. The silence continued to echo off the windows of Carla's car. After dropping Chief Evans at the police station, she headed home for a hot shower and a date with Jameson. After showering, she put on her bathrobe, went into the kitchen, grabbing Jameson, and a glass of ice.

Entering her bedroom, she turned on the television and poured Jameson into her glass. Downing the Irish whiskey in one swallow, she hoped it would help calm her nerves. However, still feeling the night's tenseness, she poured another one to numb them. After two sips, she put it on the nightstand, turned off the lamp, and closed her eyes. The last thing she heard the news anchor say before she crashed was "for Commissioner Cook and his family; this tragic event had a happy ending."

CHAPTER 6

Interrupted sleep and the Jameson effect left Carla with a bout of extreme grogginess as she awoke the next morning. Splashing cold water on her face felt refreshing and chasing the fogginess out of her mind. After toweling off, the Keurig was ready to awaken her senses. On a typical workday, the Keurig was ideal for her hurried lifestyle. At the same time, on days off, her four-cup Mr. Coffee maker suited her laid-back lifestyle.

Turning on the television, she caught the tail end of the morning news. Chief Brock Evans praised the efforts of Detective Carla McBride and Father Tim O'Brien of St. Anthony's Catholic Church. The events of last night's ordeal replayed vividly in her mind, always hard on herself, she second-guessed every decision. That's who she was, an armchair quarterback, per se. Her coffee had grown lukewarm, a trip to the microwave gave it new life. A rough twenty-four hours had taken its toll on her, and she wished for a day off. However, that wasn't to be, as a boatload of paperwork awaited her.

Carla also wanted to follow-up with the Cooks, especially Michele. Their well-being was foremost on her mind. Michele had taken a life last night, and Carla wondered how she was coping with that. Carla wondered how she would handle taking someone's life as well. Thus far in her career, she had been lucky, and until now, that thought never crossed her mind.

Arriving at the police station a little later than usual, she found her desk in the same condition as it was the day before. With paperwork piling up, it would take her most of the morning to get caught up. Even though she hated paperwork, it would give her a short break from the grind of fighting crime in the world outside the police station.

Stopping by her mailbox on the way in, she was glad to see it empty instead of those anonymous letters she received during her last case. Chief Evans handed over the Gold Fedora case to the FBI, which still pissed her off. Time healed everything supposedly, but she didn't put a lot of faith in that. A fifteen-year-old cold case that Chief Evans removed her from, still haunted her today. In that case, Penny Miracle disappeared never to be heard from again.

Even though a man died last night, elation filled Carla's soul that the incident had a happy ending for the Cook family in the short term. Long term, the Cook family had to deal with the trauma and guilt that killing someone imposes on their sanity. It was a do or die situation regardless of whether or not Jake's gun was loaded. Michele did what she thought was best and saved her and her daughter's life.

Michele agreed to meet Carla at her home that afternoon at Two PM to tie up any loose ends. After that, Carla would be off until Monday, but she also knew when one is fighting crime for a living, days off often turned into days worked. As Carla finished her last report, her phone rang. Answering it, she listened intently and then hung up. Walking down the hallway to Chief Evans' office, he had his door closed. Normally, she would barge in, but learned a valuable lesson the last time she did that and knocked instead.

"Come in, Carla." Opening the door, she immediately recognized two well-dressed gentlemen already seated across from Chief Evans. As she sat down, a sickening feeling crept into her stomach. The last time she met these same agents, Chief Evans handed over her case to them. He continued, "You remember agents Slack and Stewart from the FBI in Louisville, don't you?"

"Uh, yeah, I remember them very well. What the hell are they doing here, taking another case from me?"

"Watch your mouth, Carla. It's a professional courtesy visit. So, keep quiet and listen. Agent Slack, please begin."

"First, the FBI owes you a debt of gratitude for helping us bring in John Dickerson. Detective McBride, we appreciate the work you did along with Walt Blevins, please pass that on to him."

"Thank you, Agent Slack. Chief, I can't believe this. Why the hell are really they here?"

"Carla, I already told you once to be quiet, so button it up, or else."

As Carla slumped back in her chair, her face warmed under the fluorescent lights. Chief Evans motioned for Agent Slack to continue. "Anyway, as you know, John Dickerson, his wife, and son were taken into custody. They seized all his government, work, and personal phones, computers, and tablets. He had been under surveillance for several years for many federal charges. Still, we never had enough for an airtight case until we received a very credible tip from Al Bocconi, a retired agent. That's how we heard about your case. We told John we were ready to charge him with three counts of conspiracy to commit murder and charge him with manslaughter involving Wylie Adkins. And we told him that, if convicted, it would likely carry the death penalty. Using your evidence and what we had on him, including his involvement in a sex-trafficking business, we pressured him to give us what we needed to fight the deadly drug trade in Florida. After days of questioning and interviews, he agreed to a deal."

"A deal, are you kidding me after what he did here in Oakmont? What kind of deal?"

"If he gave us names, dates, and other information and would testify against Edwardo Cavalla, the drug lord in Florida, we threw out the conspiracy to commit murder and manslaughter charges. In return, he would enter the federal witness protection program."

"Seriously, you guys are id…"

"Carla, will you be quiet and listen?"

While nodding, her face grew warm as Agent Slack continued, "As part of the agreement, he brokered a deal for his wife and son to protect them. They already have a new identity and life in a new community separate from him. He was against it; however, that's the only way she would accept a deal."

"So, dear John gets off for the murders of Mark and Joanne Alison and Frank Ramsey, Jr., and Wylie Adkins. That doesn't seem fair, does it?"

"No, it doesn't, but we were looking at the big picture, and we had bigger fishes to fry. John was to testify next week, but when we went to arrest Edwardo Cavalla, a firefight erupted, and he escaped. With him on the loose, John would still be in danger and entered the federal witness protection program yesterday. When we apprehend Cavalla, John must testify at some point, or his witness protection program will end. Then you can arrest him on all previous charges."

"So, you don't know where he is, but he knows where we are. I'm sure he knows who I am and who Walt Blevins is, right?"

"Unfortunately, that's correct. That came out in our interviews and negotiations. John also knows who tipped us off. Persons entering the program are under stringent orders not to venture away from their new community to ensure their safety. An individual monitors a person's movement from time to time, but nothing prevents them from leaving their new community and jeopardizing their safety. Most don't; however, some have tested the waters without much success. He has a second chance at a good life, and we don't think he will risk that and try to get revenge on you or Mr. Blevins."

"A second chance at a good life, that's crap, and you know it." The agents showed no remorse for their actions. "But you can't be certain of that, can you?"

"Of course not, no program is perfect. Do you have any further questions?"

"If John were to wander or leave his safe haven, would you inform us?"

"No, that would jeopardize his safety and his participation in the program. That's all we can tell you. Do you have any further questions?"

Chief Evans quickly interjected before Carla opened

her mouth again, "No, we don't. Thank you for letting us know what was going on. We appreciate it."

Agent Slack replied, "Detective McBride, trust me, you have no reason to worry about John."

"Yeah, that's easy for you to say, have a nice freaking day!"

After Agents Slack and Stewart left, Carla got up to leave. However, Chief Evans slammed the door closed and pointed for her to sit back down. She hurled "one of those looks that could kill" at him.

"What did I do now, Chief? Those guys are idiots to think John won't come after us."

"Dammit, Carla, what the hell is wrong with you? The FBI didn't have to tell us diddly squat. They were doing us a favor because we helped them get the big guys, and you disrespected them. That will likely come back to bite us in the ass. You need to tone it down."

"But Chief, he is out there somewhere, who knows, he could be right here in Oakmont for all we know. He had three people killed, and truth be known killed Wylie because he was the one person that could still take him down. John is very psychotic and dangerous and a threat to us all."

"First, I doubt the feds would put him here; second, I agree he may be psychotic and dangerous, but that doesn't give you the right to get in a pissing match with those agents. You worry me. You've always been a hot-head when it comes to relationships, and we've talked about it many times before."

"Chief, I like to call that being tough, which I have to be, being a woman detective is difficult, you know that. I'm an excellent detective, and you know it. I don't have any anger management issues, got it?"

"The hell you don't, McBride. You need to get yourself under control before you do something stupid and end your career for good."

Furious, sweat covered his forehead. Carla knew she had gone too far and stormed out of his office. Wiping his brow, he watched her huff-and-puff down the corridor. At first, Chief Evans wanted to grab her and sit her down, but his inner common sense told him to let her go. It was something he would address later after they both cooled down. Outside the police station, taking deep breaths eased her anxiety when Jameson wasn't available.

With the meeting with Michele Cook still an hour away, she had time to waste and called Walt to see if she could stop by. She needed to talk with him, and it would give her an easy way to release her pent-upped anger. Walt was near the front of the newspaper when he saw Carla enter. Once inside his office, her face seemed flushed.

"Carla, why is your face so red?"

"I've got a sunburn, why do you think it's red?"

"Why do you always answer a question with another question? We haven't seen the sun for a week now, and people don't usually get a sunburn around here in the winter, do they, now? What's got you all in a tizzy?" After explaining her confrontation with the feds and her shouting match with Chief Evans, he continued, "Wow, guess it's not been a good day for 'the' Detective Carla McBride, has it?"

"Don't be such an asshole, Walt. Do you think I have anger management issues?"

"Well, I've noticed that you can get hot under the collar very easily, and you're a very impatient individual, and that goes hand-in-hand with anger management issues. It might be a good idea for you to take a class in conflict and anger management. It couldn't hurt, and I'm sure the police department would pay for the class."

"Yeah, I guess I've always been, what's it called, you know, a 'shoot and ask questions later' kind of person. I'll give it some thought."

"That was some issue the other day. Guess it was touch and go for a while."

"Right, you never know what's going to happen in situations like that. This one had a happy ending for the Cook family, um, that reminds me I must meet with Michele Cook. Well gotta run, say hello to my girl, Laura."

"Will do, take care, and seriously think about taking a conflict and anger management class. Maybe you can take it online or at night."

Carla offered no response and left for her meeting with Michele Cook. When Carla arrived, Michele was standing, looking out her storm door. As Carla approached the house, Michele welcomed her into the home. Michele, forty-years-old, had coal-black, short-cropped hair parted to one side. It complimented her slender face and complexion, creating her undeniable striking beauty. Greeting Carla with a handshake, she motioned her to a sitting room that overlooked their well-maintained lawn. Carla wasn't one that engaged in chit-chat or small talk and wasted no time interviewing her. After about an hour, Michele had answered all her questions.

Before leaving, Michele asked, "You know, I could really use a hug today." Facing Carla, she opened her arms, hoping for a caring and reassuring embrace.

Although Carla was not big on hugs in a professional setting, she realized Michele had just been through hell and needed support. While embracing each other, Michele could no longer hold her emotions in check, and her heartstrings erupted.

As Carla left the house, the tears she had been repressing filled her eyes; she wiped them away as she reached her car. A quick check of her phone, 3:14 PM, glared back at her. Tired and emotionally drained, the effects of the last twenty-four hours had taken its toll on her, and her tank was empty. One should never feel guilty about starting their weekend early, she thought. Besides, Jameson, her liquid lover, was calling her name.

CHAPTER 7

Alaina James Gonzalez was very outgoing, personable, and very pretty. Known merely as AJ, she was well-liked at the Oakmont Regional Medical Center and gaining respect from her peers. As an emergency room nurse, she had a special knack of calming even the most challenging patient. Her twelve-hour shift began like most, from noon on till mid-afternoon it was slow.

By late afternoon, the patient load returned to some sense of normalcy. Normal to her was being busy as hell. A major accident on the interstate sent a lot of traumas to the ER, nothing like life-threatening injuries, just a lot of cuts and broken bones. A man, late sixties, came in with chest pains, while a lady in her seventies fell breaking her hip—just usual stuff for nurses and doctors.

Nearing the end of her shift, a young man in his late twenties or early thirties came in with severe stomach pains and nausea. AJ noticed the young man patiently waiting and thought he was kind of cute; however, he was definitely not her type. She hoped the charge nurse assigned him to someone else.

Unfortunately, she was the only nurse available. Picking up his chart, she called his name. Glued to his phone, he didn't respond right away. Repeating his name, he looked around, spotting a hot nurse in blue scrubs. He sized her up and liked what he saw. Another patient sitting beside him, nudged him on the arm, and pointed toward AJ. His face lit up.

"Yeah, that's me, honey."

Ignoring his forwardness and abrasiveness, she introduced herself, keeping it professional while taking him back to the exam area. All the time, she could feel his eyes sizing her up as a possible conquest.

"Mr. Walters, hop up on the bed, I need to get some basic information from you first, take your vitals, and then Dr. Hanshaw will be in to see you as soon as possible." He complied and sat comfortably on the bed, never making direct eye contact with her beautiful green eyes. "Okay, Mr. Walters, what's your birthdate, and why did you come to the ER tonight?"

"Please call me Bryan." Ignoring his request, she wrote down his personal information as he continued, "I had mild abdominal pains late this afternoon. Several hours later, uh, they got worse. Then I felt sick to my stomach, you know nausea-like, but didn't vomit though. The pain never went away, so I'm here, glad I came in, or you would never have been my nurse, I guess it's my lucky day."

"Okay, from one to ten, with ten being the worst, how would you rate your pain right now?"

"Probably a seven, honey, yeah, a seven, baby."

"Okay, I'll need to check your pulse and blood pressure."

He extended his arm out, waiting for her to place the blood pressure cuff on his arm. As she positioned it, he inadvertently brushed her left breast. Making eye contact with her, he apologized as she pumped it up as tight as she could, he grimaced at the pressure on his arm. With her stethoscope on his forearm, she watched the gauge slowly descend. After finished, she removed the blood pressure cuff and moved away from him to prevent any further inadvertent touching. He sized her body up once more before looking into her haunting and mysterious green eyes.

"So, honey, how did I do?"

"Pulse is 64, and BP is 120 over 68. All good, you must exercise a lot."

"Yeah, I work out with weights and run two miles a day, a star football player at the university back in the day, got drafted, but my knee couldn't handle it, so, I'm in the banking business now."

Feeling a little more comfortable being a safe distance from him, she let her guard down a little engaging in a friendly conversation while waiting for the doctor to see him.

"You know, I ran cross-country in college, did okay. Anyway, I'm not from here, so, where is a good place to run?"

"The county recreational park. There is a jogging path that borders Lake Catalpa. Maybe we can go jogging together sometime. Why don't you give me your phone number, and I will call you, maybe we can have a drink afterward, maybe get to know each other, you know, hook up?"

"Umm, maybe in your wildest dreams, Romeo. Dr. Hanshaw should be in to see you soon; I hope you feel better."

Dejected, the smirky grin he had on his face quickly turned sour. Immediately shot down by AJ, it was like an arrow piercing his pride, his overzealous demeanor. As she finished with his chart, Dr. Hanshaw drew the curtain back and entered.

"What do we have here, AJ?"

"Bryan Walters. He appears to have food poisoning with a gigantic Casanova attitude, you know what I mean, don't you?"

"Yeah, I'll take it from here."

Standing outside the curtain eavesdropping, Dr. Hanshaw asked him the same questions she did. After taking care of her last patient, she clocked out and walked to her car, hoping never to see Bryan Walters again. He was a one-hundred percent jerk in her eyes and wanted nothing to do with him.

As she backed out of her parking space, another car pulled in behind her. A look in the rearview mirror, a man, shielded by the darkness of the night, stared at her. After reaching the stoplight at the entrance of the hospital campus, she glanced again in the rearview mirror. Street-lights illuminated his face; she recognized the man reflected in the rearview mirror. Her heart began to race, her left turn signal ticked to the beat of her racing heart. A glance in the rearview mirror, a flashing left-turn signal blinked in unison with hers.

Driving cautiously, the car behind her kept a safe distance from her. As she reached the hotel, she moved into the left turning lane. As she was turning into the lot, the car following her continued straight past the hotel.

Breathing a sigh of relief, she quickly entered the hotel parking lot and found the first open spot. Sitting in her car, she waited for her pulse to slow down and for her fear to subside. Several minutes had passed; her deep breathing caused her windows to fog up. A tap on her driver's side window startled her. Heart pounding, a light hit her face.

"Miss, are you okay?"

Breathing heavily, she nodded. The night security guard walked away, continuing his rounds. She exited her car and walked calmly, but quickly to the main doors of the hotel. As the doors swung open, the night manager greeted her. Before taking the elevator, she grabbed a cup of coffee to settle her nerves.

Inside her room, the scent of Bryan lingered on her scrubs. She knew the inadvertent brushing of her breast was clearly not inadvertent. The thought of him terrified her, and his lingering scent made her sick to her stomach. Removing her scrubs and undergarments, she entered the shower, hoping to rinse away his disgusting scent forever.

CHAPTER 8

A weekend of laziness and Jameson helped Carla refresh her physical and mental state. No television, no phones helped her decompress, washing away the memories of the abduction and its outcome. With situations like that, she knew how ironic it was that life and death situations could be joyous and tragic at the same time. With the past behind her, she knew the next one was just around the corner. That's how crime operated, and she had to be ready and focused on addressing it.

After finally turning on her phone Monday morning, an email from Chief Evans was foremost on her mind. She was to be at a ten o'clock meeting in his office. The details were sketchy; however, she knew Detective Bernie Kowalski would be attending as well. Bernie briefly worked with her on the Gold Fedora case at Chief Evans' insistence.

However, they didn't work on many cases together because they had the same personality and makeup, but more importantly, they didn't like each other all that much as well. Also, Carla never forgave Bernie for deciding to end the investigation of a missing girl fifteen years ago when she was a rookie police officer. The case went cold because leads dried-up, and the girl's body never surfaced. That case still haunted her to this day because of a promise she made to the missing girl's best friend.

Bernie came from a mixed racial marriage. His father was of Polish ethnicity while his mother was of African American origin. Bernie got most of his skin color from his mother while he got his father's personality and charisma. Raised as a devout Catholic attending Mass regularly and Catholic schools, he was a man of faith.

Because of his medium-brown skin color, people teased him about his Polish name. Being black and Polish was unusual, at least in Oakmont it was. He enjoyed all kinds of music, including polkas from his father's native country. He also enjoyed Polish cuisine as well as beer and bourbon. A big man, many feared him, but on the inside, he was gentle as a pussycat. Loving life as though he was dying flowed outward through his personality and charisma. His wife, Lydia, of twenty-five years, was the love of his life.

While seated in Chief Evans' office, Carla and Bernie looked at each other with bewilderment as their pulse raced. Locking eyes with them both, Chief Evans took control of the meeting.

"I called you both in here today to let you know I've enrolled you both in a conflict and anger management class. It's a night class at Flemingsville College on Wednesday from Six to Nine PM. Lord knows you both need it. The department will cover all the costs." Carla and Bernie sat stoically, not even making eye contact with each other. Silence had captured the room, finally giving way as Chief Evans continued, "Are there any questions?"

Carla said, "Seriously, we have to go to Flemingsville. Why can't we take the class at the university here?"

"I tried, but the only class available was during the day, Monday, Wednesday, and Friday at Eleven AM. Besides, I can't have you two in class three days of the week, especially that time of the day. It would be a good idea for you two to carpool that way can save on the expenses. Also, you both need to learn how to get along better, and what better way than spending time in a car as you travel to and from Flemingsville College each week."

Before Carla could respond, Bernie interjected, "Carla, I'm driving because you have a heavy lead foot and you are a bit crazy at times, I'm not sure I could survive with you driving."

"Bernie, bite me, you dickhead. You drive so slowly that a turtle could get there quicker than you could. I'm driving, end of the discussion."

"Carla, you know you are full of shit sometimes, no, all the time. Try to boss me around, and we may end up in the boxing ring."

"I could easily take you…"

A loud noise filled the room with tense silence. Chief Evans stood up behind his desk as splotches of anger painted his face, it was not a pleasant sight to witness, and both deflected the frustration in his eyes.

"Stop it, you two, you both are acting like immature teenagers, no, more like spoiled little children, and that is the reason I enrolled you both in the class. Hopefully, you will learn something. No, you better learn everything you can, and that's an order. Now, I will flip a coin to see who drives. Heads, Carla drives, tails, Bernie drives. That seems fair, doesn't it? On the other hand, don't answer that question."

Glancing at each other for a moment, they eventually acknowledged him. Flipping the coin in the air, he caught it in this right hand. Opening his hand, he showed it to them. Heads it was. Carla gave Bernie a smirky grin; he immediately flipped her the bird. The anger of Chief Evans was still in the air.

"Uh, that went really well; hopefully, you two will stay out of trouble and not kill each other. Now, get the hell out of here and leave me alone."

Bernie, disappointed in the results, tried to bargain with her, "Carla, maybe we can compromise and alternate driving, what do you say?"

"Not going to happen, Kowalski. Just suck it up like a man and get over it."

They returned to their respective desks, which fortunately for everyone else's sanity, were on opposite sides of the room. The further they were apart, the better it was for everyone. A couple of minutes had passed, and Chief Evans stopped by Carla's desk, telling her to go back to his office.

While she was walking back to his office, he proceeded to Bernie's desk and told him the same thing. Bernie walked with the chief to his office. After Bernie sat down, Chief Evans shut the door and stood behind his desk. Carla and Bernie were a little dumbfounded and confused; however, Carla would not let Bernie have the edge and spoke up first.

"Chief, now what?"

"At least until your class is over, you are now partners. It will do you both good; hopefully, you both can work together so that no one gets hurt. End of discussion. So, shake hands and get the hell out of here."

"Seriously chief, are you out of your freaking mind? We are like oil and water."

"Button it up McBride, now shake hands and makeup."

Bernie extended his hand to Carla, she reluctantly shook his hand, and they left. The news hit the station that they would be partners indefinitely, and it seemed like nobody cared. However, sentiment in the station was they deserved each other. Immediately, an office pool was created to see how long they would last or how long Chief Evans would let it go before they killed each other.

Carla sat at her desk, dejected and humiliated. Fuming mad was probably a better word to describe her demeanor. Lying on her desk was a white envelope addressed to her. Printed in black ink with no return address, it raised the hair on her neck. Anxiety was building; in her last case, she received two anonymous letters and didn't like the look of this one as well. Turning it over, she carefully slid her letter opener between the flap making a clean slice. Looking inside, it appeared to be a letter. Taking it out, she unfolded it.

The loud crash of her ten-year service award, a clear paperweight, slammed hard on her desk, silencing the muted chatter in the station. As Carla glanced around the common area, she could see that everyone was glaring at her. Utterly speechless at the image on the sheet of paper, she headed straight for Chief Evans' office. While on the phone, he noticed her quickly walking toward his office and ended the call. Waving her in, she was showing signs of anxiety, as beads of sweat dotted her forehead, she handed the sheet of paper to him.

A puzzled frown painted his face, rubbing his forehead, he exclaimed, "What the hell is this?"

"It came in the mail today, no return address. It's a sketch of a jogger with a ponytail protruding out of her hat, she has a noose around her neck, and a rose clenched between her teeth."

"I can see that, but who is it supposed to be, why was it sent to you?"

Pausing for a moment to gain her composure, she responded. "I don't know, take it to forensics, I gotta go, someone may be in danger."

"Hold on, talk to me."

"John Dickerson is behind this. In the breaking news report, when they took him into custody, he yelled about getting revenge. I took it to heart, and now this."

"Get a hold of yourself. Don't you think you're being a little paranoid? I'm sure John is nowhere near here."

"Uh, you may be right; however, he has a vast network of associates willing to carry out his revenge. Chief, I don't trust him one damn bit. Gotta go, see what forensics can come up with. I'll be fine."

Within ten minutes, she pulled in front of Laura Watson's law office. Call it great timing or karma; Laura had just delivered some documents to the receptionist. Noticing Carla enter through the door, concern painted her face as she greeted Laura with a hug.

"Let's go to your office."

"Sure, you look like you've seen a ghost. What's going on?" Laura opened the door to her office, they entered, and she closed the door behind them. "Carla, what's this all about?"

"Are you still jogging before or after work?"

"That's a strange question, but yeah. Sometimes at Lake Catalpa, sometimes at the country club, and other times at the high school track. What's going on?"

"Just be careful and be aware of your surroundings and any other people around you."

"I'm always religious about that, you know I can take care of myself, and I always have my mace with me."

"Great, just be careful, gotta run, say hello to Walt for me, will you?"

CHAPTER 9

Carla and Bernie were making the best of a bad situation. Partners needed to be close to each other and trust each other. Even though they both expected their partnership to be temporary, they moved their desks across from one another. Even that caused friction between them. Carla won out, and Bernie moved his desk.

Tuesday morning, Bernie's phone rang, rang, and rang annoying Carla. Glaring at him, she met Bernie's gaze with disgust because she knew he was purposely letting it ring, ring, and ring.

"Bernie, are you going to answer that?"

"Hey, don't get your panties in a wad."

Ignoring her obscene gesture, he finally answered the phone. Listening, he jotted down a few notes and hung up. Watching his facial expression, Carla didn't like that look; she'd seen it many times before, even on her own face.

"Hey partner, we've got a dead female body, Lake Catalpa jogging path, let's roll."

Anxiety in the pit of her stomach churned, she breathed deep trying to calm her nerves, the image on the piece of paper flashed in her mind. The conversation she had with Laura filled her every thought. Oblivious to Bernie's looming presence, the notion it could be Laura sent her pulse racing. A tap on her shoulder startled her, Bernie's eyes met the fearful expression painting Carla's face.

"Are you okay?"

"Yeah, give me a moment."

Ignoring his impatience, she pulled out her phone and dialed Laura's cell, straight to voicemail it went. Murmuring vulgarity under her breath, she dialed another number, straight to voicemail as well. Another foul murmur, her heart pounding, she called Laura's office number, voicemail spewed out her standard out-of-the-office greeting. More four-letter words under her breath sent her pulse racing out of control. Panic was controlling her thoughts. Bernie tapped her shoulder again, her face, a portrait of sheer concern, lost all color.

"We've gotta go, talk to me on the way, something's clearly upsetting you, and I need to know about it."

She nodded, and they left in her car to investigate the death of a female jogger. Her mind was still on Laura, and she was beginning to believe her worst fear might be real, that Laura was dead. Arriving at the crime scene, Carla quickly scanned the parking lot for a Mercedes with dark-tinted windows. Immediately seeing Laura's car, Carla stopped dead in her tracks. She did a quick three-hundred-sixty-degree scan of the jogging path as far as she could see, Laura was nowhere in sight. Police officers were already talking to an older couple that was out for their early morning walk—discovering the body; they called nine-one-one.

In the distance, a white sheet covered the body where JD Franklin, county coroner, hovered over it. Without warning to Bernie, Carla sprinted toward the body. Surprised and confused, he ran after her. As she got closer to the victim, adrenalin shot through her veins, and panic was taking hold of her soul. A few more steps and the body was upon her.

Gasping for air, Carla saw DJ shaking his head back-and-forth. Looking at the sheet covering the body, Carla held a glimmer of hope, the outline of the body under the sheet appeared smaller than Laura's taller frame. DJ glanced at a seasoned detective scared as hell. Bernie was still in a state of confusion as he arrived.

DJ said, "Carla, are you okay?"

"I think so. What have we got?"

"White female, blonde hair, probably in her early twenties, death by strangulation."

"You did say blonde, didn't you?"

Carla let out a big sigh of relief, breathed deeply, letting out another sigh. Surprised at her response, DJ said, "Did you think it was someone else?"

Ignoring his question, she glanced at Bernie, then back at DJ. "Nah. Bernie, why don't you go interview the couple that found her, while I tie things up here?" He nodded and slowly sauntered toward them.

DJ nodded and continued, "We found a phone in the zippered pocket of her vest; this license was with it. The victim is presumably Alaina James Gonzalez of Flemingsville. Time of death was probably between seven to nine last night."

"Flemingsville, uh, what's a pretty young thing like

her jogging here last night?"

"That's for you to find out. It looks like the perp attacked her from behind, dragged her into this tall grass, then put the ligature around her neck and tightened it. Once subdued, the perp turned her over and pulled her jogging tights down below her knees. Then the perp finished her off until she died. Forensics is doing their due diligence, but it's unlikely they will find much given where we found the body down this embankment. We'll process her during the autopsy and see what we get. There's one other thing you must see, and it's very disturbing."

"Yeah, what is it?" Raising the sheet, Carla continued, "A black rose, doesn't that mean death, DJ?"

"Something like that."

"What's printed on the strip of paper?"

"Ye who hath been bestowed a single black rose shall be granted eternal peace."

"That's pretty sick, don't you think?"

"Yeah, but that's the world we live in these days. There's something printed on the other side, and you will not like that either." Handing the black rose to Carla, she read it slowly. While giving it back to him, a chilling whiteness consumed her stoic complexion. Her pulse returned to warp speed as nerves attacked her stomach. "What do you think it means, Carla?"

"I think we are dealing with a sick, psychotic bastard, and we need to put a rush on the autopsy and analysis of all evidence. Bernie and I start a Conflict and Anger Management class on Wednesday at Flemingsville College, and I'd like to wrap this one up rather quickly."

"Wow, anger management class, imagined that."

"Screw you, DJ, make this a top priority. We have a

silk black rose on a dead girl's vagina and a fortune cookie saying there will be more, that's not good."

He shook his head back-and-forth at her while she walked toward Bernie, where he was talking to an older couple, Angie and John Whitman, who discovered the body on their early morning walk. While listening to Bernie interviewing the couple, a lady in a hot-pink spandex jogging suit was finishing her run. As the lady sprinted toward the finish line, Carla sighed and walked toward her.

"Laura, what are you doing here?"

"That's an odd question. What are you doing here?" Carla pointed toward the body still covered by a white sheet. "A dead jogger, and may have been sexually assaulted as well. You need to be careful." Laura nodded, and they shared a hug. Carla returned to where Bernie had just finished his interview with the couple.

"What was that all about, Carla?"

"Just a friend that jogs here from time to time. Anyway, I guess we start in Flemingsville at the French Colony Apartments, where Alaina Gonzalez lived. When we get back to the station, we can Google it and get an emergency contact phone number for her, you can check with authorities for any missing persons."

"Yeah, and we can use it as a test run for our class on Wednesday. I'm looking forward to it."

"Bernie, don't screw with me and don't go there, you know what I mean, right?"

"No, I don't know what you mean."

"Forget it, dickhead."

Laughing, he flashed her a quick bird. As they returned to her car, Marsh Robinson, the crime reporter for the Daily Reporter, was waiting for them. He had already taken a few pictures of the crime scene from behind the tape. Marsh knew the rules and, for now, would abide by them. Seeing them approach him, he felt like stirring things up.

"McBride and Kowalski, I didn't know you were a pair now. That's interesting; how did that happen?"

Carla said, "None of your damn business, Marsh. We'll send out a press release like we always do. That's all we have to tell you, get the hell out of our way, as we have work to do."

Marsh thought to himself, what a bitch she could be at times, or maybe she just got up on the wrong side of the bed, or maybe it was her time of the month, he didn't care what her problem was, he just wanted to do his job. Staying around for a little while, he was hoping someone had loose lips, but that didn't happen today.

Back at the police station, Carla Googled the French Colony Apartments in Flemingsville. Immediately calling the manager, it went straight to voicemail. Leaving a message, all she could do was wait for someone to return her call.

Bernie called the Flemingsville Police Department and Flemingsville College Police Department to inquire about missing persons. Bernie struck out with both law enforcement agencies and informed Carla that no one fitting AJ's description was missing.

He mumbled, "We just wait now. I hate waiting, what about you?"

"Yeah, me, too." Her phone rang, the caller ID indicated the call was from Flemingsville. "Bingo. I have a winner." She answered. "Mrs. Harold, I'm trying to get contact information for Alaina James Gonzalez, I'm investigating the death of a young woman found in

Oakmont this morning. A driver's license found at the scene belongs to her."

"Carla, are you going to put that on speaker so I can hear?"

With it on speakerphone, Bernie listened to Mrs. Harold's reply. "Oh my, I hope it's not her, she was such a pretty thing, had her whole life in front of her."

Carla replied, "Do you have an emergency contact for her?"

"Give me a minute, and I will pull her file." A file cabinet drawer opened and closed. "George Gonzalez is the only contact on her file, and here's the number." As Bernie jotted the number down, Martha continued, "Not sure what relationship he is to her, but I imagine it's her father. Anything else I can help you with?"

"We'd like to see her apartment, you know, look at pictures or other things that might help us in our investigation. Will we need a search warrant?"

"Company policy, you know how the legal people are about these kinds of things."

"Yeah, we get it. What's the apartment number?"

"Apartment twenty-five."

"Thanks, we'll get one and get back with you. Thanks for your help, and by the way, until the next of kin identifies the body, mum is the word."

"Oh, of course."

"Thank you."

The call ended, and Carla immediately dialed the number for George Gonzalez. The call went straight to voicemail. Googling him discovered he is a professor at Flemingsville College. Meanwhile, Bernie is on the phone, getting a search warrant for apartment twenty-five at the French Colony Apartments in Flemingsville.

CHAPTER 10

An hour later, they are on the road to Flemingsville with a search warrant cooperating with local law enforcement. While Carla was behind the wheel, Bernie called Martha, informing her they were on their way. The fifty-minute drive seemed like twenty-five minutes to Bernie, but again Carla was driving, and she had a heavy foot.

Pulling into the parking lot, the sign on a gate showed Martha's office was on the main level. While introducing themselves and flashing their badges, Bernie handed Martha the search warrant, looking it over, she motioned them to follow her to apartment twenty-five. On the way, Martha informed them that Alaina had not renewed her lease, and would be moving since she was a nurse at the medical center in Oakmont.

While Martha unlocked the door, they noticed an older man walking up the steps to his apartment on the opposite side of the complex. Staring at them, the man immediately recognized Detective Carla McBride from the newscast last week about the abduction in Oakmont, but not the other detective with her. Carla glanced in his direction as he quickly entered his apartment and closed the door.

Entering Alaina's apartment, they began their search. It was spotless, and nothing was out of place. The only picture sitting on an end table was a picture of Alaina's parents. A thorough search of every room, they exited with zilch. Canvassing the entire complex wouldn't take long. Bernie started on the same side as Alaina's apartment. He would work his way down, while Carla would begin with the unit where she saw the man entered his apartment earlier.

With no walkway to the opposite side, Carla took the stairs down to the first floor. Walking to the other side, she took the stairs to the third floor. Starting there, she would work her way from top to bottom, starting at apartment thirty-one.

Inside his apartment, the man watched Bernie knock on apartment twenty-six, while Carla was just a few steps away from his door. Focused on Bernie, the knock startled him, and he moved away from the curtains. Noticing the curtains moved a little, Carla remained patient, giving the man a chance to open his door. Hearing nothing, she knocked again. Finally, the door opened.

Flashing her badge, she said, "Hi, I'm Detective Carla McBride from the Oakmont Police Department. Did you know the person in apartment twenty-five?"

Eyeing Carla from head to toe, he finally replied, "Oh, you mean that pretty young fox, yeah, different, you know. I believe she was a nurse because she was always in scrubs. I saw her numerous times around the university, but she was never very friendly at all. No matter how friendly I was, she dissed me. She even went as far to call me a pervert one time, imagine that, I'm a respected professor at the university. Well, I guess the young people of today no longer respect their elders as I did. She really pissed me off. If she were my daughter, I would teach her a lesson or two. Anyway, is she in any trouble?"

"Nah, we are just trying to find her to ask her some questions about an incident in Oakmont at the medical center where she works. Did you ever see anyone enter her apartment with her?"

"Nah, she was always alone all the time I saw her. Oh, I do recall one time at the coffee shop, she sat with another hot fox, you know, they're everywhere on campus. I overheard them discussing her new job. I tried to be nice, and she told me to screw myself. Anything else I can help you with?"

Feeling his eyes ravaging her body, she responded, "Nah, that should do it, thanks for your time, Professor…"

"Don Smith."

"Okay, Professor Smith, thanks again."

"Hey, no problem, hope you find her safe and sound, and please tell her to respect her elders, especially me. Have a nice day, Detective McBride."

Carla met Bernie back down at the manager's office, informing Martha they were finished, and more than likely didn't plan on coming back. Back in Carla's car, they sat discussing their canvassing results.

"So, did you find anyone home?"

"Just the guy in apartment thirty-one, he said he just saw Alaina in passing a few times and around the university. He told me she wouldn't give him the time of day and called him a pervert a few times. Definitely a strange dude, he seemed a little nervous. I felt like he was, you know, hiding something, or maybe had a chip on his shoulder. And I could feel his eyes all over me, never made direct eye contact with me, either. Gave me the willies. You know that type, don't you?"

"No, I don't, maybe they had a history together, maybe he came on to her, she dissed him again, and again. Maybe he is a pervert and did it to her, maybe that was the only way he could get in her panties."

A look of disgust painted her face; she shook her head back-and-forth at his obscene sick theory. "Really, he was strange, I'll give you that, but a rapist and killer, I doubt it. You need to get your mind out of the gutter. You find anyone at home?"

"Nah, struck out entirely."

"Now, we have to go find George Gonzalez and let him know his daughter is dead. I hate this part the most."

"We all hate it, and it gets no easier for anyone."

Arriving at the home of George Gonzalez about ten minutes later, it was a modest house in the old section of Flemingsville. Charming bungalows, but with old-world character. Parked in the driveway was a 2007 silver Nissan Altima. Pulling in behind it, they sat for a few moments to prepare what to say to Mr. Gonzalez because it was never easy telling a father that his daughter was dead.

Walking onto a porch that spanned the width of the house, a wooden swing looked worn and lonely. Ringing the doorbell, they immediately heard footsteps across the hardwood floors as though Mr. Gonzalez was expecting them. The door swung open. Quickly flashing their badges, Mr. Gonzalez's eyes showed concern.

"Mr. Gonzalez."

"Yes, may I help you?"

"I'm Detective Kowalski, she's Detective McBride. We're from the Oakmont Police Department and have a few questions to ask you. May we come in?"

"Of course. What's this about?"

Carla said, "Do you have a daughter named Alaina?"

"Yes, Alaina James. AJ is what everyone calls her. She's a registered nurse in Oakmont."

Showing him a picture on her phone, the expression on his face answered her question. His lips quivered and his eyes glistened.

Carla said, "Maybe you should sit down and take a few minutes to compose yourself."

As he quietly sat on a sofa, he took a tissue off a side table, drying his eyes. "Yes, that's my Alaina, what happened?"

Bernie said, "This morning in Oakmont, an older couple discovered a body in the thick brush bordering Lake Catalpa. Alaina's driver's license and phone were in the zippered vest pocket on the body. We're waiting for an autopsy; however, it appears the death was by strangulation, and sexual assault is a possibility. We're sorry for your loss."

His glistening eyes showed his heartbreak. Wiping the tears away, he replied, "Thank you. AJ just started working there about two or three weeks ago in the ER department. She was commuting until she could find someone to share an apartment with, can't believe this happened to her."

Carla said, "Did she have any boyfriends, recent breakups, that kind of thing?"

"No boyfriends, my daughter was a lesbian. Not sure why she ended up that way, I guess a parent thinks they know their children when they really don't. I accepted it, and her friends knew as well. She was an only child, a free spirit like her mother. Clara, a registered nurse as well, died about five years ago of breast cancer, that's why AJ wanted to follow in her footsteps."

"Mr. Gonzalez, That should do it. If there is anything I can do, please don't hesitate to call me, here's my business card. Again, we're so sorry for your loss."

CHAPTER 11

Traveling back through Flemingsville on their way to the interstate, they scanned the cityscape just to get a sense of the city. They found the building where they would begin their Conflict and Anger Management class tomorrow evening, and Carla marked the current time down in her memory. When passing by a store called All Things Macabre, they both shook their heads in disbelief.

On their way to the interstate, they passed by the French Colony apartment complex where AJ lived. Carla just couldn't get Professor Don Smith out of her head, she had good intuition, and her intuition was telling her that this guy was hiding something. Hopefully, their paths would never cross again, and that was fine with her. Turning onto the on-ramp to the interstate, they headed back to Oakmont. Bernie broke the silence in the car. "So, AJ was a lesbian, never would have thought that."

"Why is that?"

"Ah, you know, she was a beautiful young lady and all, you know hot looking, just don't get it."

"So, are you saying lesbians can't be hot looking?"

"That's not what I meant." Changing the subject, he continued, "You know, many people in the station think you are a lesbian because of the way you carry yourself, are you?"

"I will not dignify that with an answer, dickhead. And, you think I'm not smoking hot, do you?"

"Um, guess that come out the wrong way. Let's just say if I were fifteen years younger and not married, I'd be asking you out and see where that goes."

"Listen, dickhead; you'd be way out of your league, so get that thought out of your mind."

A blast from the radio smashed the silence inside the car. "Well, I guess we start at the medical center and see what we can discover. That may not be easy with all those things about HIPAA these days."

"Yeah, maybe not, but we'll push the envelope and see what happens. If we need a warrant, we'll get one."

The rest of the trip home was a silent one other than Bernie making a call to the regional medical center to see if the CEO was in today. It was always best to start at the top because they should know the HIPAA rules better than anyone.

Entering the medical center, they identified themselves while flashing their badges. Bernie asked for Jonathan Nicholas, CEO of the regional medical center. Waiting in the reception area with every Tom, Dick, and Harry in the world tested their patience. It didn't bother them, because in their line of work, they had already encountered just about every Tom, Dick, and Harry before anyway. Several minutes elapsed before a well-dressed gentleman approached them. After standing up, they flashed their badges, and exchanged pleasantries with him.

"Detectives, nice to meet you. How may I help you today?"

"Mr. Nicholas, can we go somewhere with a little more privacy?"

"Of course, just follow me."

Following him down a long corridor, they turned the corner to another long hallway. Finally, Mr. Nicholas stopped and motioned them to enter his office. Carla and Bernie sat in the well-appointed leather chairs across from his desk. Mr. Nicholas closed the door and sat across from them. "Now, what did you want to see me about?"

Carla said, "Do you have an employee named Alaina James Gonzalez? His questioning eyes met their curious gaze. "According to her father, she took a job in the emergency department two weeks ago."

"Let me see." After a few keystrokes, he pulled up a list of employees by department, he replied, "Yes, we do. What's this about?"

"We are sorry to tell you this, but a young lady was found dead this morning at the county recreational park. A license on the body identified her as Ms. Gonzalez."

"Oh my, I'm so sorry to hear that. I understand from her supervisor; she had a lot of promise of being a great nurse someday. You know, I like to get to know our employees and remember her telling me she might even want to be an ER doctor one day. What a shock. So, how may I help you? You have my full cooperation."

Bernie replied, "Thank you, sir. We'll need a list of all employees that worked with her in the ER. We mean everyone, including doctors, nurses, orderlies, house-keeping, anyone that might have had contact with her."

"Right, anything else?"

"We are just getting started. We'll need a list of people that went through the ER during her shifts. Just names, we don't care why they were there. That will be enough to get us started. Can you do that without us getting a warrant?"

"Tell you what, let me call our legal department, I'll get back with you when I have an answer."

Carla interjected, "Listen, sir, the sooner we get the names, the sooner we catch the asshole that killed her, so call now. We will wait right here until you get an answer."

"Yeah, yeah, okay."

"Thank you."

"Would you mind stepping outside for a moment?"

Carla fired back, "Uh, we'll just sit right here."

Nodding, he immediately called the hospital counsel, and ten minutes later, they walked out with their list. Carla scanned the list, knowing they had their work cut out for them. There were pages and pages of people that went through the ER during her shifts, and she had only worked there two weeks or so until someone ended her life.

"Pardon the pun Bernie, but we're looking for a needle in a haystack, don't you think?"

"Funny, let's get started."

Back at the station, they began reviewing the list of employees and patients that AJ interacted with, and it was daunting. Interviews based on the employee's schedule and the human resources availability created issues for the investigation. Bernie contacted Jonathon

Nicholas to explain what they needed to rule out every employee AJ had contact with as suspects.

He transferred Bernie to human resources; an hour later, Bernie received an email with a schedule of interviews for the weekend. Bernie relayed the list of employees to forensics and tech services to get as much information as possible on each employee before the interviews began on Friday afternoon.

Carla retrieved her email, and one caught her eye. It was from the coroner about Alaina James Gonzalez. The report attached confirmed the manner of death as strangulation; however, no sexual assault occurred as previously thought. That would suggest that something interrupted the attacker, and he tightened the ligature tighter and tighter to keep her from screaming. Of course, that was only an assumption.

The killer was likely someone strong, big, and agile because she also had three cracked ribs contributing to her inability to fight back. There wasn't any DNA found under her fingernails, or anywhere else on her body. None of this was what they wanted to hear, and they still didn't have the analysis of the black silk rose yet.

Meeting with Chief Evans, they brought him up to speed on the case. Returning to their desk, they began the arduous task of reviewing each list. Assuming it was a male perpetrator, they separated them by male and female using first names. They believed the killer was likely on one of those lists. AJ was new in town and had only been in contact with the people on the list.

Based on the coroner's report, the suspect now was likely a male, and they compiled a list of the male employees and patients based on their first name and would start there. They gave the list to forensics and the techies to work their magic.

Patience was not a strength for Carla or Bernie, but somehow, they would have to manage their impatience the best they could. Bernie glanced at the big clock on the wall, and five o'clock was approaching fast. Carla glanced at the clock as well and then at Bernie. A smile crossed his face.

"What?"

"Carla, we'll be off duty in thirty minutes. Do you want to get a drink somewhere, chill out since we will be spending a lot of time together? Besides, we are in a waiting game, and I'd rather have something to drink to clear my mind. What do you say?"

"Well, Bernie Kowalski, what would your wife say about that?"

"Nothing, it's police business. Besides, you know, you may not be my type after all."

"Okay, then what is your type?"

"Listen, McBride, do you want to get a drink or not?"

"Sure, but you are buying."

"How about McGruder's?"

"Perfect. Jameson, my liquid lover, will be there."

"Liquid lover, what the hell is that all about?"

CHAPTER 12

After a few hours of bonding and booze at McGruder's, Carla and Bernie put the past behind them and pledged to be the best partners as possible. Arriving a few minutes apart the next morning, a ton of documents awaited them. Employees in the ER would be first since it was the shortest list.

After separately reviewing the information from forensics on the employees, they met in the conference room to discuss and compare their notes. The meeting didn't take long because the information showed there weren't any employees with criminal records. However, that didn't mean these employees couldn't have committed this horrendous crime; it was just unlikely. Furthermore, their due diligence was necessary to eliminate the employees as persons of interest.

Chief Evans had sent a press release to all media, and that meant Marsh Robinson from the Daily Reporter would soon be calling. The newspaper had a short brief about the body, but no name or anything else until they received the press release. It was just a matter of time until he called Carla. Her desk phone rang while she was in the ladies' room, so Bernie answered it. He could see from the caller ID that it was likely Marsh Robinson. He knew Carla tried to avoid him as much as possible, so he would take care of him and have a little fun as well and put it on speaker.

"Marsh Robinson at the *Daily Reporter*. Where is Detective McBride?"

"None of your business. How may I help you?"

"The press release, about the body found at Lake Catalpa, didn't provide much information about the victim. I wanted to ask her a few questions for my story, and get a quote or two."

"Listen, dude, she's not taking any questions today. If you want to ask me any questions, go right ahead, but I'm not answering any as well."

Marsh knew he was getting nowhere with Detective Kowalski and replied, "I'll call her back some other time, thank you."

Hearing Bernie ending a phone call, Carla asked, "Who was that?"

"Your boyfriend, you know, Marsh from the Daily Reporter, he wanted to ask you a few questions. I told him you were not taking any questions today. I told him he could ask me some if he wanted to, but I wasn't answering any today either. He said he would call back some other time when you weren't so busy."

"Cool, you might make a good partner after all."

"Yeah, you owe me one."

Throwing him the thumbs-up gesture, she nodded and called the coroner to get further information on the autopsy. The only thing DJ had to add was that in his professional opinion, the perpetrator was likely someone at least six feet or so, and weighing at least two-hundred pounds or more. Being hit with such force, it probably cracked her ribs, rendering her unable to fight back.

He informed her that the attacker might have been a football player at one time. At least that narrowed the suspect list down considerably. Running with that theory, Bernie notified Jonathon Nicholas they would be over to speak with him again and suggested the emergency room director be present when they arrived. Checking in with the receptionist, she gave them directions to his office. When they arrived, the director of emergency services was ready to answer their questions.

"Detectives McBride and Kowalski, nice to see you again. Meet Josh London, our emergency room director."

"Nice to meet you, detectives, Jonathon said you wanted to ask me questions about the employees in ER that worked with AJ. Shoot, I want to help find this sicko as much as you do, she had a promising future. How may I help?"

Carla said, "Josh, do you have any male employees about six feet or so, and weighing at least two-hundred pounds or more, maybe a former football player?"

"Yeah, the only person that fits that description is Perry Desmond, I believe he was a linebacker at the university, but that was at least fifteen years ago. He is one of our male nurses, a damn good one at that."

Bernie asked, "Is he working today?"

"Yes, he is, he likes to pick up extra shifts. We had someone call in sick today, and he came in."

Carla said, "May we talk with him?"

"Yeah, but I doubt he's your guy, he has two kids, and his wife died a year ago. The kids are his life, and he wouldn't do something like this to jeopardize losing them."

Carla quickly responded, "We'll make that determination, would you please get him?"

"Of course, I'll be back with him in a minute."

Several minutes later, Josh returned with Perry Desmond, and right away, a sour expression graced Carla and Bernie's face. Perry fit the description initially; however, it was unlikely this severely overweight man with a noticeable limp could generate the force that pummeled AJ. Besides, he had a credible alibi the night she died. Perry told them he moonlights at a nursing home. While Carla was questioning him, Bernie called the nursing home verifying his alibi. As Perry left, Carla and Bernie sat dejected, searching for answers.

Taking advantage of the moment, Carla inquired, "Josh, did you work the night of AJ's last shift?"

"No, I work Monday through Friday, day shift."

Bernie said, "Tell us more about AJ, working habits, any complaints, um, was there anything brought to your attention about her that may help us?"

"Well, the only thing that comes to mind is what her mentor, Jackie Elder, said in passing one day. She told me she thought AJ was a little too friendly with some patients, especially males. Jackie worked that night, and maybe she might have information that would be helpful."

Carla said, "Is she working today?"

"Sorry, not until Friday."

Carla insistent on talking with her today asked, "Where does she live or what is her phone number? We must see her today."

"Tell you what, let me call her and see if she can come in today."

Carla said, "Thanks, we appreciate your cooperation."

Stepping out of the office, he returned a few minutes later, informing them she would meet with them in about thirty minutes.

Nodding, Bernie said, "We'll get a cup of coffee in the coffee shop and wait; let us know when she gets here."

While waiting for Jackie Elder to arrive, Carla and Bernie ordered coffee in the canteen discussing the case and their upcoming anger management class that night. Carla wasn't looking forward to it even though it might help her manage her impatience. Bernie, on the other hand, couldn't wait. Changing the subject, Bernie said, "Carla, you were actually nice to Josh, what's up with that?"

"Just trying to be a little more diplomatic, you know, uh, perceived a little differently."

"Well, maybe it's me wearing off on you, um, my charming personality and charisma."

"You are full of it and not just today, bite me."

Interrupting their friendly bantering, Josh said, "Jackie Elder is here and waiting in Jonathon's office."

Carla continued her bantering with Bernie. "It's every day, dickhead." Then she directed her attention to Josh. "We'll be right there."

Reaching Jonathon's office, Jackie sat waiting patiently for Carla and Bernie. Seeing them in the doorway, Jonathan motioned them in. Jackie rose to meet them.

"Nice to meet you, detectives, how may I help?"

Carla said, "How about we sit down. This could take a few minutes, okay?" Jackie and Jonathon returned to their chairs. "Thank you for coming in today. Now, Josh mentioned to us you told him you thought AJ was getting too friendly with patients. Tell us about that."

"AJ was great with patients, keeping them calm and at ease; however, it concerned me that some patients might perceive her personality differently. Usually, it would involve the male patients. She had a way of joking with them to make them feel at ease. However, they might take it the wrong way, you know, like maybe she was interested in them."

Carla interjected, "Doubt that, according to her father, she was a lesbian." It surprised both Jackie and Jonathon. Carla continued, "Is there any particular incident that stands out?"

"Yeah, it was AJ's Sunday shift, I guess her last one. It's so terrible what happened to her. Anyway, this good-looking guy came in about eleven that night, probably at least six feet tall, probably two-hundred pounds or more. AJ got him. Took his vitals and information on why he was here. I was in the exam area next to her and heard a little of the conversation. I believe he asked her for her phone number so that they could have a drink sometime. She said something to him, like maybe in your wildest dreams, Romeo. AJ dissed him big time, and he didn't like his ego getting crushed. She left, and Dr. Hanshaw took over."

Carla said, "Did she see him again?"

"Uh, I don't think so. Dr. Hanshaw finished with him, and she handled two other patients before her shift was over. AJ said in passing, he thought he was God's gift to women and that he was hitting on her big time, but she wasn't interested."

Carla said, "Who is this guy; we need all the information we can get?"

"His name is the best we can do, you know, HIPAA," said Jonathon. "Josh can pull up those records for you."

After a few keystrokes, Josh responded, "The patient's name is Bryan D. Walters."

Bernie said, "Thank you all; we appreciate your help, especially you, Ms. Elder."

CHAPTER 13

Back at the police station, Carla and Bernie Googled Bryan D. Walters, immediately his information loaded. He was a first-team All American in football several years back at the University of Kentucky. As an All-American linebacker, he signed a free-agent contract with the Cincinnati Bengals after he graduated. After being cut by the Bengals, the Cleveland Browns signed him to a free agent contract only to release him. His old knee injury did him in. They reviewed other information and discovered that Bryan D. Walters is the son of Bryan A. Walters, CEO of First Bank Trust and Savings, and a city commissioner as well.

With a solid lead, they left to visit Bryan A. Walters at First Bank Trust and Savings about his son. After a five-minute drive, they entered the bank and approached the receptionist identifying themselves while flashing their badges. Bernie asked the receptionist if Mr. Walters was in; she made a quick call and asked them to sit in the waiting area.

Expecting a man in his fifties, a much younger man,

probably late twenties or early thirties, approached and greeted them. They noticed that this man was favoring his right knee.

"Mr. Walters, I'm Detective Carla McBride, and this is my partner, Detective Bernie Kowalski, we liked to ask you a few questions about Alaina Gonzalez."

"Who?"

Carla replied, "Alaina Gonzalez, a nurse in the ER at the medical center, does that ring a bell?"

Shaking his head back-and-forth, he replied, "Let's go to my office, where it's more private to talk about this situation."

Bernie said, "Good idea, Romeo."

After entering his office, he motioned them to take a seat. While sitting behind his desk, bewilderment painted his face. "Detectives, I don't believe I know who she is, so, why are you here?"

Carla said, "Oh, I believe you do know her. You met her at the ER Sunday night. According to the information we have, she worked up your chart. You asked her for her phone number, and she blew you off. Do you remember that, Romeo?"

"Oh, I'd forgotten about that, yeah, I do remember her. I came in with stomach pains, and she took my information. Then the doctor examined me and gave me a prescription for food poisoning. I never saw her again. Did something happen to her?"

Bernie said, "She's dead, found at the jogging track at Lake Catalpa Tuesday morning. According to personnel that worked that Sunday night, they overheard you recommending that location to her since she was looking for a place to run. Now, she turns up dead there. Hard to believe that it is a mere coincidence, don't you think?"

"Look, I had nothing to do with her death. She seemed like a nice person and well, very hot. I mentioned to her about the Lake Catalpa jogging path, and I asked for her phone number, but that was it. Obviously, she wasn't interested, and I left it at that. Not the first time someone dissed me."

Carla said, "Where were you Sunday evening between Seven and Nine PM?"

"Home watching the NFL."

Bernie said, "Can anyone verify that?"

"Unfortunately, no, I was home alone as usual. Like I said, I had nothing to do with that nurse's death. Come on, detectives, I've never been in any trouble in my entire life."

Carla said, "We're just checking out leads. You seem to be favoring your right knee, what's wrong with it?"

"I'm a jogger. Tripped on something the other night. Fell scraping it, plus, it's sensitive from an old football injury."

Bernie said, "Where do you jog?"

"Mostly where I live. But occasionally, I jog around Lake Catalpa, but that's been a while. Anything else I may help you with?"

Carla replied, "That should do it, for now, Mr. Walters. Thank you for your time; we'll see ourselves out. And, by the way, don't leave town."

"Your welcome, if I can be of any further help, please let me know. Have a nice day, detectives."

Back in the car, they both felt that this guy was hiding something. Having two hours before they had to leave for Flemingsville, Carla had a hunch she wanted to check out at the crime scene before going to class. Carla knew forensics wasn't perfect, that you never know what you can find out the second time around just as she did in the Gold Fedora case. Arriving at Lake Catalpa, they parked as close as possible to the jogging path and walked the rest of the way to where AJ was found.

Looking around, Bernie said, "What are we looking for?"

"Remember Bryan favored his right knee, said he tripped jogging."

"Yeah, so, are we looking for where he may have fallen?"

"Sort of, let's imagine AJ jogging here in the early evening. Where we are standing would be the darkest area on the jogging path. Her body was lying down there with her feet only visible from the path. That probably meant the attacker was hiding behind those trees over there, or maybe, he was jogging behind her."

"Okay, then what?"

"She is jogging on the side where the path borders the lake. She passes the trees, Bryan takes off tackling her so hard that they hit the ground, she is struggling to breathe because she had the breath knocked out of her. He has control and places the ligature around her neck and tightens it. She is still struggling to breathe and can't scream for help."

"Yeah, I guess that's possible."

"Bryan turned her over and pulled down her jogging pants. Not realizing she is dead, he panics, and that's why there was no sexual assault. He leaves the black rose and then takes off jogging around the path until he reaches his car."

"Great theory, and you might be right, but what are we looking for?"

"Let's look for any rocks or hard objects he may have

hit with his knee when falling to the ground. If that happened, something could be in the brush or rolled down the embankment."

Looking around in the brush a few feet to the right and then to the left, nothing caught their attention. Carla kept telling Bernie that something was here, but maybe they had to think out of the box. Retracing their steps, they ended up back where AJ was found. Looking toward the rocky shoreline, Bernie noticed something that didn't seem right, kind of out of place.

Down the embankment toward the lake was a small block of wood, like a piece of treated lumber used to support decks. It looked out of place because there weren't any other pieces of wood on the rocky shoreline below. Walking down the embankment, Carla put rubber gloves on and picked it up. Looking it over, there appeared to be some black fibers embedded in it. Further examination showed there was also some discoloration on the corner where the dark fibers were embedded. It looked similar to dried blood.

"Great job, Bernie. This block of wood could be what we need to put Bryan Walters away. Maybe we just found that needle in the haystack."

After returning to Carla's car and placing the block of wood in an evidence bag, they headed back to the police station to log it in as evidence and requesting that forensics examine and test it for DNA. Carla instructed Sherry to put a rush on it. Everything Carla turned in was a rush job. The big clock on the wall indicated it was time for them to leave for Flemingsville for their class that evening.

CHAPTER 14

Arriving ten minutes early in front of the building that housed their class, Bernie shook his head back-and-forth at Carla as they exited her car. After a short walk up one flight of steps and down a short walkway, the building was upon them. Entering through a set of double doors, they took a right, and their class-room was the first door on the left.

The lecture hall was small and dimly lit like a small movie theatre. It appeared to have about forty seats. Choosing seats in the middle of the last row gave them a good view of everyone else. She felt right at home because when she attended Sunday Mass, that's where she sat in the back pew. If she received a call during church, she could exit without too much distraction. That would work here as well because of the rear exit.

Even though the lighting in the room was inadequate, bright lights illuminated the lecture podium. Entering the lecture hall, a man took the podium like a veteran professor. Carla recognized him the moment the lights hit his face. She whispered to Bernie, "That's the guy I told you about in apartment thirty-one. This class will be interesting if I might say. Remember, I thought he was hiding something, I still do."

"Carla, I can't wait for you…"

"Good evening class, I'm Professor Don Smith. You can call me, Professor Don, if you like. This is Conflict and Anger Management 101; if you are not here to learn how to manage your anger, confrontation, and conflict better, then you should leave now. This class is about you, and only you. I'm here to facilitate the discussion so you can better manage both, no textbook is required. This class is about student interaction and role-playing. So, I hope everyone is ready to learn. For me to get to know you and for you to get to know your classmates, we will begin with a simple introductory exercise. First, everyone must choose a new seat and sit beside someone you don't know."

Every individual got up, looked around, and chose a new seat. Carla moved one row down while Bernie went for a chair in the second row. "Now, I want you to introduce yourself to individuals seated near you." A few minutes went by, and the chatter echoed off the walls. "Okay, now that we got that out of the way. Each of you will take two minutes to introduce yourself to all of us. Please tell us your name, occupation, why you are here, and what you want to get out of the class. Normally, I would start in the front; however, tonight, we will start in the back. The gentleman in the last row, first seat on the left, will start us off. Then we will begin with the first person in the next row going right to left. Please pay attention and be ready when it's your turn. Stand up and speak loudly. The man in the last row may now begin this important exercise."

"Hi, everyone. I'm Ken Edmunds, human resources director of Macron Industries. I deal with conflict and confrontation every day in my job, and I want to learn more, so I can teach employees how to handle it better. If I can do this, my job gets a little easier."

Professor Smith replied, "Great, next."

The introductions continued, and finally, the person next to Carla stood up and informed the class of her information and sat back down. Carla wasn't paying much attention to any of the introductions because her mind was still on Alaina Gonzalez because she didn't deserve to die that way; no one did. Oblivious to what was going on, Professor Don noticed Carla staring into nothingness.

Professor Don said, "Next." Carla was still in another world. Students were staring at her, and she paid no attention to them or Professor Don. Agitated, Professor Don said, "Next." Carla felt the lady next to her tap her on the arm; she finally realized that it was her turn. Standing up, Professor Don recognized her.

"Hi everyone, my apologies, I was doing a little daydreaming." She heard some snickering in the background. "Okay, folks, button it up, you can't tell me you've never daydreamed in class or at work before. So, get over it. Anyway, I'm Detective Carla McBride of the Oakmont Police Department." That got some oohs and awes from the class. "I'm here because my chief thinks I have anger issues. Well, folks, I don't, so this class is probably a waste of taxpayer funds. Next."

Agitated at Carla's lack of respect for the class,

Professor Don stepped in front of the podium to address her. "Detective McBride, since you have disrupted this class already, would you please tell us why you were daydreaming?"

"Seriously, it's none of your business; it's my private thoughts."

"Detective McBride, haven't we met before?"

"You already know that, so, why did you ask me that?"

"Tell the class how we know each other."

"I was conducting what turned out to be a death investigation of a young lady who lived across from you, isn't that right, professor?"

"Class, I think you can see why Detective McBride really needs this class. It's amazing that she ever solves any cases at all with that kind of condescending attitude. Who's next?"

Fuming inside, she wanted to fire back at him; however, she decided differently and returned to her chair with egg on her face. Finally, it was Bernie's turn. He stood up and introduced himself and that Carla was his partner. You could hear multiple people mumble "lucky you" throughout the lecture hall.

When the introductions ended, Professor Don addressed the class. "Okay, everyone, thank you for being so honest tonight. Honesty is a big part of what you will learn in managing conflict and anger. That will be it for tonight. Next week we will begin with some role-playing, which should be very interesting."

Silence captivated them on the trip back to Oakmont, and Carla couldn't wait to get home and taste Jameson, her liquid lover. A stiff drink was what she needed to wash away the embarrassment she suffered at the hands of Professor Don, and Jameson Irish Whiskey would fit the bill. As her head hit the pillow, her last thought was about how she would get even with him before the semester ended.

CHAPTER 15

While Jameson washed away the bad memories from last night's class and confrontation with Professor Don, a long hot shower would wash away any staleness leftover from the previous day. Reflecting on last night, she felt she got the best of him in the beginning, but he got the last word in, and that pissed her off to no means. She still couldn't get it out of her mind that Professor Don was hiding something from his past. Hell, maybe even who he was, or who he had been. For a moment, she also thought that he looked similar to John Dickerson.

However, she put that thought out of her mind because John was younger and in a witness protection program somewhere. Besides, she needed to focus her energies on finding who murdered Alaina James Gonzalez. Bryan Walters was a person of interest, and she hoped something on the piece of wood they found yesterday implicated him.

Carla arrived at the police station in a very cheerful mood. As she walked to her desk, her colleagues kept their eyes glued on her like some Greek Goddess. Maybe it was Nike, the Greek Goddess of Victory. Confident and strutting her stuff this morning, she was ready to kick ass, taking no prisoners. As she sat at her desk facing Bernie, who was already hard at work, she sent a grin of superiority his way.

Even though he had just flipped her the bird, she was still ready to have a great day, and hopefully, solve the Black Rose case. It all came to a crashing halt as Chief Evans appeared at her desk. Looking disgusted, he had a mean scowl on his face, which usually meant all hell would break loose real soon. Placing his hands on her desk, he softly but forcefully said, "Both of you, in my office now!"

Wondering what got him all bent out of shape so early in the day, they entered his office. She thought maybe he got up on the wrong side of the bed or perhaps he wanted some last night and his wife said no. Regardless of what it was, they knew he was freaking pissed at them, or for that matter, maybe the whole damn world today. The slamming of the door echoed into the common area.

Motioning them to take a seat, he addressed them with anger in his voice. "Marching into First Bank Trust and Savings and accusing Bryan 'The Crusher' Walters of having something to do with that jogger found in the park, what the hell is going on with you two?"

As she often did, Carla spoke when she shouldn't have. "Chief, that jogger has a name, Alaina James Gonzalez, everyone called her AJ."

"Button it up McBride; I'll let you know when you can speak. Do you even know who Bryan Walters is? Son of Bryan A. Walters, CEO of First Bank Trust and

Savings and the most powerful city commissioner. His son is a legend in this community. First-team All American linebacker and pro with the Bengals and Browns. If he hadn't screwed up when he was a sophomore and then messed up his knee in his senior year, he'd be playing in the NFL today. What were you guys thinking? Please explain what the hell is going on, will you, Carla?"

As Bernie remained silent, Carla replied, "We interviewed Jackie Elder, AJ's mentor in the ER, and she told us about her next to the last patient Sunday night, that being Bryan Walters. She said that AJ told her he was coming on to her and wanted her phone number, she wanted no part of it. She dissed him, and he didn't like that."

"And that's a reason to accuse him of attempted rape and murder."

"Chief, he met the criteria based on the coroner's report, and we followed through on it."

"You screwed up, Carla You should have come to me immediately, we could have handled this a little differently."

"Okay, okay. You mentioned about Bryan screwing up as a sophomore, what's that about?"

"It's nothing. It's one of those 'he said-she said' issues. The cheerleader acknowledged consensual sex with him the first time. But he was evidently, horny as hell, and wanted more to celebrate a big victory. She said no, the second time around. He didn't listen and continued anyway, and she gave in to him. A few weeks later, she accused him of rape. We arrested him, but eventually, all charges were dropped probably because of an undisclosed financial settlement. Had he been convicted, his professional career was toast."

"So, he has a wild streak in him, even more reason that he could be our man."

"I don't think so since then he has been a model citizen and has done well at the bank. Why screw all that up by being dissed by some little nurse."

"Chief, she has a name, and if Bryan is our man, we'll get him. We found additional evidence at the crime scene. If it turns out as we think, we'll need to get a DNA sample from the All-American boy."

"His DNA is already on file from the previous 'he said-she said' issue."

"Okay, but don't you really mean rape, because it was rape when the cheerleader said no, right?"

"Carla, watch your mouth. Now, how about class last night, how did that go?"

Bernie snickered and chimed in, "As I expected chief, Carla, and the professor had a lively conversation, you know what I mean, don't you? In the end, Professor Don got the best of her."

"Shit, Carla, when are you ever going to learn to be quiet and be less authoritarian? I don't want to hear anything bad coming from that professor at Flemingsville College; you got it? Don't answer that question; just get the hell out of here. I need to go smooth things over with Mayor James and Commissioner Walters."

CHAPTER 16

When Carla and Bernie left the chief's office and returned to their respective desks, her message light was flashing rapidly. She hit the button, listened, and hung up very quickly. Without saying a word to Bernie, Carla bolted. She was on a mission, and her destination was the forensic department. Bernie, realizing that, sprinted after her. Sherry was waiting for Carla as she entered the lab.

"Sherry, you got something?"

"Yeah, as you suspected. We found synthetic fibers embedded in the piece of wood. The fibers are generic and probably came from any jogging pants sold in thousands of stores or online. What's more interesting was what else we found. Skin probably from an abrasion was embedded in the wood. However, something already came back on the black silk rose found on her body that may be more important."

"That's fascinating, Sherry, what is it?

"DNA."

"Tell me it belongs to Bryan D. Walters."

"You wish, it's a match to a dead man. You ever heard of Hank Fisher?"

"Yeah, it rings a bell, do you have anything else on this Hank Fisher?"

"Report says he, along with Charles Brown, died in a boating accident over two years ago. Their bodies were never found."

"Are you sure?"

"Ran it twice, the same result. Sorry to burst your bubble Carla, but that's all we found. It looks like you've got your work cut out for you looking for a dead man now. Good luck with that."

"Shit, that's it, I've got to call Al Bocconi now. Thanks." Sherry nodded and went on about her business.

"Carla, who the hell is Al Bocconi?"

Ignoring Bernie's question, Carla remembered where she heard Hank Fisher's name before. He and Charles Brown surfaced during her last case, the Gold Fedora. Hank Fisher, aka Frog and Charles Brown, aka Peanuts, were members of Alpha Tango Special Forces with Spike, Tater, Rocky, and Casanova. She explained everything to Bernie. Who's who and who's dead.

"Bernie, we need to go see the chief and let him know this case has really turned bizarre, plus I need to apologize to him about this morning. We also need to pay a visit to Bryan 'The Crusher' Walters and apologize to him as well."

"Is this really Detective Carla McBride I'm talking with, wanting to apologize to the chief and Bryan Walters?"

Rather than responding verbally, Carla shot him the bird. Bernie shook his head back-and-forth, grinning ear-to-ear. After meeting with Chief Evans, Carla returned to her desk where everybody was staring at her because the look on her face said she just got her ass reamed. Ignoring her co-workers, Carla sat down, staring at her phone. Her voicemail light lit up, she hit the button and listened. At first, she thought to herself that it was probably Hank Fisher calling her from the bottom of the Gulf of Mexico; however, it was Marsh Robinson from the Daily Reporter. She was no mood to call him back; however, she knew he was relentless.

At first, she wasn't going to tell him they had DNA belonging to a dead man at the bottom of the Gulf of Mexico. But the more she thought about it, maybe she should tell him that. He wouldn't believe her if she did, so why not have a little fun with him. She called and explained her cockamamie story, and as she thought, he just laughed and told her when she had something concrete, to call him back.

Finding Al Bocconi's phone number, she dialed it. The call went straight to a standard voicemail message. Evidently, he had never personalized his voicemail greeting since they last spoke. She left him a message to call her as soon as possible. She put her hands to her face to hide a single tear in her eye. The Gold Fedora case had taken its toll on her, and now it was rearing its ugly head all over again.

Opening her laptop, she Googled Hank Fisher. After her search information loaded, she found what she was looking for, the story about the boating accident. It was straightforward, just as Al had told her several weeks ago. The boat exploded, scattering the wreckage everywhere. There weren't any bodies or body parts found in the area. Hank Fisher and his friend, Charles Brown, were never found or heard of again until possibly now.

Feeling overwhelmed, she redialed Al Bocconi. It went straight to voicemail as before. She Googled him and the most recent information loaded. As her eyes flew open, she searched again with the same result. Four-letter expletives filled the common area interrupting the peacefulness.

An obituary of Al Bocconi was on her screen. Below the obituary was a news story. It read Al, along with his dog, Rocket, died in a hit-and-run accident one morning before daylight. He was out jogging with his dog when the accident happened. There weren't any witnesses, and the death investigation was ongoing. End of the story and Al Bocconi as well. Closing her laptop, she put her head down on her desk until Bernie tapped her on the arm.

"What's going on in that little brain of yours?"

"Not a damn thing…not a damn thing."

She informed him that Al Bocconi had turned up dead in a suspicious hit-and-run accident in Pensacola, Florida. She hoped that Al could shed some light on Hank Fisher. Now, she was hunting for a dead man, and the only possible person that could have helped her was Al Bocconi, and he was now dead.

As far as Carla knew, the only other living member of Alpha Tango Special Forces was in a federal witness protection program somewhere. She knew Chief Evans wasn't going to like it, but she needed to meet with FBI Agents Slack and Stewart again.

CHAPTER 17

Laura and Walt spent time each evening planning their wedding, finally settling on the second Saturday of April next year. A late afternoon wedding at the Memorial Gazebo overlooking Lake Catalpa would be the perfect setting for their wedding ceremony. Avondale Country Club would be the ideal spot for the reception under a big tent accented with twinkling lights nestled in the ceiling like shining stars raining down from the heavens.

Reservations for all aspects of the wedding were complete. Laura, a non-practicing Catholic, had chosen Father Tim O'Brien of St. Anthony's to preside over their ceremony during a full Mass. Baptized in St. Peter's Episcopal Church, Walt hadn't been to church in a very long time. So, the choice was perfect for the wedding. Now, they just had to fine-tune everything and wait for their big day to arrive.

Walt had just returned from the Kentucky Press Association's annual convention, where the Daily Reporter took top honors in their circulation category. First in

General Excellence, sounded damn sweet to him and Chad Atley, his boss in Altmont. Walt expected his newspaper to be at the top every year, and nothing else would be acceptable. It had been a long drought for his newspaper since it even finished in the top three, so this award was especially sweet.

The Daily Reporter was also up for the best overall property of the year honors in the company. Their series on the Gold Fedora case, which was top-notch, told the whole story of Mark and Joanne Alison's murders as well as the subsequent murders of Frank Ramsey, Jr., and Wylie Adkins. The paper, especially Walt Blevins and Editor Todd Hailey, helped bring John Dickerson, a powerful senator from Florida, to justice even though it didn't turn out as they hoped.

With a storybook romance, Laura and Walt were the talk of the town. Many in town thought they had the perfect relationship. And in many ways, their lives strangely resembled Mark and Joanne Alison. Laura was an up-and-coming lawyer while Walt was quickly becoming a rising star in the community as well as in the American Newspaper Company. Life was good, and they had their whole future in front of them.

Ever since Carla involved Walt in the Gold Fedora case, she had the run of the newspaper. She didn't bother checking in with the receptionist anymore when visiting him, and today would be no different. Opening the main doors, she went straight to his office. Seeing Carla in the doorway, he motioned her to sit down. After replying to an important email, he said, "Sometimes, I feel like you are on my payroll."

"Walt, you couldn't afford me."

He laughed and shook his head back-and-forth.

"What's on your mind? I know you are not here to check on the wedding plans for Laura and me, are you?"

"No, but I want to hear about them after we finish. Do you remember the two members of the Alpha Tango presumed dead in a boating accident?"

"Yeah, what about them?"

"Do you remember the lady jogger murdered in the park, AJ Gonzalez?" Walt nodded as she continued, "Well, there was male DNA found on her body. Anyway, guess whose DNA it is?"

"I don't have time for a guessing game."

"Ah, Mr. Publisher, don't be such a sour puss. Anyway, we thought it might belong to Bryan D. Walters; a patient AJ saw in ER a couple of nights before she died. However, we were wrong. It belongs to Hank Fisher, aka Frog of Alpha Tango, yep, a dead man."

"How is that even possible?"

"I don't know, but we will find out."

His ears perked up, and he grinned, "Did I just hear we; does that mean we are a team again?"

"Yeah, I guess so, but you must play by my rules, no playing cop. I need your help in finding out as much as possible about the boating accident and Hank Fisher and Charles Brown. Maybe your sister papers in Florida can help us just like they did with John Dickerson."

"Yeah, I'll have Todd make some calls, and we will go from there, how's that sound?"

"Great, I always knew you were a team player, now, how about telling me about those wedding plans?"

"I'm sure you have spoken with Laura since you are her maid of honor and helped with picking out her gown, so what else do you want to know?"

"Who's the best man, Mr. Publisher?"

"Best friend back home, Huey Carlson, we've been friends since grade school."

"I thought maybe it would be Chris since he will be your brother-in-law."

"No, but he understands why it's not him. By the way, did you and Chris ever have a thing for each other?"

"Nah, Chris is like a brother to me, besides I don't have time for relationships, and if I did, it would never last long with my unpredictable work schedule and all."

"Don't sell yourself short, I've seen the way he looks at you, it's not a brother-sister kind of look. I think he has had a crush on you for a long time, and at the Christmas celebration, I saw how you looked at him as well. Don't let time pass you by; life is too short not to fall in love with someone. I finally found my soulmate, maybe Chris is yours."

Like always, she changed the subject so she wouldn't have to address that. "Hey, thanks for helping me get information on Peanuts and Frog, gotta run, say hello to my girl Laura, will ya?"

"Will do, hey, would you want to come over tonight and have dinner with us? Chris will stop by as well, plus one other couple. Amelia and Zakk Wolfe, I think Amelia works with Laura. We hope to complete our wedding plans and would like your input."

"Thanks, maybe I will, but don't get your hopes up, I've got to catch a killer, and well, you know me. Oh, one other thing I forgot to tell you."

"What's that?"

"Al Bocconi, the retired FBI agent we talked to, well, he's now dead. A suspicious hit-and-run accident while out on a jog one morning. No witnesses and no suspects. It seems like everybody in Alpha Tango is dead except dear old John Dickerson, who, by the way, is in a federal witness protection program."

"Really, where?"

"Only the feds know, and they said it was none of our business."

"Holy shit, and now you have DNA from a dead man show up, what the hell is going on and what's next?"

A shrug of the shoulders, she closed her eyes and shook her head back-and-forth. After leaving the newspaper, anxiety crashed her soul.

CHAPTER 18

With Bryan Walters no longer a suspect, all that Carla and Bernie had to go on was a black rose and a dead man's DNA. The black rose found on AJ could have been purchased anywhere. A Google search showed that a few stores in Oakmont carried them.

Their first stop was All Thinks Macabre in downtown. The regional company had stores in several communities throughout Central and Eastern Kentucky. They had noticed the one in Flemingsville the other day and would check it out next week before class. They felt there was no need to make a special trip today just for that.

The murder occurred in Oakmont, and that's where they would start. All Things Macabre had everything black. It was more like a specialty clothing store. If you wanted black clothes, this was undoubtedly the place to find them. They had a section where you could find accessories for the macabre in you. That's where they found the black roses. A salesclerk noticed Carla and

Bernie browsing around and approached them, "May I help you with anything?"

Carla said, "Black Roses, are they a big seller here?"

"Yeah, and not just around Halloween."

Carla said, "Really, what kind of person would buy them?"

"Just about anyone, I know that's hard to believe since they are a symbol of death and other morbid things. You know, some people buy them as gag gifts when they hit that over the hill age, isn't that the big five-o?"

Bernie said, "Anymore, I think it could be the big four-o as well. Did anyone purchase any in the last week or so?"

"Let me see; we just got a new order last month. Umm, we ordered a dozen, and that's what we still have. So, I guess not."

Bernie said, "Okay, thank you for your time, and by the way, here's my card. If someone comes in to purchase any, would you please let us know?"

Nodding, she read Bernie's business card. "Wow, so you're a detective, that's pretty cool. You all come back."

Next up was Dark World. Browsing around the store, they could tell this place was weird. It was more about macabre items rather than what was at All Things Macabre. The store had bizarre things ranging from dangling eyeballs to even soda in black cans with weird names such as Black Blood Cola, which filled the shelves. Finally, they found the black roses. A strange-looking guy approached them.

"May I help you find something for the weird friend in your life?"

Bernie said, "We're not into weird, but we are into black roses."

"Groovy, man. We got them as you can see. How many do you want?"

Bernie said, "We're not here to buy, we need information. Did anyone buy a bunch of them lately?"

"Uh, let's see, um, no, man. People are usually buying just one, you know…"

"Yeah, I know, for the big one."

"Right, man, you're pretty cool."

"Well, thank you, here's my card in case anyone comes in wanting to buy several."

"Whoa, Detective Bernie Kowalski, that's heavy stuff. You're the first cop I've had in here that's interested in a black rose, now that's cool."

As they were leaving, Carla said, "Bernie, you should have bought one and made that kid's day."

"I can't believe what is becoming of the young kids today. I think the world is in a real heap of trouble if you know what I mean. What's next?"

"I think it's time for lunch. Is McGruder's okay with you, partner?"

"Sounds good."

A short time later, they entered McGruder's and sat in the booth at the front of the pub near the main entrance. Carla always liked to sit there because she could still see who's coming and going. It was at the height of lunch hour, and the place was busy as hell, and they were lucky they even got a booth. She already knew what she would order while Bernie took his time, but in the end, he always ordered the same thing.

Seeing them come in and take the corner booth, a waitress approached them. "Hi, I'm Mandy, are you both ready to order?"

Carla said, "Rueben, house chips and unsweetened iced tea with lemon."

"What may I get you, sir?"

"Fish and chips, extra tartar sauce, and sweet tea."

"You got it; I'll put your order in and be right back with your drinks."

It had been a while since Carla had been in McGruder's. She had painful memories of Sam, who used to work there. Because Rocky was dead, she might never know what happened to her.

Their lunches arrived, and Carla dived into her Reuben. Bernie, on the other hand, just picked at his fish and chips. While eating in silence, they enjoyed people watching and the downtime. They watched people from all walks of life taking time out of their day for a nice lunch and a break from the rat race. After they finished their meals, they headed back into the real world to solve real crimes, especially the Black Rose case.

As they went out the main door, two men entered from the side door and bellied-up to the bar. They ordered Smithwick's Irish Ale and checked out all the badges that adorned the walls and the coat of arms flags that hung from the metal trusses above.

CHAPTER 19

Walt's research turned up the same material as Carla's research, which was mostly about the accident and the search for their bodies. He searched by each name, the business name, by scuba diving companies, fishing excursions, anything that might turn up some credible information. Reading through multiple search pages, he found a story about the number of excursion companies going under in Florida because of competition and the recession. One story caught his eye. The story featured one company that was struggling to survive, Fisher Excursions and More owned by Hank Fisher and Charles Brown.

In the story, Hank Fisher explained to the reporter how challenging the business had become because of the Great Recession. The interview touched on the many reasons for the struggling industry. He explained his business was also feeling pressure from their bank because they were behind on mortgage payments. Also, in the story, Hank Fisher told the reporter that if the business climate didn't improve in the months ahead, they would likely have to close their business. And most likely, if they couldn't sell their boat, the bank would take it over, and they would have to file bankruptcy.

After noticing the date of the story, Walt wondered whether they planned the accident to alleviate their financial commitments. He wondered if these guys would do that to free themselves from debt. Anything was possible; after all, they were members of a special forces unit and were very resourceful. It was a crazy theory, he thought, but he knew desperate people took desperate measures to survive.

Thinking out of the box, if Hank Fisher and Charles Brown faked their deaths, they must have had an accomplice in helping them begin a new life somewhere else. John Dickerson flashed in his mind. Being a powerful senator and real estate developer, he certainly would have the resources to do it. He remembered from their conversation with Al Bocconi that they were like brothers and would do anything for each other.

Searching Alpha Tango again, not much was available on the special forces unit; however, scrolling further down the search list revealed one item that caught his attention. Alpha and Tango Excursions in Bayside, Texas, was created in 2009 at the height of the Great Recession and raised a red flag in his mind. It was about the same time that Hank Fisher, aka Frog, and Charles Brown, aka Peanuts, presumably died in a boating accident. The story listed Grayson Hewitt and Parker Bowen as current owners of the business; however, there weren't any pictures of them.

A more advanced search using Hank Fisher, Charles Brown, John Dickerson, and Fisher Excursions and More revealed a story published several years ago. He opened up the news story and read where Hank Fisher, Charles Brown, and John Dickerson, aka Casanova, had joined together to form Fisher Excursions and More. A photo in the story identified the three of them in the company's boat, Easy Living. That was a connection; John Dickerson was a silent partner in the business. Walt downloaded the complete story, including the photo.

Walt performed a search on Al Bocconi again; the story about the hit-and-run accident followed his obit. A recent photo of Al was just below the headline that read; Retired FBI Agent Found Dead. As an ongoing investigation, no one had come forward, and apparently, there weren't any witnesses. His dog, Rocket, died in the accident as well. At the end of the story, if anyone had information, they should call Detective Jimmy Ramirez at the following number. He printed and downloaded that story as well.

Leaning back in his chair and massaging his temples, he pondered all the possibilities no matter how farfetched they were. First, every member of Alpha Tango except John was dead, or so it seemed. Walt wrote down assumptions and created an organizational chart for Alpha Tango. Al had told them that Casanova, Peanuts, and Frog were extremely tight, like brothers, and because of that, they likely started an excursion company together.

He put them on one side of the paper. Then he listed Spike, Tater, and Rocky beside them. Six names across a sheet of copier paper, landscape style. Spike, Tater, and Rocky were all dead. Staging Peanuts and Frog's deaths would eliminate their financial obligations. With the help of John, they could begin a new life somewhere safe and debt-free.

Al tipped off the FBI about John Dickerson. Taken into custody on multiple charges, John agreed to testify against Edwardo Cavalla, and gets immunity and entered the federal witness protection program until he can testify against Cavalla. Al conveniently ends up dead from a hit-and-run accident. He concluded that if his theory that Peanuts and Frog were alive, then maybe they were carrying out a request from John to seek revenge on Al for tipping off the FBI. That tip destroyed John's life and ambitions of possibly running for Governor of Florida as well as President of the United States one day.

Thinking about his cockamamie theory, he laughed out loud at such a possibility. As quickly as he enjoyed his preposterous laugh, a flushed-face replaced his humor as his attitude turned somber-like. Fear drifted in and out of his mind realizing that if Hank Fisher and Charles Brown were alive, then anyone associated with him and Carla could be in real danger.

CHAPTER 20

While waiting for guests to arrive for an evening of friendship, Laura and Walt were already enjoying a glass of Silver Oak Cabernet and rehashing the unimportant things in their day. Laura had a way of easing his fears; just the sight of her changed a sour attitude to one of gratitude and happiness. With Laura wearing tight-fitting designer jeans and a form-fitting knit blouse, Walt's face lit up, chasing away all concerns facing him.

Her straight and silky dark hair resting on her adequate, but firm breasts created fantasies in his mind. As he stared at her haunting green eyes, he planted a soft-sultry kiss on her lips. She smiled and moved in for a much deeper kiss of passion and fire. As he tasted her sexiness, the doorbell chimed, and they released to cool the fires burning inside. The doorbell sounded again; she gazed into his eyes and smiled. He knew that smile and that sparkle in her eyes was a signal of a night of sensual pleasure.

While Laura walked to answer the door, Walt positioned himself behind the bar separating the kitchen from the great room; he needed time to cool his jets down. Expecting Amelia and Zakk because they were always early, Carla surprised her. She was never early for anything social, but business was another story. Giving Carla a big-time sisterly hug, Laura directed her to the bar fronting the kitchen where Walt was preparing drinks. It was the focal point of gatherings at Laura and Walt's home.

"So nice to see my girl again, what can I get you to drink?"

"Jameson would be nice."

Walt was on his game, a Jameson on the rocks sat on the bar as she approached. Carla and Walt greeted each other with high-fives, a tradition after teaming up to solve the Gold Fedora case, and now they were a team again.

"Hey, Walt, did you find out anything on what we talked about yesterday?"

"Working on it. Let's keep tonight strictly a social evening. No business stuff tonight."

"Okay, sourpuss."

Laura arrived at the bar where she caught Walt with two fingers to his lips, hushing Carla. Laura asked, "Now, what are you two discussing? Come on now; we don't keep secrets from each other."

"Of course, as always, not a word to anyone. I thought we had a sure suspect in the jogger killed near Lake Catalpa; however, forensics discovered DNA belonging to a man that's been dead for several years."

Laughing immediately, Laura choked on her drink and coughed a few times. "Seriously, if that's true, that's not a good thing." Simultaneously, Carla and Walt acknowledged her, while remnants of concern slowly traveled across their brow. "I guess that answers that question. Carla, why do you need Walt's help?"

Chimes filled the room, saving Carla. Answering the door, Laura expected Amelia and Zakk; however, it was her brother, Chris. Hugging him, she planted a soft kiss on his cheek. Laura and Chris were very tight as a brother and sister could be. Since their parents died years ago by a drunk driver, all they had growing up was each other. Standing at the bar, Carla smiled, lighting up Chris's face. Walking over to the bar, he gave Walt a friendly handshake. Chris and Walt were becoming more like brothers than good friends.

Facing Carla, hoping for a hug, she extended her hand. Dejected, Chris reciprocated. He knew Carla was not the hugging type unless she was in a serious relationship with someone. She had always been like that even though they had known each other for many years. Their relationship was more like Laura and Chris, brother and sister style. Carla was a mysterious woman, and Chris knew their relationship might never move beyond what they had now.

Laura's cell phone rang, interrupting the quiet and reserved conversation. She answered and stepped away to have a private conversation. Ending the call, she rejoined everyone, still solving the world's problems. Laura informed them that Amelia and Zakk had to cancel, their two-year-old son, Chase, was sick.

"I'm sorry you guys won't get to meet them, maybe another time. It's just the four us, so let's enjoy each other's company."

Chris enjoying a glass of Silver Oak Cabernet, interjected, "Sounds good to me, how about you, Carla?"

"Yeah, why not. I'm off duty, and hopefully, nothing will happen tonight like before Christmas."

Walt responded, "Well, you better knock on wood."

Rolling her eyes and flipping him an indiscreet bird, the conversation continued while enjoying their drinks. Everyone was becoming more relaxed while reminiscing about their golf outing back in the fall and what went down that day. Although it wasn't funny at the time because of Joanne Alison's death, they could laugh about it now and tease one another, especially about Walt being a person of interest.

The conversation moved to the great room where a modern steel and glass coffee table separated two eclectic chairs from the love seat. Laura and Walt purposely left wedding planner books and packages in those chairs. Suggesting that Carla and Chris sit on the love seat, Laura removed the stuff in the chairs after they were situated on the love seat.

Appetizers were moved to the coffee table to keep Carla and Chris there. The Laura-Walt conspiracy was working perfectly, Carla and Chris were having a private conversation by themselves. Recognizing this, Laura and Walt retreated to the kitchen to refresh everyone's drink. While in the kitchen, they couldn't help eavesdropping on the discussion on the loveseat.

"Carla, you know our relationship has been more like a brother-sister one for a long time. I want more than that, and I'd like to change that and take you out on an actual date."

"Chris." A big sigh filled the loveseat. "Chris, I love you as a brother and enjoy being with you, but I'm not good for you. I've got baggage, and my work consumes every waking moment of my life, I guess I'm obsessed with fighting crime and have no time for serious relationships."

"Yeah, I understand that, but I would play second fiddle to your work if you just gave me a chance. Maybe we could have lunch or dinner sometime, only the two of us and talk about it. What do you say?"

"Let me think about it. Why don't you call me next week, and we'll see where that takes us, okay?"

"Great, just give me a chance."

As Laura and Walt were returning to their chair, Chris was wiping a big smile off his face. They thought for a moment their conspiracy plan was working, Carla and Chris were acting like a couple rather than like a sibling relationship.

Laura said, "Carla, what are you two talking about; it looked rather serious, don't hold out on us?"

"Oh, just reminiscing again. Guess I better run, I've got a busy day tomorrow chasing down leads, and whatever might surface. You never know in my business what it might be. Could be something good or maybe not, you never know."

Chris interjected, "Yeah, I should run as well. Thanks for a great evening. Carla, may I walk you out?"

"What a gentleman you are Chris, thank you."

CHAPTER 21

Arriving at the police station bright and early, Carla, wearing a big and different attitude after last night's needed diversion, waited for Bernie to arrive. Working without him, she researched her only lead, a dead man named Hank Fisher. Unfortunately, the material found in her previous searches wasn't of much help. There were multiple reports of the accident, but nothing new was out there.

While waiting for Bernie, who never watched the clock, she turned her focus to the black silk rose. Her searches revealed information across the board, which was of no help to her until one story popped-up piquing her interest. Fifteen years ago, a man obsessed with a younger woman, left one on her windshield several nights in a row. Eventually, police staked out her house and caught the individual. It was a strange story of obsession; he just wanted her attention. Weird, she thought and shook her head back-and-forth. Fully engrossed in the story, she hadn't noticed Bernie staring at her.

She murmured to herself, "What a sick, dark obsession."

"Carla, did you say something about a sick, dark obsession?"

"Didn't see you come in. Just reading about black roses and came upon this story where a man was obsessed with a young woman. Police caught him, and he said he didn't mean to harm or frighten her. He just wanted her attention."

"Yeah, that's pretty sick. What else did you find out about black roses?"

"Not much, just that it symbolizes death, destruction, darkness, and all those weird psychotic things. I also did a little research on our dead man, had a fishing and diving business, legit by all standards, and get this; his partner was none other than Charles Brown. This whole accident is weird."

"In what way?"

"If it was a fishing excursion, what happened to their clientele? If it wasn't, what were they doing that far out partying, wasting fuel, and other things? That business is very expensive and all, so maybe they planned the accident and faked their deaths."

"Have you checked your mailbox yet today?"

"No, I usually wait until about Ten AM, but if you want to, by all means, have at it."

Bernie left to go pick up their mail. At the same time, Carla continued to search the web for anything connected to black roses, AJ Gonzalez, Hank Fisher, or Charles Brown. She couldn't believe how many individuals named Charles Brown were out there. Bernie returned, holding a small package and showed it to her.

"Just toss it on the desk, I'll open it later after I finish my due diligence."

Tossing it on her desk, he said, "You might want to look at it now."

"Why?"

"Just look at it, I have a bad feeling."

Looking at him strangely, she picked up the manila envelope staring at the address label or lack of one. Different colored letters and numbers, which had been cut out and pasted on it, formed the address label. Creepy, she thought, turning it over, tape sealed the envelope rather than the usual way with the metal clasp. Being careful not to contaminate it, but then again, Bernie had already done that when he took it out of her mailbox. Feeling it, she immediately knew it was more than just a letter; it contained something oblong.

While outlining the contents of the package, a scary thought crossed her mind. Using a letter opener, she slipped it carefully under the flap. Opening it, she peeked inside; its contents left her breathless. As her pulse skyrocketed, a ghastly shade of pale painted her otherwise rosy complexion. Turning it upside down, she shook it gently, letting the contents of the envelope fall out onto her desk.

A black rose with a strip of paper shook her to her core. Catching her breath, she shook the envelope up and down to see if anything else would fall out, but nothing did. Returning her attention to the black rose on her desk, she picked it up, reading the message on the strip of paper.

It read… *Ye who hath received a single black rose shall be granted eternal peace.*

Sheer fright captured her face. Bernie stared in

silence, trying to find something to say to her that would help her manage the fear erupting in her soul. Identical, or so it seemed, to the one left on AJ Gonzalez's body, Carla had lost it. Shaking, she murmured something indiscernible under her breath. In all her years of police work and close calls, nothing had shaken her soul as this did.

Getting up, she ran to the ladies' restroom to settle her nerves, collect her thoughts, and gain her composure. Once inside, the reflection in the mirror revealed a vulnerable, frazzled, and frightened woman. Her thoughts careened off the deepest recesses of her brain; her eyes glistened with tears of unfriendly fright. Nothing had penetrated her soul like this ever before.

Five minutes later, she returned to her desk, where Bernie was examining the black rose. Her color somewhat normal now warmed her face, but inside she was shaking and silently crying. Emotionally drained and distraught, she realized for the first time, her vulnerability, and that she was human after all.

The black rose of death scared the living hell out of her. In a state of shock, she reflected on her life. Maybe it was time to live life rather than letting her career rule her every waking moment. She thought about what she and Chris had talked about last night. Her face appeared lifeless and cold; her catatonic state grabbed Bernie's soul.

"Are you okay?"

"Hell no, I'm not okay, I need to get out of here. Let Chief Evans know that I'm taking the remainder of the day off and why. Please take this black rose to forensics to have it analyzed. Then visit All Things Macabre and the Dark World again; see if anyone bought them lately. I'll call you later after I've had time to pull myself together. I don't think I have to tell you what I'm feeling right now, do I?" Bernie looked for words to say; he had none. "Right, I didn't think so."

Grabbing her purse, she quickly left the station. Noticing her surroundings, she unlocked her car and stared at the windshield as her eyes and mind played tricks on her. Blinking her eyes, the black rose she thought she saw lying on her windshield wiper disappeared. A knock on the window scared her, she pulled out her service weapon without looking and pointed it at the window. Bernie yelled and stepped back. The engine fired up, putting it in gear, she gunned the accelerator squealing the tires as she left the parking lot.

CHAPTER 22

Paranoia controlled her every thought while fear attacked her soul. With her service weapon ready, Carla unlocked her apartment door, silently counted to three, and slowly pushed the door open. Sunlight filled the room, glancing around, nothing looked any different than when she left that morning. Continuing throughout her apartment, she murmured "all clear" after checking each room. A big cleansing sigh did little to calm her anxieties.

Still shaking, Jameson, her liquid lover, gleamed at her from the bar, which separated the living space from the kitchen. A two-fingered pour swirled around the bottom of her glass. Its caramel aroma soothed her senses. Jameson's intoxicating love met her lips, numbing her fears temporarily. After a long sip, she carried it to her bedroom, placing it on the nightstand. From sheer exhaustion and fright, her head crashed hard on her pillow. Staring at the ceiling, muted shades of daylight faded into the shadows of darkness in her subconscious.

While breathing peacefully, dreams gushed from the furthest recesses of her brain. A journey through her early childhood, a happy childhood she thought, created a curious smile on her face. She had no worries back then as she does now. Life was fun; however, today, an artificial black rose with a morbid fortune-cookie message changed all that. Happy dreams paused as that black rose took center stage in her mind. *No... Nooo... Noooooo* echoed off the walls of her subconscious reality.

A bittersweet dream took her to the day when her mom died. Then they fast-forwarded to when her father raised her protecting her from all the evil in the world. In a millisecond, her whole life passed in front of her. Suddenly, her happy dreams crashed hard. Her worst nightmare began as she sat all alone in a pitch-black movie theatre, paralyzed in her seat, her horror flick was about to roll.

In the opening scene, Carla was sleeping in her bed peacefully without a worry. As glass splattered on the hardwood floors, her eyes, wide open and fixated, peered through the thick, murky darkness. In the hallway leading to her bedroom, heavy breathing and footsteps moved closer, grinding the glass into the hardwood floor.

"Who's there?"

Thumping footsteps crunching the broken glass was the only response. A dead eerie silence swarmed around her as she searched for calmness.

"Who's there?" she repeated.

Heavy breathing and crunching footsteps grew louder, louder, and louder.

In the second scene, a life-altering deadly response stood in the doorway. Pulsating demonic eyes bored holes through her soul. As moon rays illuminated the room with muted shades of light, a hulk of a beast growled ferociously, clenching a black rose between his fluorescent-like teeth. A glowing red liquid, resembling blood, flowed from the petals of the black rose.

As it traveled down the stem onto the floor, the substance formed a crimson river rushing toward her bed. Her heart reverberated violently; her lungs searched for calmness. In an almost calming and soothing voice, Carla asked, "Who are you? What do you want?" Silence responded as the crimson river inched closer to her soul. "Stop, or I will blast the hell out of you." The deafening silence roared even louder.

On the big screen, in the final scene, the crimson river began flowing upon her bed. While holding a long-serrated knife, the beast sloshed violently through the crimson river toward her. As the crimson river encompassed her, the serrated blade of death hovered above her. Pulling her Glock from underneath her pillow, she emptied the magazine into the beast's brain. Unfazed by its firepower, the creature continued his quest for the ultimate revenge, his final game prize. In one quick downward motion, death was seconds from stealing her soul. With her darkened pupils fixated on the faceless beast, "No...o...o...o...o...o" echoed off the walls waking her up from her nightmare, her horror flick.

Quickly rising in her bed, her erratic respiration begged furiously for life. Although the beast, the crimson river, and the blade of death had vanished, parked in her subconsciousness, they waited for a sequel. On the night-stand, Jameson glowed; the pain screamed as it went down. The cold sweat of fear and desperation in her clothes clung to her trembling body. After drawing her knees up to her chest, fear invaded her innermost thoughts. A subdued silence eventually surrounded her with peace and tranquility. Cautiously, getting out of the bed, and grabbing her Glock, she moved throughout her apartment, whispering, "All clear...all clear...all clear."

Running back to her bathroom, she placed her Glock on the vanity. As the water fell from the rainfall shower-head, she rushed in fully clothed. Realizing what she had done, her wet clothes landed in the corner of the shower. The steaming hot water soaked her hair while the glass doors grew cloudy and cold. As the steam dissipated, the demons holding her naked vulnerability hostage swirled into the sewers of death.

After stepping out of the shower, her favorite fluffy white robe covered her shivering soul. Still shaking from the horrific nightmare, with her Glock in hand, she went to the kitchen for more of Jameson. His calming amber liquid soothed her soul, numbed her fears.

While back in her bedroom, she placed her Glock on the nightstand, picking up her phone, she dialed a friend's number. After two rings, the call was answered. After a very short conversation, she hung up. Ten minutes later, her doorbell rang. Her eye to the peephole, Chris stared back at her. Opening the door, a fragile and fractured woman, trying to save her soul, trembled in front of him. A fluffy white robe covered the naked and vulnerable woman he was desperate to love. Never seeing her in such a state of fear before, he searched for the right words to comfort her.

As she stood shivering in front of him, incoherent babbling crushed his soul, and his comforting words were not enough to ease her fears. While holding her close to his body, his arms loved her as she silently cried. Caressing her back and soothing her soul, the shape of her body loved his touch. Although weak and vulnerable, what she needed was a brotherly-like friend to get her through the night. Continuing to hold her close, he comforted her easing the deep personal crisis haunting her.

On the threshold of a deep and dark place in her life, he carried her to the bedroom. Laying her on the bed, he covered her with a comforter as she repeatedly whimpered, "All clear... all clear... all clear." While sitting in a lounge chair, her pain and despair weighed heavy on his soul. As he prayed to God, her whimpering gave way to shallow breathing as muted pale light faded into soothing shades of dark peacefulness.

CHAPTER 23

Somehow that night, Carla felt safe, and she slept soundly without any repercussions from the dark nightmare of yesterday afternoon. Freshly brewed coffee permeated her senses, the smell of a new day eased her fears. Opening her eyes, she tried to focus on the individual sitting in the lounge chair in her bedroom.

At first, she didn't remember much from last night, and out of instinct, she reached for her Glock on the nightstand, not knowing who was sitting there. As her vision improved and fogginess in her mind cleared, she recognized the man that came to her rescue. Her mind recollected what she went through last night. She remembered calling Chris and him holding her tight, comforting her. Although all the details of last night's ordeal were still a little foggy in her mind, the things she remembered brought a smile to her face.

"Carla, how do you feel this morning? Last night you were, let's just say, I've never seen you so distraught and desperate, what happened?"

Drawing her knees to her chest, she rested her chin on her knees and stared at him. He held up his coffee cup, she nodded. Going to the kitchen, he poured her a cup of coffee and returned to her bedroom. Taking the cup of coffee in both hands, she put it to her lips and smelled its freshness. Taking a sip, she glanced at him and smiled.

It was the first smile her face had seen since yesterday, and it felt good. Taking another sip of the coffee, she awakened even more. The events of last night resurfaced. She remembered taking off her clothes in the shower, then putting on her fluffy white robe over her naked and vulnerable wet body. Realizing she was still naked underneath sent thoughts through her mind, she wondered if he took advantage of her last night.

"Thank you so much for coming over last night. I don't believe I could have stayed here alone after what I went through yesterday. You are my knight in shining armor. Did anything…"

"Nothing happened last night if that's what you are wondering. You should know me better than that. Now, tell me what happened because you looked as though you had experienced the kiss of death."

"Let me get some more coffee in me and some breakfast, then we will talk."

"You got it, stay in bed, and I'll bring you another cup of coffee, then I will fix you breakfast. Omelet, how does that sound?"

"Yeah, I'd like that."

Chris quickly went to the kitchen and returned with another cup of coffee. Handing it to her, he returned to the kitchen to make breakfast. Opening the fridge, he shook his head back-and-forth, she had nothing that would make a good omelet. Returning to her bedroom, she was sitting in the lounger now, smiling and recovering. Her radiant complexion was beginning to shine through as some sense of normalcy was returning to her body.

Smiling at her, he said, "Can't believe you don't have breakfast items in your fridge. I'll need to make a quick trip to the store; then, I'll fix us that gourmet breakfast I promised you. I'll lock the door on my way out and text you when I'm back, and you can let me in."

In a soft, but scratchy tone of voice, she replied, "Yeah…of course."

While gone, she took another shower to wash away any remnants remaining of yesterday's horrific nightmare. After a relaxing shower, she dried off and chose her favorite pale-yellow lounging pants to wear while a white form-fitting blouse perfectly complimented her pants. While looking at herself in the mirror, a smile crossed her face as she appeared to be almost back to normal.

Her phone dinged, a knock on the door followed. Realizing it was Chris, she opened the door, and he carried two bags of groceries into the kitchen.

"Now, you look like the Carla McBride that I know."

"Thanks, bro, I'm feeling much better." A vulnerability was still lingering inside her body, letting her guard down, she continued, "Come here."

Chris approached her, wondering what this was all about. She opened her arms, he approached her, and their bodies gently touched for a moment. She released his hug and softly planted a kiss on his cheek.

"What was that for?"

"Just a thank you, may I get you anything or help you?"

"Do you have any more coffee? I'll need a cup while I'm fixing breakfast."

Pouring him a cup, she handed it to him. After taking a few sips, he put it down and began preparing breakfast. As he was chopping the onions, sweet peppers, and mushrooms, she watched him with delight. She thought to herself; he knew what he was doing. He would be a good catch for any woman, but not her because she cherished their relationship the way it was.

Within about ten minutes, he plated the omelet with bacon and wheat toast. Butter and jam were already on the table with small glasses of orange juice. In a very playful and jovial mood, he bowed and extended his arm. "Madam, breakfast is served. Do you need anything else?"

"Looks like you got it all covered, where did you learn to cook like that?"

"Nowhere special, trial, and error mostly."

"Well, thanks for everything, I've not had a breakfast like this in, I don't know when."

"Well, you're welcome. Now shut up and enjoy."

Nodding, she sent a brotherly-sisterly-like smile at him. As she was eating, her mind drifted back to yesterday, only letting the good things enter her mind, her childhood, and her parents made her smile. Her thoughts then turned to Chris. He was a super guy, and she was lucky to have him in her life, and she cherished that. Knowing he could have taken advantage of her last night and didn't, that meant the world to her.

With breakfast finished, dishes off the table and in the dishwasher, Carla sat stretched out on her loveseat, while Chris sat across from her. Both still had coffee to finish. Turning on the television, she flipped channels until she reached the Today Show. Although they were oblivious to the weekend hosts, an eerie, peaceful silence captured the room.

"Okay, Carla, now that you have your belly full of my gourmet breakfast, tell me what happened yesterday. I've never seen you like that before. You can trust me; you know that."

"What happened yesterday, well, I thought would never happen in my wildest dreams. I've never experienced the fright that grabbed my soul yesterday. I've been punched and shot at, but what happened yesterday scared the living shit out of me."

"Just take your time, and if you don't want to tell me, that's okay."

"No, I need to get it off my chest. You know the female jogger killed in the park last week. Well, whoever committed that horrendous act, placed a black rose on her vagina. He never violated her. Somehow it was a message, uh, maybe a message to me. By the way, none of this has been made public. Obviously, the couple that discovered her know about it, but we haven't released it to the public or press and probably won't until we're ready. So, it is very confidential."

"You have my word, what you tell me stays here."

"Thanks. My partner and I visited all the shops that carried black roses to see if we could get a solid lead. However, we struck out because you can buy them just about everywhere, and online. So, yesterday in my mail, I received a mysterious package with a weird demented label. It wasn't a label per se, but rather cut out letters and numbers, all different colors and sizes, pasted on the manila envelope, really kind of creepy. When I opened it, a black rose fell onto my desk; it was identical to the black rose found on the jogger. You know it's a symbol of death. Taped to it was a strip of paper like you'd find in a fortune cookie. It read… ye who hath received a single black rose shall be granted eternal peace. I panicked. It scared me like never before. I had to get out of there and came home."

Carla went to the kitchen to hide her fear and poured herself another cup of coffee and returned to the loveseat smiling at Chris. After taking a few sips of the coffee, she continued, "I told my partner, Bernie, to take the envelope and the black rose to forensics and then meet with Chief Evans to inform him what was going on. When I got home, I lost it. I was a nervous wreck and collapsed on the bed, crying myself to sleep. I dreamed about my childhood, my life flashed by me at lightning speed and then abruptly stopped. Now, what's next is the hard part."

"If you need another break, stop and compose yourself. Take all the time you need; we have all day."

"No, I need to get past this, if I'm going to catch who did this. When my dreams stopped, a black rose appeared in front of me. I screamed in my sleep, and it quickly dissipated. Happy dreams ended, and the nightmare began with a huge man like a big beast standing in my doorway. He was clinching a black rose between his teeth, blood was dripping from the black rose, and he was coming toward me. I pulled my Glock from under my pillow and emptied it into his brain, creating a large hole, causing a river of blood to flow toward me. Sloshing through the river of blood, he continued toward me, wielding a large serrated knife. He swung his arm down to kill me; that's when I woke up screaming and shivering from a cold sweat, I was utterly mortified."

Chris wanted to hold her tight, taking a chance, he

moved from the chair to the loveseat sitting beside her. Putting his arm around her shoulders, he massaged her neck. At first, she flinched and thought about taking his arm away. However, she knew he would never take advantage of her and embraced his expressions of concern.

Carla continued, "That's why I needed someone here to stay with me and keep me safe. You're my big brother, and that's who I needed, but more importantly, who I wanted. It was a life-altering moment. I know I'm obsessed with my career and putting criminals away. I haven't taken time off in months. I even considered quitting, but that's not who I am. I just need time off. I'm taking some needed R-and-R."

"Good for you."

"Hey, listen…um…what are you doing the rest of the day? Can you get away?"

"Remember, I'm the boss, what do you have in mind?"

"Not sure, but let's just take a ride. I don't care where or what we do. Let's just call it a play day. I need you to be with me today. What do you say?"

"Sure, I would need to stop by my apartment, take a shower and change clothes, yeah, why not. It's a date."

"I really wouldn't call it that, bro."

"Oh, well, at least you're smiling, play day it is."

While she was getting dressed, he notified his assistant he would be out of the office today. After a quick stop by his apartment, a quick shower and a change of clothes, he was ready for whatever the day would bring.

"Okay, where do you want to go?"

"Surprise me, I'm all yours, of course, in a brotherly-sisterly way."

"Um, do you really want to get away? I mean away, like a long weekend, separate rooms, of course."

"As I said, I'm all yours. I need to decompress and try to forget the darkness I've been through."

"Okay, let me make a few calls, see what I can come up with."

While Chris went to his bedroom to make some calls in private, she moved around his living room looking at photos, well just about anything she could see. Books he's read, magazines on the table. His place didn't look like a bachelor pad at all; she noticed he had style, and it was a style she liked.

Oblivious to him standing in the doorway, she examined his personal life on display. He cleared his throat, demanding her attention. Glancing in his direction, she smiled as he admired her beauty. He had a shit-eating grin across his face.

"What?"

"Nothing. Let me pack a bag, and then we will stop back at your place because you'll have to pack enough clothes for three days. Sound good?"

"Like I said, bro, I'm all yours. What are you waiting for?"

CHAPTER 24

After about a five-hour ride, on Interstate 64, the exit for Lewisburg, West Virginia, was upon them. Turning right off the ramp, they proceeded toward downtown. After making a left on E. Washington Street, the General Lewis Inn was three blocks away from the historic downtown area.

Upon entering the hotel, they approached the quaint reservation desk where an older gentleman was on the phone. Noticing Carla and Chris approaching him, he ended the call and greeted them.

"Hi, I'm Chris Abbott. I called this morning to reserve two rooms. She's Carla McBride, um, here's my confirmation number."

"Let me check, just a minute." Nodding, Chris waited patiently. "Mr. Abbott, I must apologize. It appears there was a mix-up on the reservations, and we only have one room available with two double beds. Does that work for you?"

"Sir, uh, that is a problem. We are not a couple, you

know, we're more like brother and sister. Uh, we need separate rooms."

"Once again, I apologize. I can call other hotels in the area to see if they're any rooms available, is that okay with you?"

"We really wanted to stay here since it's within walking distance from the historic downtown area."

Carla, in her usual, but abrupt personality interrupted the conversation. "Sir, we'll take it."

"Are you sure about that?"

"Yes, you could have taken advantage of me last night, and you didn't. I trust you, and we will make it work, besides if you try something, I'll just have to kill you."

With a confused look on his face, the desk clerk responded, "Well, okay now. Um, may I have a credit card and identification, please?"

Receiving their room key, they headed down the hallway to Room 107. Opening the door was like entering the past. The room had two antique beds with complimenting furniture. Their room was small, but still had a small loveseat facing the television. A small bathroom was adequate for their stay. After putting their bags on the bed, they headed for the bar just off the lobby. The small and inviting bar was the perfect spot to relax with a drink after their five-hour journey through Kentucky and West Virginia.

The bar area, complemented with antiques and civil war memorabilia, was empty, and that suited them just fine. An older gentleman tending bar placed drink napkins in front of them. Carla scanned the bottles on a shelf behind the bar to see if Jameson was there. Standing tall, Carla smiled. He was there, and that was all that mattered to her. Chris, more of a beer drinker, surveyed the beers they had on tap.

"What may I get you, folks?"

"The lady will have a Jameson on the rocks. What kind of beers do you have on tap?"

"We don't have many, your usual ones. Miller Lite, Coors Lite, Bud Lite, Bud, Michelob Ultra, and a local craft beer."

"May I get a sample of the local craft beer? And you better make that a double shot of Jameson on the rocks for the lovely lady."

"Very well, coming right up. Here are some snacks to munch on."

"Thank you, sir."

Their drinks arrived, and each savored a sip while munching on Chex Mix and pretzels. Chris liked the local craft beer and ordered a pint. Carla continued to scan the hotel and lose herself in the moment. This trip was exactly what she needed to re-energize.

Chris explained to Carla the history of the inn, which was named after General Andrew Lewis, and built on a civil war site, opening in 1929. The eastern end of the building was a brick residence built in the 1800s while they designed and built the western section in 1928. According to some historians, three different ghosts roam some of the rooms.

"Haunted, are you kidding me?"

"Well, that's what their website says."

"Do you believe everything on the internet?"

"No, but let's ask the bartender."

"Sir, I read that ghosts roam this hotel, is that true?"

"So, they say, Rooms 206 and 208 are supposedly haunted by The Lady in White. Hope you are not in either of those rooms, it could be a restless night. And supposedly, Rueben, a black slave, roams the main dining hall each night. The oak beams supporting the ceiling are supposedly from the oak tree he was hung from a long time ago."

"There you have it, Carla. Ghosts are in the house." Directing his gaze toward the bartender, he held both glasses in the air. "When our drinks come, let's grab them and explore this place. If the rooms are open, we're allowed to enter them, even the haunted ones."

"Sounds good, bro."

"I wish you wouldn't call me that."

"If I didn't, then people would think we are a couple, can't have that, can we?"

"Okay, sis, you win."

Before they explored the hotel, they made dinner reservations. Even though snow blanketed Lewisburg and the temperatures were below freezing, they went out on the patio to experience the ambiance of Lewisburg. Breathing the refreshing coolness of the air, Carla was fascinated by the amount of snow on the ground. Surprised how beautiful the undisturbed bluish-white snow was, it touched her emotional vulnerability.

With dinner two hours away, another round of drinks would put them in the right mood for an evening of worry-free relaxation. With her phone off-limits, and until now, she had ignored it completely. However, curiosity was getting the best of her and turned on her phone to listen to her messages. Two were from Walt, a couple from Laura, a couple from Bernie, and one was from Wanda Jordan, aka Daisy, who worked at Whisman's, a local bar, in Oakmont.

Daisy had bolted from Oakmont because she feared

for her life after learning that her one-night stand, Spike, died at the hands of Rocky. After working with Carla to create a sketch of Rocky, Daisy fled north to Vermont to stay with relatives because she feared for her life. Her message was seeking Carla's advice, whether it was safe to return to Oakmont and her old job. Believing it was safe, she dialed Daisy's number, which went straight to her voicemail. After leaving her a message, she turned off her phone. It was time to relax with Jameson, her liquid lover, and of course, Chris, her brotherly friend until it was time for dinner. After a nice quiet meal, their room with double beds would provide a sanctuary for winding down.

A relaxing hot shower was just what they both needed to cap off the night. Carla had first dibs and took her time cleansing herself from yesterday's life-altering events. After her shower, she came out of the bathroom dressed in a pair of yellow lounging pants with a white V-neck blouse caressing her sexiness. It was a wow moment for Chris. Until now, he had never experienced her in this manner, displaying her sexuality in his face. Speechless, no words could describe what he was feeling. His shock-n-awe smile said it all.

"What?"

"Uh, noth…nothing. I guess, um, I guess I better get my shower now, likely a cold one."

Rolling her eyes, she gave him a flirtatious little smile while taking a seat on the loveseat. After Chris finished his shower and got dressed, he sat beside her on the loveseat. For a moment, the silence was awkward, but still very peaceful at the same time. Turning on the television to break the silence, he picked a movie on HBO to watch. Knowing anything having to do with law enforcement was a bad idea; he chose a romantic comedy instead.

Sitting on the loveseat, they finished their nightcaps they brought from the restaurant. With the effects of a long day and several drinks, her head fell gently on his shoulder. Within a few seconds, her eyes closed, and she was purring like a baby kitten. Continuing to comfort her after the long day, he put his arm around her savoring this rare moment of intimacy he had longed for. It wasn't long till his eyes drooped and knew it wouldn't be long before he fell asleep as well. Picking her up, he carried her to the bed, laid her down, and covered her with a blanket in hopes she would have a peaceful night.

"Sweet dreams, my love."

Already in a deep sleep-like trance, she whispered, "You, too…my love."

Morning came quickly for them. Carla had the best sleep she'd had in a long time. While stretching and yawning, the aroma of brewed coffee filled the room. Wondering what all the commotion coming from the bathroom was, she was about to get out of bed when Chris appeared in front of her looking refreshed and ready for the day. She was still stretching and yawning to awaken fully. Smiling at him, she laid in the bed, hiding her sensuality.

"Hey, how did you sleep last night?"

"Like a baby. Thank you for all you have done."

He nodded. "Coffee in bed?"

"Sure, you are such a romantic, can't believe someone hasn't snatched you up by now."

"I guess you could say, uh, the right person just hasn't come along yet." A moment went by, and he prepared her coffee. "Here's your cup of coffee just the way you like it. You want an extra pillow so you can sit up while drinking your coffee?"

"That would be nice, thank you."

Sitting up, the taste of coffee filled her soul with warmth and love. While admiring her stunning beauty in such a vulnerable woman, he tasted the coffee and smiled. Remembering her display of sexuality last night, he couldn't get that image out of his mind, or take his eyes off her. While savoring the coffee, his fantasizing trance couldn't be hidden.

"Chris, are you okay? How did you sleep last night?"

"Alone."

"Real funny, bro."

"I meant good…yeah, yeah, really good."

"You're such a jokester, you know."

"Nah, just a hopeless romantic."

"You'll find the right person one day, and then it will be all over for you."

Under his breath, he whispered, "I think I already have."

"What did you just say?"

"Oh, nothing. Do you want breakfast in bed? We can order room service if you like?"

"Nah, let's eat downstairs. It will just take me a few minutes to get ready."

"Yeah, sounds great."

After breakfast, they stopped at the registration desk to ask for some brochures about the community and places they should see. Behind the registration desk, a middle-aged lady was busy on the phone, helping other customers. Not in a hurry, they waited for her to end the call. Carla noticed the lady was attractive and in great shape. The badge she was wearing identified her as

Alicia Maddox, assistant manager. Coal-black hair styled almost like Pink surrounded her pretty face. For some odd reason, Carla thought she recognized her, which was strange because she had never been to Lewisburg before. Given her traumatic events of the last few days, about everyone she encountered looked like someone she knew or had seen before.

Alicia gave them a shortlist of places to visit. The Greenbrier Sporting Club, and The Snead golf course, along with The Greenbrier Resort was at the top of the list. Carla noticed her professionalism, her customer service skills, and knew the hotel was fortunate to have her.

Chris thanked her and out they went to explore what Lewisburg and the Greenbrier Valley offered. Local retail outlets, artist shops along with interesting local eateries dotted the cityscape giving the town its unique charm. After strolling up and down the streets of the historic city, they finished the day off with dinner and drinks at the General Lewis Inn.

After a peaceful night, the next morning, they took Alicia's advice and visited the Greenbrier Resort for a classic lunch at Draper's Café. After touring the historical hotel and famous bunker, a ride through the Greenbrier Sporting Club capped off their visit to White Sulphur Springs.

The General Lewis Inn, with its charming amenities and ambiance, was just what Carla needed to decompress and forget her life-altering experience with an artificial black rose. Her time with Chris in Lewisburg was one of the best times she'd had in her life. During that time, she saw Chris from a whole different perspective. She was beginning to realize he just might be her knight in shining armor. However, falling in love with him was very risky. She cherished their current brotherly-sisterly relationship and didn't want to lose that by loving him in a whole different way. Besides when she returned to Oakmont, her priority was finding Alaina Gonzalez's killer, and bringing that person to justice.

CHAPTER 25

Walt still couldn't get his fiction-like theory out of this mind. The whole concept of Peanuts and Frog faking their death, or Pseudocide to avoid financial ruin was not that crazy. Bennie Wint had pulled it off in 1989 to escape a dangerous South Carolina drug ring. He started a new life in North Carolina, but eventually, it caught up with him twenty years later at a traffic stop.

Now, Hank Fisher, aka Frog, had risen from the dead because forensics identified his DNA from evidence collected from the crime scene in the death of AJ Gonzalez. The more he thought about his theory, the more he believed it had merit. Then Al Bocconi conveniently died from a hit-and-run accident; nothing was making sense to him.

Dialing Carla's office number, it went straight to her voicemail. Her greeting said she would be out of the office until Tuesday and to direct any information to her partner, Bernie Kowalski. Walt had never met him before and didn't feel comfortable presenting his cockamamie theory to him without her. He didn't leave a message for her and hung up. The more he thought about it, he redialed Carla's number leaving her a detailed message, and he needed to talk to her as soon as she returned.

By afternoon, Carla hadn't returned his call. He figured she just hadn't listened to her messages yet or returning any calls today. With his theory foremost on his mind, Walt took Carla's advice and called Detective Kowalski to pitch it to him. After calling the police department's main number, the receptionist transferred him to Kowalski's extension. Going straight to voicemail, he left him a message to call him about Hank Fisher. He figured that would get his attention. It did, and about fifteen minutes later, Walt's phone rang. He recognized the caller ID and answered in his usual professional manner.

After putting the call on speakerphone, Bernie's voice filled his office. "Mr. Blevins, this is Detective Kowalski. I'm returning your call. You have information about a dead guy named Hank Fisher. I can't wait to hear this."

"Detective Kowalski, Carla asked me to research him, and since I can't reach her, I'd like to discuss what I found out with you. Can we meet today sometime?"

"Okay, umm, this better be good. I've got to tie up some loose ends on another case. It will be about forty-five minutes before I can meet with you, does that work for you?"

"Yeah, see you then."

Having extra time before Detective Kowalski arrived, he decided to call Alpha and Tango Excursions to see what he could find out. Switching off his caller ID, he crossed his fingers and dialed the number, hoping he could pull this off. Putting it on speakerphone, he waited for someone to answer. Finally, a young lady with a Hispanic accent greeted him.

"Isabella, my name is Hank Farris. Is Mr. Hewitt or Mr. Bowen in today?"

"No, sir, they left last week. Said they'd be gone for about two weeks or more. Said they had some business to take care of in Florida. After that, they would head north for some vacation time. They said they would check in from time to time. Do you want to leave a message? I can give it to them when they check in with me."

Walt thought for a moment; however, his better judgment told him not to leave a message and a number. He informed Isabella he would call back in two weeks when they returned. After hanging up, his phone immediately rang. For a moment, he didn't know what to think since it happened so fast; however, it was the receptionist's desk calling to inform him that Detective Kowalski had arrived. The receptionist escorted him to his office, where Walt was waiting for him. After exchanging pleasantries, Walt motioned him to take a seat. Closing his office door, Walt sat across from him and began.

"Detective Kowalski, thank you for coming over, as I said, Carla asked me to do some research. By the way, is she okay? I tried calling her twice and went straight to voicemail both times."

"Uh, she took a few days off, and that's all I know. By the way, please call me Bernie." Walt nodded, and Bernie continued, "Let's get started, I'm a busy man, so this better be good."

"Please have an open mind about what I'm going to tell you."

During Walt's story, Bernie is shaking his head back-and-forth. A few times, he even laughed under his breath.

Finally, after about ten minutes, he finished as Bernie stilled showed signs of disbelief.

"Well, what do you think?"

"That's some theory you got there. And what do you want me to do about it?"

"I know it sounds crazy, but the timeline fits, and you have DNA from a dead man in your most recent case. How do you explain that?"

"We can't, at least not yet."

"If Hank Fisher was alive, couldn't you?"

"Well, yeah. How are you going to prove it?"

"I'm not; you are."

"Really, and how will I do that, hotshot publisher?"

"I think you can start by calling the detective assigned to the case involving the death of Al Bocconi. Something's just not right about that. The story indicated the investigation is ongoing. Maybe you can get a little more information than was published in the newspaper. Police don't always tell the media everything; isn't that right?"

"Yeah, say I do that, then what?"

"Use your years of experience and intuition. See if they found the vehicle that ran Al down. He lived in a rural area, he jogs one morning and then he is a victim of a hit and run. Don't you find that a little odd?"

"So, you think Hank Fisher and Charles Brown rose from the dead as Grayson Hewitt and Parker Bowen in Bayside, Texas. They leave to go to Florida and take out Al Bocconi. Then Hank's DNA ends up at the crime scene here in Oakmont."

"My guess is they owe John Dickerson a big debt. John wants revenge for Al ratting on him. Use all your resources to find out as much as you can about Hewitt and Bowen. What do you have to lose?"

"I don't know; it's a pretty wild theory and all. If you are wrong, it might make me look like a fool. If you are so sure about this, why don't you call?"

"Um, I thought about that, but with you being in the law enforcement brotherhood, you likely would have a better chance of getting additional information I couldn't."

"Good point there, give me the information, and I will think about it."

"Thanks, if anything, do it for Carla's sake, will you do that?" Bernie nodded and left.

CHAPTER 26

Sitting at his desk at the police station, Bernie kept thinking of the last thing Walt said to him. Please do it for Carla's sake. He thought about her reaction when the black rose fell out of the manila envelope. He'd never seen that look on her face before. Taking Walt's advice, Bernie dialed the number for Detective Jimmy Ramirez of the Escambia County Sheriff Department and waited patiently for an answer. Finally, someone answered, and he put the call on speakerphone.

"Detective Ramirez, this is Detective Bernie Kowalski from the Oakmont Police Department in Kentucky. I want to ask you a few questions regarding a hit-and-run case of yours involving Al Bocconi."

"Why is a detective in Kentucky interested in this case?"

"It may be linked to the murder of a young woman here."

"How so?"

"DNA found at our crime scene is from an individual

that previously lived in the Pensacola area until he was declared dead in a boating accident about two years ago. Does the name Hank Fisher ring a bell with you?"

"Yeah, I remember the name, what does it have to do with our case?"

"I'll explain, just bear with me for a moment. Do you have any leads, suspects, or the vehicle that hit him?"

"Um, yeah, we did find a wrecked vehicle with no plates several miles on the other side of town. Someone evidently lost control and hit a tree."

"What about the driver?"

"We figured it was a DUI, and the driver left the scene. Likely to turn up later when the person sobered up. May I put you on hold for a minute, I have another call?"

"Yeah, no problem."

A minute elapsed, and he returned to his conversation with Bernie. "Detective Kowalski, our case just got interesting. The car used in the hit-and-run accident belonged to Hank Fisher, the guy that died in the boating accident. Furthermore, there was blood on the front grill hood belonging to Al Bocconi. We have the vehicle that killed him, and it now appears it was not an accident."

"We have DNA from Hank Fisher, and you have a car belonging to him. You've heard the name John Dickerson before, haven't you?"

"Who hasn't down here, isn't he in a federal witness protection program? What's the connection?"

"Yes, he's in the program; however, your victim, Al Bocconi, was instrumental in bringing him down. Now, Al shows up dead. Fisher's car is involved in the hit-and-run. And, now, Fisher's DNA shows up at our crime scene. That's not a coincidence, is it?"

"Doesn't sound like it."

"We believe Hank Fisher and Charles Brown, aided by John Dickerson, faked their death to get out from under financial ruin or something far worse. We think they're now living in Bayside, Texas, as Grayson Hewitt and Parker Bowen, and operating a fishing excursion company."

"Whew, that's some theory, so how may we help?"

"Let us know of any further developments and keep an eye out for them."

After ending the call, Bernie logged into the police system databases and searched for Grayson Hewitt. Nothing appeared. He searched for Parker Bowen, the same result. Other than the information that Walt gave him on them, nothing else came up. He remembered Walt telling him he called the number for the Alpha and Tango Excursions and talked with a young lady named Isabella, who was very cooperative. What the heck, Bernie thought he would call her and see what else he could get out of her. Turning off his caller ID on his cell phone, he dialed the number putting the call on speaker, a few rings later, a young lady answered.

"Alpha and Tango Excursions, this is Isabella, how may I help you?"

"Isabella, that's such a pretty name."

"Thank you, sir. You want to book an excursion?"

"No, honey, is Grayson Hewitt or Parker Bowen in today?"

"No, they're on vacation for at least two weeks or more."

"Um, lucky them, I wish I could get a vacation sometime. Anyway, I knew them from when we served together in the Army. It's been at least twenty years since

I last saw them and was wondering what they look like now. Your website doesn't have any pictures of them on it, do you know how I could get one?"

"That's right, Grayson and Parker didn't want them on there, don't know why, though. Anyway, I have a picture of them and me on my phone. Give me your number, and I will text it to you."

"Uh, how about an email address, would you email it to me?"

"Si, that will work."

"Email it to polishdude@gmail.com."

"Si, it's on its way, anything else I may help you with?"

"Nah, when they get back, will you have them contact me at that email address?"

"Okay, have a nice day, sir."

"You too, honey, and I love your name."

"Gracias."

Isabella's email came through right away. He opened it on his laptop and viewed it. Then he took the picture Walt gave him from the article that had a picture of Hank, Charles, and John. Under his breath, he said, "Well, I'll be damned. They sure look the same as Hank Fisher and Charles Brown."

Immediately calling Walt, it went straight to voice-mail. Leaving a message, it was getting late, and he called it a day. At home, some good Polish food served up with a Yuengling Lager from America's oldest brewery in Pottsville, Pennsylvania, awaited him.

CHAPTER 27

Arriving at Carla's apartment in mid-afternoon, Chris gathered her bags from the trunk and walked her to her door. While unlocking the door, she asked him to stay for a few minutes more. The remains of a troubling nightmare still lingered in the apartment, having him there helped her chase away any darkness that remained. Once inside her apartment, he placed her bags inside her bedroom and stared at her, wondering what was next.

As she glanced at him, his thoughts returned to the past few days he spent with the girl of his dreams, while she decompressed with her big brother, as she called him. Regardless of how each felt about their relationship, they would remember the past few days for a long time. In many ways, he hoped it would have been more than a family-like event, but she wasn't ready.

On the other hand, she saw him in a whole different way. She realized more now than ever, if she were ever to get serious again with someone, she would want someone just like him, but not him. The friendship they had was too much of a risk, especially if they became romantically involved, and it didn't work out.

Chris wanted to stay, but also knew he should leave. Noticing a confused expression crossing his face, she approached him and planted a brief thank-you kiss on his cheek. His face lit up and asked, "What was that for?"

"For being there for me the past few days and now, will you stay with me a little longer?"

He nodded, and they sat on her loveseat together, talking and laughing for hours. He fixed a late lunch, BLT sandwich with a fried egg. She noticed again how adept he was in the kitchen. A leisurely lunch eased any remaining fears left in her apartment. Cleaning up the table, he put the dishes in the dishwasher.

"I guess it's time I leave, are you going to be okay?"

"Yeah, I'll be fine. Thank you so much for being here for me. You know you're an angel and a saint to me. You mean the world to me, bro."

"Thanks, if you need me, let me know, okay?"

Nodding, she walked him to the door where there was an awkward moment of silence. Both were standing, looking at each as if they both didn't want their time together to end. He grabbed the doorknob to open the door and was startled by her hand, grasping his arm. Turning around, she hugged him. Releasing her arms, she stood on her tiptoes, gently planting another soft kiss on his cheek. Looking deep in her eyes, he had other thoughts and knew this wasn't the right time to make a move. She was still vulnerable, and he would not take advantage of her under any circumstance.

He left with thoughts of what could have been, while she went about her day; however, she couldn't get him off her mind. Deep inside her soul, something told her not to let him go. Life was too short not to experience his love and devotion for her. She shook her head back-and-forth saying out loud. "Get a hold of yourself, Carla, that's nonsense."

Again, she reflected on the past few days; the black rose, the nightmare, her most previous cases. The good and the bad; however, everything came back to Chris. She needed someone to talk to about him, and that was an easy choice. Laura answered, putting the call on speaker.

"Hey, detective, why haven't you been answering my calls? Funny thing is my brother wasn't answering my calls either. What's going on with you?"

"Hey, I'm sorry. Things got weird on Friday, and my world got turned upside down. I had to get away where I could sort things out."

"Yeah." Carla informed her about the black rose, and the nightmare, and how it scared her, she lost it and needed help. "Carla, why didn't you let me help?"

"You're my best friend and all, but you've got enough going on planning the big wedding, your job and all. I didn't want to bother you. I needed my big brother, so I called Chris."

"So, that's why he wasn't calling me back as well."

"Yeah, um, probably so. Chris is a saint, you know. He came over and comforted me and stayed the night."

"Go on, tell me more, did you…you know?"

"Don't get any wild ideas, nothing happened. I needed to get away, and Chris took me to this nice quaint town in West Virginia named Lewisburg. We stayed at a place called The General Lewis Inn and had to end up staying in the same room." She can hear Laura mumbling something, "No, we didn't if that's what you are thinking. It had double beds, and we made it work. I've had one of the best times of my life with him these past few days."

"And, what else?"

"Chris was a perfect gentleman. Never once did he try to take advantage of me in my vulnerable state of mind. He had opportunities, and had he tried, I probably would have succumbed to him. I just needed his love in a non-sexual way and to be protected, and he did that."

"You know, I've seen first-hand how you act around each other, how you look at each other. It's doesn't take a rocket scientist to see you both have feelings for each other. Why don't you give him a chance?"

"I'm not good with relationships, and what we have now, you know, works for me. I don't want to ruin that and hurt him, and ruining the friendship we have now, maybe forever. It's too much of a risk, and one I don't want to take."

"Why don't you guys go out to dinner and talk honestly? Dutch date, no strings attached. Discuss your relationship and be honest with each other. You never know where that might lead you."

"Yeah, maybe I will give it some thought, well, thanks so much sis, talk to you soon."

CHAPTER 28

A cup of hot coffee sat on the Keurig as Walt settled in his office, getting ready to start the day. The first order of the day was his email, see which ones were important and returned those that were. His voicemail was the next item in his daily routine. One by one, he listened to each one and, based on importance, either saved them or deleted them. It was the last message that got his attention.

Bernie had called last night after he had left for the day, leaving him a message about his discoveries from his research on Al, Grayson, and Parker. He suggested they meet this morning to discuss his findings. After speaking with Bernie, they agreed to meet at Walt's office at Eleven AM. Before he realized it, Bernie had arrived. The receptionist took him to Walt's office, where he was waiting for him in the doorway. After they entered, Walt closed the door.

Sitting across from each other, Walt got right to it. "Good morning, Detective Kowalski."

"Can we dispense with the detective greeting shit, just call me Bernie, will you?"

"Of course, Bernie, it is. Before we get to your discoveries, have you heard from Carla?"

"Yeah, she left me a voicemail, said everything's fine, she will return to work tomorrow."

"That's not like her, you know, not answering her voicemails, what's really going on with her?"

Not thinking clearly, he said, "She received a black rose in the mail last week, freaked her out big time. She needed space and took time off. Now, don't tell her I told you, she'll be pissed." Walt, a little confused, nodded just the same. "I called Detective Ramirez as you suggested. Make a long story short. The hit-and-run case is ongoing, and they found a wrecked car without any plates on the other side of town. Registered to Hank Fisher, forensics identified it as the car that killed Al Bocconi. I explained your theory, and at first, he laughed. But when I told them about his DNA showing up at our crime scene, he had a different tune. They currently have no suspects in the ongoing investigation, and he said he would keep us informed of any new developments."

"Alright, that's great, anything else?"

"Yeah, I called Alpha and Tango Excursions as well and charmed young Isabella into giving us more information. I told her I was an old friend of Grayson and Parker from the Army and hadn't seen them for a while. I asked her if she had any photos of them since there weren't any on their website. And of course, she did. She sent me a photo of her with Grayson Hewitt and Parker Bowen. Well, Hank Fisher and Charles Brown resemble Grayson and Parker. Here's the photo Isabella sent to me."

Studying the photo, the two individuals resembled Hank Fisher and Charles Brown.

"Great work, now, what's next?"

"We keep our eyes open for any car with Texas plates here in Oakmont."

"Okay, maybe tomorrow when Carla returns to work, can we get together and brainstorm?"

"Sounds good, but don't you have a business to run?"

"Give every employee empowerment and the tools; it runs itself."

"Well, gotta run. I'm checking out the places again that sell black roses to see if I can find out anything else."

"Hope you find something."

"Me too, especially for Carla's sake."

Walt returned to his newspaper world while Bernie searched for where the black rose came from. Questioning the workers at each place, he purchased one black rose from each location. Back at the police station, he gave them to forensics to examine, hoping for a match to the ones already in evidence.

Forensics didn't take very long and returned them to Bernie. They explained to him there was a difference in the stem length and the material used to make the rose. More than likely, they were purchased somewhere other than Oakmont. That was not the news he wanted to hear.

CHAPTER 29

Returning to work early on Wednesday, Carla was refreshed and looking more like herself than the person she was last week. Jameson, hot showers, and Chris had washed away her demons. She was ready to tackle crime again. Bernie greeted her as if nothing had happened. He was his usual self, and she dished it right back at him. They were becoming more like permanent partners than temporary ones. Settled in at their workstations, Bernie continued staring at her.

"What is it, dickhead?"

As a beaming smile crossed his face, he said, "Oh nothing."

"Right, what…?"

"Your buddy Walt and I met yesterday because he couldn't get a hold of you."

"Look, Walt is not my buddy."

"Whatever. Carla, hell, I couldn't even get a hold of you. What happened to you?"

Once again, she had to relive that painful night, but

the more she talked about it, the easier it was to forget it. Listening intently with a caring ear, concerned painted his face.

"Dammit McBride, why didn't you call me? I could have helped you."

"I appreciate that, but my big brother rescued me, and that's what I really wanted and needed."

"I didn't know you had a brother."

"I don't. I have a great friend that is like one. That's the relationship we have, nothing else. We went away for a few days, and nothing happened."

"Didn't insinuate that it did."

"Screw you, let's talk about something else, bring me up to speed on everything."

While walking by her workstation, Chief Evans said, "Glad to have you back, McBride."

"Thanks, glad to be back. Okay, Bernie, now, where were we?"

"Tell you what, Walt wants to meet with us today and discuss our findings and brainstorm. Are you okay with that?"

"Sure, when?"

"We agreed, ten-thirty at this office this morning. What's with you and Walt?"

"It's complicated, and I'll leave it at that. Why don't you drive today and tonight to our class? It will do me good to see things from a different perspective."

"Damn, something really happened to you while you were off, I like it."

"Hey, let's just say, I see things in a different light now and don't ask why, dickhead."

"Now, that's my girl."

Waiting for their meeting, she went to her mailbox to

see what surprises she might have. It's empty, and she sighed. No surprises and no more black roses in her mailbox today. Returning to her desk, she cleaned it up a little even though not much was out of place. A visit to forensics didn't provide her any more information than she already had. She asked to see the black rose she received last week, and the one left on AJ. The evidence clerk retrieved it, and she signed the log.

Taking each black rose out of the evidence bag, she held them in her hands. A black rose threw her for a loop and jolted her soul. The one she received was an exact match to the one left on AJ. As she held them, she hoped something good would happen; that maybe she would get a vibe from her guardian angel. However, that didn't occur. Placing them back in the evidence bag, she signed them back in and returned to her desk.

While they left to meet with Walt, she remained silent, observing the world from a different viewpoint in the passenger seat. Announcing themselves to the registration desk, they immediately went to Walt's office, where he was waiting on them.

"Come on in, guys, and take a seat."

Immediately, Carla noticed one wall looked just like it did during the Gold Fedora case. Now, they were doing the same thing for the Black Rose case.

Carla said, "What do we have here, Walt? I see two sides of Alpha Tango. Which one is the evil side?"

"Carla, both sides are evil. The one with Casanova, Peanuts, and Frog gets the prize for the worst. Remember, Al told us they were extremely tight, and that likely continued after they got out of the army. The one picture showed the three of them when they formed Fisher Excursions and More. John was likely a silent partner.

And if Peanuts and Frog are alive, which the picture that Isabella sent Bernie proved, then the three of them are the only ones alive out of Alpha Tango, and now they are back together."

"Okay, that makes sense. What else?"

"Keep an open mind. John Dickerson, aka Casanova, wherever he is, contacted Peanuts and Frog through a public email server and ordered them to take out Al because he tipped off the FBI, and he wanted revenge. Al probably was the only honest one among Alpha Tango. Frog had an old car in storage and used it to kill Al, then made it look like a drunk driver stole the car and wrecked it. Police find out it's registered to Hank Fisher, who's supposed to be dead. Their case, in many ways, is dead in the water as well unless we can find them."

"Okay, go on."

"John wants revenge on everyone that brought him down. Hank Fisher and Charles Brown are carrying it out because he doesn't want to risk his witness protection program. All records show that they are dead, so they become invisible to the world. At least until Hank's DNA turned up here."

"But, Walt, why kill AJ?"

"That's the thousand-dollar question. I'm sure we'll connect the dots, maybe they're connected somehow. Anyway, I understand you received a black rose in the mail, and it freaked you out."

As Carla gave Bernie an in-your-face-bird, Bernie interjected, "So, much for keeping a secret, Mr. Publisher."

"Bernie, don't worry about it, Walt would have found out, anyway."

Walt feeling all red-faced said, "It just slipped out,

I'm sorry. Anyway, Hank Fisher, aka, Frog and Charles Brown, aka, Peanuts may be in Oakmont or were at least here at some point. Not sure what they will do next."

Bernie said, "I don't like where this is going. You both may be in danger, maybe me, too."

"Guys, I don't think he would go after us, too risky. He might go after something else or someone, um, we both love. Shit, oh no, not her, not Laura."

Bernie said, "Who's Laura?"

"My fiancée."

"Walt, that's it. He wants to make us suffer by doing something to Laura, who we both love dearly. John wants us both to suffer the way he is suffering now without his wife and son in his life, and for everything else, we did to him."

"But how would he know her?"

"My guess is Frank Ramsey, aka Spike told Wylie Adkins, aka Rocky, and he told Casanova. Spike saw you with her multiple times and just put two and two together. They likely had their eye on her long ago."

CHAPTER 30

ear seized Walt's face; his eyes turned glassy while uncertainty crushed his soul. His heart was racing so fast and thumping so loud as if it was lying outside of his chest. The thought of something happening to Laura was too much for him to handle. He had waited all his life for someone like her to come into his life. His fiancé, his future wife, and someday, the mother of his child might just be the next target. Heavy silence hovered over them.

Carla and Bernie sat stoically, staring at themselves as if they were attending a funeral of a best friend. Carla hoped she was wrong, but she had no other explanation or theory. Maybe it was instinct or intuition that caused her to jump to that conclusion; however, she was sure that Laura was in danger. They stared at Walt as he struggled with this latest theory.

Walt broke the silence as he tried to reel in his emotions, "Carla, seriously, do you really think that? Maybe you returned to work too soon."

"I'm sorry, Walt, but it just makes sense. Do you have a better theory?"

"Well, uh, no, but I don't want to believe that either."

"Me neither, we both love her very much."

"Then, what's next, Carla?"

"Well, one thing for sure is we can't tell her. However, as inconspicuously as possible, we need to caution her to be very careful in everything she does."

After several hours, they felt they had made progress. Unfortunately for everyone, their progress ended on a sour note. Walt had to see Laura, he wanted to tell her, but he knew he couldn't. Bernie suggested that they call it a day since it was close to lunchtime. Suggesting to Carla that they have lunch at McGruder's again, she declined. It brought back too many bad memories, especially about Sam. She suggested they head back to the police station, and check-in before going to Flemingsville. Then they could have a late lunch before they visited All Things Macabre and then to their class.

Walt, needing to be with Laura, invited her to lunch at the Apollo Café. Meeting her at her office, they walked together to the café. She thought that was nonsense but gave in to him. After arriving, they grabbed the only booth left near the front window. As they ate, Walt couldn't get over that she may be the target of John's revenge. She thought he was acting a little weird, but he was like that sometimes. It was something Laura would have to get used to. She thought of the wedding vows they would say to each other. Notably, the "for better or worse, in sickness and in health, till death do us part."

Eerie silence between them was creating an awkward moment. Laura asked, "Are you okay; you seem distant or preoccupied?"

"No, um, yeah, yeah, I'm fine. I just wanted to have lunch with you today, see your lovely face, hold your hand, and kiss your lips."

"Walt, you know you are such a romantic guy. That's the one thing I love about you the most. I love you so much; I can't imagine life without you."

"Me neither, love you, too."

Holding hands and enjoying the moment, they were oblivious to anyone coming or going through the doors. Several individuals left from a table in the back of the café. When those individuals passed by them on their way out, two men entered taking that same table. It had a line of sight that allowed the two men to watch them without being seen. Laura and Walt finished their lunch and left without noticing either of them.

While Laura and Walt were at lunch, Bernie and Carla were on their way to Flemingsville. With Bernie driving, Carla was observing the scenery as she had never done before. Riding shotgun gave her a different perspective on everything. Bernie was finally getting to drive and on his terms. Even though he was driving five miles under the speed limit, she didn't seem to mind and threw him a smile. Arriving in Flemingsville, they stopped at The Pig and Whistle. Famous for its cheeseburgers and fries, their lunch lived up to its reputation.

After lunch, they headed downtown to All Things Macabre to check out the black roses they had in stock. Pulling in front of the store, they entered, and a chime sounded. It was dark inside, just like the one in Oakmont. The layout of the store appeared to be identical to the one in Oakmont. They weren't there to buy anything other than a black rose that forensics could examine and compare to the others in evidence.

Carla was hoping this one would match the one she recently received. Since the layout was identical to the Oakmont store, they knew where to find them and immediately spotted them. Bernie had already picked one black rose from the display. A young lady with a pierced ring below her lower lip finally came out of the storage room and approached them.

"Hi, I'm Serena, what may I help you find?"

Bernie said, "I think we found what we came in for."

"I see a black rose. Is there anything else you need for your deep or dark lady?"

"No, and my lady is not deep nor dark."

Carla interjected, "Is this the only black roses you have?"

"No, we have more expensive ones behind the counter. We don't put them out unless someone asks for them specifically. I'll go get one and show it to you." She returned with a much higher quality black rose, showing it to them. "This is the best there is, just feel the material in the rose petals."

Carla recognized this black rose as it appeared to be identical to the one she received last week. Bernie asked, "How many of these do you have?"

"We have two left out of the six we ordered."

Carla said, "Did anyone buy several of these in the last month?"

"Yeah, a female college student purchased four of them two weeks ago. I thought it was strange for a college student to waste twenty dollars on them. Maybe her parents had a bunch of money to waste. I wouldn't even spend five dollars for one of them; they're a waste of money."

Bernie said, "What did she look like?

"You know, like every other girl on campus, just take your pick, and that would be her."

Bernie said, "Of course, is there anything else you can tell us?"

"Listen, are you going to buy anything or not?"

A little pissed-off at Serena, Bernie fired back, "Hey, is that any way to treat your customers?

"Sorry, I'm a little on edge today, a big test tomorrow."

"That's better; I'll take one of each. One for the deep and dark lady in my life, the cheap one for the dark mistress I have on the side."

"Well, okay, now. Will that be cash or credit, sir?"

"Cash and a receipt in case either of my ladies wanted to return them." They walked out, and Carla just shook her head back-and-forth and laughed. "What are you laughing for, McBride?"

"Bernie, you're such a dickhead, you know."

"Yeah, I know, but if you can't have any fun in life, why even live. You should learn to live a little more before it's too late, you'll regret it if you don't. Why don't you take some risks now and then?"

Carla rolled her eyes at him, "So, are you a shrink now?"

"Nah, just want to live every day like I'm dying, you know, like the Tim McGraw song Live Like You Were Dying? You should listen to it sometime."

"Seriously, let's go to class, thank goodness we only have five left after tonight."

"Lead the way, partner."

CHAPTER 31

Entering the small lecture hall, Carla shook it up a little, sitting in the front row where she could get a better look at Professor Don. And she was hoping he would pick her to do role-playing because she wanted to get the last word in tonight. Bernie sat three rows up from her near the center all by himself. The rest of the class entered, and within minutes, everyone was present and ready for the class to start.

Professor Don stood just outside the entrance engrossed in a conversation with a lady, probably a colleague of his or someone he was banging. Carla could tell by their actions; their conversation had nothing to do with education. Although she could barely hear them, he told her he would see her tonight. The lady left, and he took the lighted podium. Right off, she noticed that the professor's mustache and goatee were full-grown now and made him look even older than before.

"Good evening, I hope everyone is ready for a little fun tonight. Remember, to be honest, be yourself, and have fun. But before we start any role-playing, let's discuss the twelve ways of managing and diffusing conflict and confrontation used in the Dale Carnegie Training. Who would like to start? And so, that we get to know each other better, stand up and tell us your name again."

A lady in a gray business suit immediately stood up, and Professor Don recognized her, "Great, remember to tell us your name and what you do."

"Hi everyone, I'm Bonnie Prater, and I'm a branch manager at a local bank. In my opinion, the most important action in diffusing conflict is a good listener. You know, really listening to those involved before saying anything at all."

"Great point, Bonnie. Listening is crucial to managing conflict. Thank you. Let's hear from somebody else, and if no one volunteers, I'll pick someone at random. I've always believed those who volunteer are the most prepared and can control the situation. Who wants to be next?"

Bernie was ready to get it over with and stood up, "Hi, I'm Detective Bernie Kowalski with the Oakmont Police Department."

Carla couldn't hold back and murmured, "Can't wait on this one."

Professor Don heard Carla's little blurb, "Detective McBride, do you have something to share with the class?"

"Um…no, sorry, professor."

"Detective Kowalski, please continue. Hopefully, your partner will keep her comments to herself and give you the floor."

"As I was saying, remaining calm, no matter what the circumstances are, is extremely important. In my line of work, every situation can escalate to something dangerous."

"Another great answer, thank you, detective. Alright, who's next?"

A man sitting by Bernie stood up, "Hi, everyone. I'm Gary Elliott, and I'm in human resources at a large regional food processing plant. Admitting that you are wrong is very important as well. It can ease the tension and allow the other person to feel better."

"You guys really know your stuff, great answer, Mr. Elliott. Don't be scared, who's next?"

Over the next hour, eight other classmates stood up and expressed their opinion or belief about which of the twelve strategies were most important. The discussion was professional, entertaining, and calm. Professor Don was eating it up, and the class seemed to have fun as well. Just what he wanted because it made his job that much easier.

"Okay, class. We have one more to discuss, and after that, we can take a break. Who is next?" A moment of silence goes by, and no one is volunteering. "Okay, then. I'll just pick, uh…"

Immediately Carla stood up, "I'm Detective Carla McBride with the Oakmont Police Department. Everything you have said is important. In my opinion, first and foremost, is observing and watching for warning signs, then use any or all of the other eleven reasons to diffuse the situation without it escalating any further."

"Detective McBride, you hit the nail on the head, would you please elaborate?"

"Yeah, an example would be noticing a co-worker using conversational jabs, sarcasm, rudeness, or passive-aggressive behavior with someone. Before acting, take the time to observe and listen to them. Then you can decide the best course of action to diffuse it before it reaches the conflict stage."

"Excellent, Detective McBride. Thank you. Let's take a fifteen-minute break, and when we resume, it's role-playing time."

The lecture hall quickly emptied into the main common area; most people just stood around and talked, while some relieved themselves. With it freezing outside, Carla and Bernie walked down the long corridor that led to the main lecture hall. Inside, a guest speaker was talking about the Great Recession. The event was part of the college's Symposium on America's Recovery from the Great Recession. They peeked through two glass windows in the door to observe the speaker using his hands while talking. Having seen enough, they walked back to the lecture hall.

"Bernie, it seems like everybody these days has a solution to the world's problems and issues. The problem, you know, is that today's solutions will become tomorrow's problems. Kind of what goes around eventually comes back around."

"Wow, that's pretty insightful."

"That's just the way it is."

"Yeah, I guess so. Your answer at the end of the class was fantastic. I'm sure you impressed Professor Don with all your bullshit."

"Wasn't BS, dickhead. I've had that training before, use it every day on the job."

"Guess you are returning to your normal self."

"Let's head back to class and get this shit over with."

The class resumed with only enough time for two role-playing skits. Since no one was interested in volunteering, Professor Don chose individuals that hadn't taken part in the class thus far.

Traveling back to Oakmont seemed like an eternity for Carla as Bernie was moving his usual speed, which aggravated the hell out of her. Neither was talking, so he turned on the satellite radio. Bernie liked all genres and picked an easy-listening station because it matched the mood in the car. Soon, Bernie started singing and stopped, "Carla, that's the song I was telling you about, the one by Tim McGraw, Live Like You Were Dying. Just listen to the lyrics."

"Okay, but it's just a song."

"Yeah, but country songs are about living, dying, and all the struggles in people's lives. You know, actual events in the singer's life sometimes are the basis for the song."

"Shut up so I can listen, dickhead."

She heard the first three lines of the song, and then her mind wandered as the lyrics took her back to the black rose incident. How it freaked her out, brought her to her knees. Then she thought about Chris, her big brother, that came to her rescue. The three days she spent with him had been unbelievable, one of the best times in her life.

Suddenly, Bernie swerved to miss something in the road, causing her head to hit the window, waking her up from a dream-like trance just in time to hear the end of the song. Listening to the lyrics, she thought about the message of the song. Before she realized it, they were at the police station. They chatted for a few moments, and each left to go home. Bernie was going back to his deep and dark wife of twenty-five years. At the same time,

Carla was going home to an apartment filled with emptiness and loneliness.

Carla always had Jameson to turn to when she arrived
home. He was her liquid lover and confidant for now.
Pouring a double shot of him, she prepared for a good
night's sleep. Taking care of things in the bathroom, she
came out dressed in yellow sheer-like lounging pants with
a form-fitting long-sleeved white blouse. Looking at her
reflection in the mirror, she thought of the night she wore
this same outfit in front of Chris and didn't give it a second
thought. She remembered his expression. It was a look of
awesomeness and wonderment. Her reflection in the
mirror told her why. That night she was a stunning red-
headed Irish woman flaunting her sexuality right in his
face. She thought any other man would have acted, but he
didn't. They had that special relationship that wouldn't
allow it. He respected that, and that meant the world to her.

A few sips of Jameson and it was lights out. The
remainder would have to wait for another day. A deep
sleep enveloped her body and inner soul. Dreams came
fast and furious. Pleasant dreams, dreams of happiness.
One moment she was riding a merry-go-round at the park
with her friends, and the next, she was on vacation with
her parents as a teenager.

Then her first kiss and her sixteenth birthday party
flashed in front of her. Her senior prom and the all-night
party held at her high school floated in front of her. Then
graduation day and remembering how proud her parents
were that day. Then off to college. Pledge week and then
joining a sorority. Football games and tailgating. College
graduation ceremonies and parties.

Dreams moved at warp speed. She was in the police

academy, then graduation, and becoming a rookie police officer, and later a bad-ass detective. Those were the happy times, and more dreams of happiness flew throughout her mind. Subconsciously, she was waiting for them to end, but they didn't. Dreams of golfing with Laura, Walt, and Chris, her big bro as she called him and dinners with Laura, her Bestie.

Then her dreams moved in slow-motion and finally came to a halt. She was back at the General Lewis Inn, where she was coming out of the bathroom. Chris was staring at her beauty and sexuality. He couldn't resist her any longer, picking her up he placed her on the bed. His kisses were soft and then exploring. In a trance, she accepted his love and affection.

Primal urge and instinct overcame them, and explosions of heat, lust, and passion made them wholesome and one. Neither could resist their desires to explore each other's wants and needs. Her dreams took her to new heights of sexuality. She was in another world, a world of happiness, love, and peace.

Awake now, she looked towards the ceiling, drawing her knees to her chest, she moaned and groaned, trying to catch her breath. Her clothes soaked in a sultry hot sweat clung to her sensual, silky skin. Glancing at her cell phone, Two AM glared back. She turned on the nightstand lamp to see if Jameson was still alive. He was, she picked-up the glass, took a sip, and then downed his amber life.

Her heart was still pounding. Her wet clothes clung to her innocence. Standing in her bathroom, she removed them, turned on the shower. She entered to cool her primal desires burning inside. Exhausted from her dreams, she toweled off and crawled back in bed. As she lay naked under the blanket, she drifted off to another happy dream world to the tune of "*Live Like You Were Dying*" dancing in her head.

Morning came quickly. Surprised to find herself naked, she tried to remember how that might have happened because she remembered having on a nightgown when she crawled into bed last night. Jameson was gone. Entering the bathroom, she could see her clothes lying on the floor. Reaching down to pick them up, the dampness from the sweat of her erotic dreams lingered throughout them.

Turning on the shower, she wanted to clear the grogginess still holding on to her body. After toweling off, she put her fluffy robe on, then to the kitchen to brew coffee. While it was brewing, she opened the fridge, the eggs, bacon, and orange juice that Chris bought last week remained ready for an encore. The smell of the omelet still lingered in the air while his scent flowed out from the fridge. Smiling, moments of her dreams slowly flashed in her head. After pouring herself a cup of coffee, she was eager to begin a new day in her life.

Enjoying her coffee, the events of the past week flooded her mind. As she reflected on the good and bad in her life, Tim McGraw's song kept dancing in her head. Carla knew life was passing her by, and she didn't like what she saw in the mirror of her future self. Something had to change, and that would start today. Putting her phone on speaker, she dialed Laura's phone number and waited for her to answer.

"Carla, what are you calling so early for?"

"Laura, I just wanted to hear your voice. Is Walt there?"

"Ah, yes. um, did you want to speak to him?"

"No, just tell him I said hi."

"Okay, um, are you okay?"

"Ah, yeah, I'm fine, gotta run. Love you."

"Love you, too."

Ending that call, she left her phone on speaker and dialed another number waiting for someone to answer it.

"Carla, so nice to hear from you. How are—"

Before Chris could finish his sentence, she interrupted him as she always did, "Chris, lunch today, Sunroom at the club, won't take no for an answer. See you then."

Chris couldn't believe what he just heard, "Well, okay…"

Not letting him get another word in edgewise, she ended the call. Her life would change today for the better. Living life as if there was no tomorrow was the first item on her menu, she would place that order today and embrace it.

CHAPTER 32

Random expressions moved up and down Carla's face. She had many things on her mind as she battled her emotions of happiness and uncertainty. Bothered by many things, she had many questions, but no answers. Was her intuition that Laura was in danger, correct? Did John Dickerson really have revenge on this mind? Where were Hank Fisher and Charles Brown? What was Hank Fisher's DNA doing at two different crime scenes in two different states? Where was John Dickerson, and where was his wife, Gina, and her son, Landon? Like Jeopardy, but in reverse. Many questions appeared on the board, and she just had to find the correct answers or lose this psychotic game to John Dickerson, who promised revenge.

Bernie sat across from her reviewing files and reports, and his expression never changed, he was an even keel kind of man, his disposition was one of calmness. She remembered the ride home the other night and the song Bernie, sort of lived his life by. Looking up the lyrics, she realized the meaning of them, how life, good or bad, can change in an instant. Someone once told her, we're all a phone call away from a tragedy that will change your life forever.

Before the most important lunch in her life, she had an out-of-the-box hunch she wanted to explore with Patsy Groves, the police department's sketch artist. Gina Dickerson was foremost on her mind and in a witness protection program. Meeting Alicia Maddox at the General Lewis Inn in Lewisburg, she looked very familiar to her.

Carla was hoping Patsy could prove one of her burning questions, whether Gina Dickerson transformed herself into Alicia Maddox and living in Lewisburg. If her hunch panned out, she wasn't sure how to use her discovery or whether it had anything to do with her current investigation; however, her intuition was telling her it would come in handy sometime in the future.

Lunch with Chris would be the first step in really living her life like she was dying. Committing to loving Chris was scary to her, but she realized it was now worth the risk. The black rose was a wakeup call. After lunch, she and Bernie would re-visit the Oakmont location of All Things Macabre. Bernie had already given the black roses he bought in Flemingsville to forensics to examine and compare with the ones already in the evidence locker.

Patsy, gifted as a sketch artist at facial recognition and reconstruction, could make something out of nothing. Carla was hoping she could transform a picture of Gina from her description of Alicia Maddox. Carla had emailed Patsy the most recent photo of Gina saved from the publishing company's website. At her workstation,

Patsy was ready to transform Gina into Alicia Maddox, if that was possible.

"So, you want me to take this photo and transform it into a different person based on your description of the person you met in Lewisburg, is that what you want?"

"Correct. So, why don't you begin by removing all her hair? Okay, now would you give her a new hairstyle like the singer, Pink?"

"Okay, I must go online and pull several photos of her. It will just be a minute. She has several styles."

Pulling up several pictures of Pink, Patsy showed them to Carla. After studying the hairstyles, she pointed out the one she wanted. Patsy made one click and nodded.

"Color the hair, dark black." Another click, Patsy waited for further instructions. "Add a pair of glasses, black frames, that fit just below her eyebrows. We're getting close. Thinner eyebrows, please."

"Now, is that her?"

"Something's missing; Gina Dickerson was a little heavier. The lady at the hotel was the same height, but much thinner, closer to about one-hundred pounds."

"Okay, um, let's reduce her facial features by about fifteen percent and see what we get. How's that?"

"Damn, that's her, the lady at the hotel, um, Alicia Maddox, please print that out for me and the picture of Gina we started with."

"You got it, anything else?"

"Not today, maybe later. I need to be sure of my hunch on this first. And mum is the word on this, thanks."

Patsy nodded. Carla put the two pictures in a manila

folder and returned to her desk. At this point in proving her hunch, she would keep it a secret. She knew partners shouldn't keep each other out of the loop and any information about their cases; however, this was a hunch she wasn't ready to share with Bernie until it became relevant.

Her phone chimed, lunch in fifteen minutes at Avondale Country Club with Chris, appeared on the screen. She wasn't sure how this lunch would go; she hadn't practiced or even thought about what she wanted to say. As her pulse raced, second-guessing thoughts crept into her soul.

Arriving at the country club a few minutes early, she walked up the steps to enter the country club by the Sunroom. Looking through the windows, she liked what she saw—iced tea with lemon positioned above the cloth napkins while salads were ready on the placemat. Three yellow roses on the table created an intimate atmosphere. Carla, in many ways, wanted this lunch to be special. Somehow, Chris had taken the initiative to set that mood.

Entering the mansion, Chris immediately greeted her, then showed her to the Sunroom and pulled out her chair for her. He sat across from her, admiring her beauty. For a moment or so, silence created awkwardness until he raised his drink for a toast. Following his lead, their glasses met in the center of the table.

"Cheers to us, thank you for suggesting we have lunch. I had salads ready for us. Once we finish them, we will enjoy our famous penne pasta with marinara sauce. Is that okay with you? If not, we'll order something different."

"That's fine; everything is perfect, didn't know you were a mind reader."

"I'm not, but I think I know you pretty well. So, why

are we having lunch today? Don't take that the wrong way. It thrilled me that you suggested, no, told me we're having lunch today. I would love to have lunch with you every day for the rest of my life."

Blushing a little, she replied, "You've always been a big brother to me, and I love you in that relationship. I love what we have. When I need you, you're always there for me and all. Umm, this past weekend was one of the best times of my life. I finally realized that life is short, and my life may be passing me by. This lunch is about living my life as I should've a long time ago. So…"

Carrie, their server, suddenly arrived to retrieve their salad dishes, interrupting her. "Are you guys ready for the penne pasta, more bread, and iced tea?"

"Carrie, um, that would be great, thank you."

"As I was saying Chris, uh, I want to throw our brother-sister relationship out the door and start all over. I know it's risky, and if it doesn't work, we could lose what we have now, and that would crush both of us."

Again, Carrie arrived with the penne pasta dish and interrupted their conversation. "Here you go, enjoy." Chris nodded. "You're welcome, boss."

"Anyway, Chris, I don't want either of us to get hurt. You have a concerned look on your face, what are you thinking?"

"Yeah, I get it. I understand the risks, but I'm willing to take them. I've been waiting for this for a long time. We'll just have to make sure it works. So, where do we start?"

"Right here, lunch every week, just like today. Dinner each Saturday, I get to pick the place. Then we will see where it goes. We need to take it nice and slow, and that goes for any intimate physical part of our relationship. Chris, I saw how you looked at me last weekend. You want me terribly, but I need time to make sure it's what I want, and I'll let you know when I'm ready for you. Are you okay with those terms?"

"I'll do my best, but you were so damn hot in your jammies, you're hard to resist."

"Well, I'll do my best not to tantalize you too much."

"Deal, we better eat our pasta before it gets cold."

Finished with their lunch, he walked her out to her car and opened the door for her. After closing it, he turned to walk away. She lowered the window, unsure of what she was going to do.

"Hey, come here for a minute." He turned around and leaned down toward her. "Come closer." Leaning in closer, she planted a soft kiss on his lips. It wasn't a lingering kiss, just a sweet kiss that said I'm beginning to love you differently. She pulled her head away and smiled.

"What was that for?"

With a smile on her face, she replied, "I guess it's time I acted like your girlfriend instead of your sister. Will you call me tonight so we can talk?"

Nodding, he watched her drive up the road to fight crime. While entering the mansion, he couldn't wipe the smile off his face. Carrie had been cleaning off the table in the Sunroom and witnessed everything. She just smiled at him and winked. Still wearing an ear-to-ear smile, a colorful warmness covered his face. Looking at Carrie with that big smile, he sarcastically said, "What?"

Carrie just rolled her eyes and laughed, "Nothing, boss, nothing."

CHAPTER 33

Arranging to meet at All Things Macabre at One-thirty PM, Bernie waited in his car outside the store until Carla arrived. Entering the store, they noticed two people browsing around. At the counter was the same person who helped Bernie the other day. A young lady named Alex greeted them at the checkout counter. Although Bernie had just been in there last week, he flashed his badge and introduced Carla.

"I was in here the other day and purchased one of the black roses you have on display back there. We were in Flemingsville yesterday and stopped in that store. I assume the same person or company owns both stores, is that correct?" Alex nodded. "Well, um, that store had some other black roses behind the counter that were more expensive. Do you carry them?"

"Normally, we have them, but over a week ago or so, we sold the last ones we had. We have another shipment coming in soon, and if you leave me your name and number, I can call you when they come in."

"Nah, that won't be necessary. We're just here for information. Who bought the roses?"

"Uh, two men, they bought all we had, I believe it was two or three."

"What did they look like?"

"Maybe early fifties, one small guy, say around five feet, five inches, while the other was about six feet, two inches or so."

Pointing at the wall behind the counter, Bernie asked, "Does that camera work?"

"Yeah, but it rewrites after seven days, sorry."

Bernie pulled out his phone and brought up a photo and showed it to her. "Is this them?"

"Could be, but not sure, didn't pay that much attention to them."

"Okay, thank you."

Nodding, Alex left to attend to another customer. Even though they got the information they came for, visiting the Dark World would cover all their bases and due diligence. Carla left her car parked in front of All Things Macabre and let Bernie drive to Dark World, and it was a bust.

Dropping Carla off at her car, he went back to the police station, while she went to visit Laura. Waiting in the law firm reception area, she heard footsteps coming down the hallway. Laura waved her back to her office, where she sat across from her. Unsure what prompted this unexpected visit, Laura looked a little puzzled as Carla sat in silence, gazing around the office.

Before Laura could ask a question, Carla blurted out, "I had lunch with Chris today."

"So."

"No, I really had lunch with him, not as that brother-sister thing, more like the other kind of thing."

"What do you mean? You are not making any sense."

Looking giddy like a teenager in love, she said, "I took your advice, well maybe Bernie's too. Chris and I will take it slow and see where our relationship goes."

"That's it, um, you're in love with my brother, I knew it."

"Not in love, um, yeah, I guess I am in love with him. The time I spent in Lewisburg with him was special."

Hugging her, Carla told her everything. Even her erotic dream from last night. Every…last…detail. Laura looked at her and saw a different person. A person that seemed happy, but more importantly, letting happiness enter her life once and for all.

"It's about time; how did he react?"

"Um, let's just say he was stunned and speechless. He walked me out to my car and opened the door for me like the gentleman that he is. As he walked away, I rolled down my window and asked him to come closer. He did, and I planted a soft kiss on his lips, I guess it was our first real kiss of the next chapter of our lives."

"You go, girl, what's next?"

"Gonna have lunch each Wednesday and dinner on Saturday. Take it slow until we're sure we can handle this new relationship. I hope we will be compatible. We're both taking risks hoping that it will work."

"It will, I see it in both of your eyes when you're together."

"I hope you are right, Laura."

"Hey, let me ask you a question on a different subject."

"Shoot."

"Since there have not been any other incidents at Lake Catalpa, is it safe for me to jog there?"

"I would stay away from there; the old high school track would be better since more people use it, and it's just safer, especially in the morning."

"Thanks, that's what I thought, but I wanted to get your opinion. Walt will join me when he can."

"Great, guess it's time for me to get back to solving crimes, see you later, love you."

"Love you back."

CHAPTER 34

After sharing a hug, Carla returned to the police station to focus on the case, aptly named the Black Rose. At her desk, she opened a manila folder and stared at the two photos inside. One was of Gina Dickerson, while the other was a sketch using Gina Dickerson's picture. The woman Patsy created looked eerie similar to Alicia Maddox, assistant manager at the General Lewis Inn. At least it did to her and Patsy, Alicia Maddox could be Gina Dickerson. Then the other question, more important than any, was it related to her current case involving the murder of AJ Gonzalez, and the black rose?

Who was Alicia Maddox she kept asking herself? A quick Google search revealed who she was, or at least what was on the internet. It stated she was born and raised in a small town of White Sulphur Springs, West Virginia. Smaller than Lewisburg, White Sulphur was more famous because of The Greenbrier Resort. The resort was luxury and relaxation at its best. First-class-everything and very expensive she found out.

According to the internet, Alicia went to local schools throughout her early education, graduating with honors from East Greenbrier High School. She then attended West Virginia Wesleyan University majoring in business administration with a minor in hotel management. After graduation, she landed a job in her hometown at The Greenbrier Resort, where she worked until her recent appointment as assistant manager at the General Lewis Inn.

According to the internet, she had been an assistant manager at the General Lewis Inn for over two years now. Carla wondered why someone would leave The Greenbrier Resort for the General Lewis Inn. Undoubtedly, The Greenbrier Resort paid more money than her current job. However, money wasn't everything to some people, maybe the history and mystique of the General Lewis Inn attracted her. Why Alicia would leave America's resort for an old historic hotel in Lewisburg raised a red flag in her mind.

Further down the list was some personal information. The information stated she was married to Gary Maddox, a coal operator in White Sulphur Springs, for about twenty years. They divorced three years ago, and maybe that's why she left The Greenbrier Resort. There was no mention of any children raising a red flag. Carla knew placing credible information on the internet was necessary for people entering the federal witness protection program.

To test that, she searched for Gary Maddox. As she expected, he was supposedly legit, according to the internet. She printed all the information she found and placed it in her secret manila folder with information for Alicia

Maddox, or Gina Dickerson. In her mind, they were the same person, but only time would tell if she was right. She put the file folder in her desk drawer and locked it for safekeeping when and if she ever needed it.

Carla recounted her day oblivious to what was going on around her, even ignoring Bernie's antics. By her account, which was the only one that mattered, she had had a great day. She had decided that Alicia Maddox was Gina Dickerson until otherwise proven differently. She was tucked away in a West Virginia town living her new life. When she and Chris met her at the General Lewis Inn, she looked happy and thankful that she was alive.

Carla finally realized that her relationship with Chris was no longer the brother-sister thing she felt safe with; it was now much more. She started that today with a kiss, a real kiss that sealed the deal. How fast the relationship would proceed was up to her because Chris was ready to take it to the next level. Today, she finally discovered she was in love with a man she had always loved. However, today, it was a different type of love.

"Carla…Carla…Carla! Earth to Carla. What is going—"

"Bernie, I can hear you, what do you want, dickhead?"

"What are you so preoccupied about?"

"Everything, uh, I started living my life like I was dying."

"Well, good for you. Have a great evening and a drink on me."

"You too, partner. I'm heading out as well, see you tomorrow."

Once again, Bernie was heading home to the woman

of his dreams. Every night he would greet his wife with a big hug and a kiss. She would serve him a wholesome Polish meal, and then he would sleep with the love of his life. He was a happy man, and it was easy for Carla to see why he loved life so much.

All Carla had, for now, was Jameson, her imaginary lover posing as a glass of whiskey. An empty glass still sat on the counter from last night's journey through her subconscious world. She gave Jameson a new life on the rocks as she poured him into the glass. Taking him to the loveseat, she took a sip of his amber love. He tasted good but not as good as Chris's sensual lips. It was almost the perfect ending to her day. Having Chris would make it perfect. But she's the one that wanted to take it slow and easy until they were sure this new relationship was real and going to work.

The nightly news would inform her of the day's top events, while Wheel of Fortune and Jeopardy would challenge her brain until Chris called. Around Eight PM, he called, and they talked for almost two hours. Joking and laughing just getting to know each other better as a couple and finally finding real love. Even though Jameson was hovering next to her lips, it was not him she wanted to taste. Jameson was slowly replacing Chris as her big brother instead of her liquid lover.

The evening had passed, and Carla crawled in bed with Jameson. She sat the half-empty glass on the nightstand. Her lamp gave way to darkness. Closing her eyes, she escaped to a state of bliss. Dreams began to surface; her subconscious embraced them. Like previous nights, dreams of happiness took her to her youth, growing up in Oakmont. Temporarily, images of the black rose hid in her subconscious world, waiting to threaten her soul. Her dreams put her and Chris in their room at the General Lewis Inn, as passionate, sultry, love quenched her raging hormones in her subconscious world.

CHAPTER 35

ike most mornings, Carla and Bernie reviewed notes and evidence hoping something new would jumpstart the Black Rose case. Frustration was taking its toll on them. While rubbing his temples to relax his thoughts, Bernie's phone rang, startling him. Answering it, he listened to the caller, then immediately ended the call.

"Carla, we've got a situation at the courthouse."

"Great, that's all we need while we're deep into finding AJ's killer."

"There's no time to chit-chat, let's go."

"Damn, I was hoping we would have a slow day to end the week, so much for that."

"Sorry, partner, but crime doesn't take days off."

Arriving at the county courthouse, a lady in her forties was pacing back and forth, wringing her hands. Approaching her, they identified themselves with badges flashing. The lady introduced herself as Dabney Larson. Frazzled didn't describe a look of sheer concern plastered on her face. A nervous person, to begin with, Dabney was always thinking the worst when a situation developed, whether it be job-related or in her personal life. She was a worrier, plain, and simple.

Bernie said, "Ma'am, what's going on?"

"Judge Ashley Harrington, uh, is thirty minutes late for the first item on the docket. She, um, hadn't called, uh, and that's not like her, you know. I didn't know what to do, umm, or who else to call, so I called you guys."

Carla responded, "Dabney, just calm down, slow down, please."

"Okay, but, uh, I just know some perp has got her, oh my…"

"Let's go over there and sit down; you need to calm down if we're going to help you." Nodding, she sat on a bench just outside the courtroom. Directing her gaze at Bernie, Carla said, "Why don't you go in the courtroom and see what the situation looks like there. Talk to both lawyers and anybody else that's in there."

"Sure, you're better at calming down whacko people like her, good luck with this one."

"Now, Bernie, you're not playing nice."

Turning her attention back to Dabney, she was wringing her hands repeatedly. "Dabney, take several deep breaths, and let's start from the beginning."

"She's never late, never. She's always early, always. Uh, I didn't worry until about ten minutes before her first case. I called her husband, who is out of town, but he didn't pick up my call. As it got closer and closer and still no Judge Harrington, uh, I started to panic. After another ten minutes, I called you guys. I know something has happened to her; I just know it."

"We don't know that, so, please stay calm. What's the first case about?"

"You remember the allegedly DUI case about six months ago, where the son of a powerful bank president and state senator, hit an SUV killing the mother and her unborn son."

"Yeah, I remember, go on."

"Her husband, Adam Prescott, an army corporal deployed in Afghanistan at the time of the accident, was very unhappy with the plea deal the defendant made. Judge Harrington was to announce his sentence this morning."

"Okay, where is Mr. Prescott now?"

"I'm not sure, he lives in Oakmont, being treated at the Veteran's Hospital in Lexington for PTSD."

"Okay, what else can you tell me?"

"I don't know, Detective McBride, she's a judge, and no matter how she rules, she will make someone mad. You're going to find her, aren't you?"

"Unfortunately, until we get any further information that proves she is missing, we have to sit tight. We must look at any possibility of who might want to harm her. Is there anything else that you can think of at this moment?"

"Nothing else, I know her very well, and this is not like her at all. I know something has happened to her. I just know someone has her. You have to…"

"Dabney, we will do everything we can to bring this to a safe conclusion. We'll check for accidents, you know, check hospitals before we jump to conclusions that Mr. Prescott has her, and you need to remain calm if you want to help us, can you do that?"

Nodding, she continued sitting on the bench, wringing her hands. Bernie returned from the courtroom drama informing Carla that both lawyers expected the defendant to receive the lightest possible sentence because of his father's influence. And that Adam Prescott had planned to be here today for the sentencing. When he didn't show, his lawyer called his cell, went straight to voicemail.

"So, Carla, Adam Prescott, who is suffering from PTSD, kidnapped the judge thinking it would get her to issue the maximum sentence. Goes off the deep end because he's got nothing to lose."

"Could be, have you heard anything, you know about any accidents, or maybe she had an emergency and went to the hospital for treatment?"

Bernie had already checked with the police officers outside the courthouse, and there were no active accidents in the area. Calling the regional medical center, Judge Harrington was not a patient at the moment. That left them with only one hunch to play, and that was Adam Prescott.

"Bernie, guess we need to talk to his lawyer. Go get him."

"Don't have to, here he comes now."

Bernie motioned for Adam Prescott's lawyer to meet with them. His lawyer slowly approached them with a casual attitude as Bernie was still waving at him. "Mr. Brody, this is my partner, Detective Carla McBride."

"Nice to meet you, how may I help you?"

Carla asked, "Mr. Brody, where is your client?"

"I don't know, I talked to him this morning, and he seemed just fine. You know he has his moments with PTSD, he said he would be here."

Carla replied, "What time was that?"

"Uh, I guess it was around seven-thirty."

Carla asked, "Do you know where he lives?"

"See those apartments above Amsbury's Clothing, that's where he lives. I've already been there, and no one answered the door."

Carla responded, "Doesn't mean he's not there. Bernie, go visit Amsbury's and see if we can get in his apartment and check things out."

"On it, partner."

"He's not in there, and his car is gone," responded Mr. Brody.

"Maybe not, but if he abducted the judge, we might find something in there that drove him off the edge. Now, does Mr. Prescott work?"

"He is employed at Goodwin's Commercial Services. Got that job through temp services. Seemed to be doing just fine."

Bernie visited Don Amsbury and persuaded him to let him search Adam Prescott's apartment. Bernie knocked on the door several times, but no one answered. Mr. Amsbury unlocked the door and backed out of the way. With his service weapon drawn, he entered the apartment. The loft-style apartment had a bedroom off to the left, the door was open, and he could see that no one was in there. Across from the bedroom was a small bathroom. It was clear—the loft area, which included a small kitchenette and living area, was all clear as well. There was no sign of Adam Prescott anywhere.

Looking around the apartment for anything or a clue that would have caused him to abduct the judge, he saw nothing in the loft area. Walking back to the bedroom, he couldn't find anything that would be a reason Adam would do this. That left the tiny bathroom, as soon as Bernie entered the bathroom, a picture of an ultrasound on the bathroom mirror grabbed his attention.

Written on it was Adam Prescott, Jr., January 27, 2012. Bernie glanced at his digital watch, then grabbed the picture. Running out of the apartment and down a flight of stairs, he quickly assessed any on-coming traffic. Once safe, he sprinted across the street to the courthouse, where Carla was finishing up with Mr. Brody.

Out of breath and sweating a little, he held the picture toward Carla. "Look at this, it probably drove him off the edge, caused him to do something this stupid."

One look at the photo gave them their answer to why he presumably abducted the judge, and she handed it to Mr. Brody. He shook his head back-and-forth and said, "Damn, so, today was when his son was supposed to be born. And that probably drove him off the edge. Now, what, detectives?"

"Bernie, we've got to find him before it's too late. We'll start with his employer."

Wasting no time, they arrived at Goodwin's Commercial Services in the Oakmont Park Office Complex off the bypass. Entering the business, they identified themselves as they flashed their badges. Asking for the plant manager, a few minutes later, Ted Fox greeted them. Inquiring whether Adam Prescott was working today, Mr. Fox shook his head back-and-forth.

After a brief discussion of where he might be, Mr. Fox informed them of the original building that housed the business. Although it was a shot in the dark, their intuition told them to start there. Securing the keys for the vacant building, they left, hoping he was there, that Judge Ashley Harrington was there and alive.

CHAPTER 36

rriving at the original building that once housed Goodwin's Commercial Services, the door was already ajar. Near the main entrance was a beat-up truck, presumably owned by Adam Prescott. It was empty; Bernie placed his hand on the hood, which was still warm. Carla called for backup and EMS in silent mode. Spooking a former Army corporal with PTSD could have unintended and tragic consequences, something they were hoping to avoid. Putting on their Kevlar vests, neither of them had a good feeling about this hostage situation since Adam Prescott had nothing to lose.

A peek inside the door, nothing but darkness met their eyes. With service weapons drawn, flashlights beaming, Carla called out his name and identified themselves. Silence. On her count, they entered an atmosphere of deep uncertainty. Dead silence continued throughout the building, while the musty air stood still.

She called out his name again; faint breathing in the distance grabbed their attention. Finally, a broken and unstable voice murmured under his breath. Unstable emotions were clearly controlling Adam Prescott. As they moved closer, his breathing grew heavier.

"Mr. Prescott, this is Detective McBride, please let us help you."

"Go away…or…uh, the judge dies."

Carla responded, "We're here to help you."

"Can you bring my wife and son back?"

"No, we can't, and you know that. And neither can Judge Harrington. So, just let her go, and we will get you some help."

"Nobody can help me, the VA couldn't, and you can't, someone has to pay for taking my wife and son, Adam Jr., away from me. She was all I had, and that bastard stole her from me along with my unborn son."

"Adam, take it easy."

Silence had once again captured the building creating an atmosphere of tragic uncertainty. Breathing became more labored, drowning out their soft footsteps as they approached Adam and Judge Harrington. Carla motioned Bernie to continue working towards Adam's voice. A beam of light faded across Adam's body, then landing on Judge Harrington. Gagged and bound to a metal folding chair, fear painted her face. Behind the judge, Adam pressed his weapon to her head, and she flinched, letting out a feeble murmur. He pushed it harder against her temple and whispered, "Shut up."

Nodding, Judge Harrington grew quiet. Carla did her best to keep the conversation going while Bernie positioned himself for a clean shot if it came down to that. Inching closer, Carla made another attempt at communicating with him. Adam's breathing grew heavier and heavier.

Startling Carla, he said, "Don't come near me, nobody can help me. I already told you that."

"Okay. Tell you what, Adam. I'm going to walk towards you slowly. I'll put my gun down, and you do the same."

"Stop, or she dies."

"Then you'll die, do you want that?"

"I don't know, uh, what I want anymore."

Apparently, Adam's emotions were out of bounds; Carla knew this hostage situation was heading in the wrong direction, and very fast. Meanwhile, Bernie was in position, ready to take a shot. Eerie silence catapulted throughout the building as she inched closer and closer to Adam.

Carla and Bernie had not been partners very long, making communication in these situations somewhat tricky, especially in unfamiliar darkness. However, they had talked enough about the ways they would communicate in these situations. She hoped he remembered, and they would be on the same page.

Suddenly, Carla turned off her flashlight, waited five seconds, and turned it back on. Their moment of truth had arrived. Creeping slowly, a quick beam of light hit Adam's eyes, startling him. Shielding his eyes gave Carla her chance to move in. While she crept toward him, her misstep sent an empty paint can rolling across the concrete floor, whispering vulgarity under her breath, she froze.

Reacting to the noise, Adam fired an errant shot in her direction ricocheting off a metal support post; echoes continued to bounce from wall to wall. During all this surreal commotion, Judge Harrington had rocked the chair, falling forward to the floor away from Adam.

Boom...Boom!

Adam returned fire, Bernie grunted as he grabbed his shoulder, then his leg, his weapon dropped to the floor. Darkness and silence filled the building again. Carla's light blinded Adam, shielding his eyes, he fired erratically in her direction. Moving the beam of light from his face to his torso, Carla took aim.

*Boom...boom...*thundered off the walls followed by a thud and a clang of metal, shining her flashlight on Adam's body, a bloody silhouette of death laid on the floor. His weapon was a few inches from his outstretched hand. With her gun still in kill mode, she crept toward him, kicking his gun out of the way. Checking for a pulse, she breathed a big sigh of relief.

Hurrying to aide Bernie, blood oozed from his left shoulder onto her hand. EMS had been on standby and rushed in. After stabilizing Bernie, they rushed him to the hospital where he would undergo surgery to his left shoulder, the superficial wound to the left leg would not require surgery. Police officers already on the scene attended to Judge Harrington, who refused treatment.

Visiting the hospital, ER personnel informed Carla that Bernie was still in surgery, and confirmed that his injuries were not life threatening. Hoping to meet his wife, she asked for her. Carla was informed that Bernie's wife had been visiting relatives in Tennessee and was on her way to the hospital. Waiting until he was out of surgery and in recovery, Carla returned to the police station to wrap things up.

Paperwork could wait until tomorrow or even the next day. She knew the events of the day would put her on desk duty until an internal investigation was completed, and that suited her just fine. A night with

Jameson would help her attempt to erase the heartbreak and emotional rollercoaster she was riding if that was even possible. Until today, she had never taken another human life before. Adam Prescott, unfortunately, was her first kill, and guilt began to punish her soul.

CHAPTER 37

Jameson was willing, waiting for Carla when she arrived at her lonely apartment. The bottle of Irish Whiskey had several ounces of life remaining, and then it would be dead, just like Adam Prescott. She hoped that would be enough to erase the horrible events of today. She had fired her weapon many times before, and wounding criminals that needed to be stopped. However, today, she took a human life for the first time. Even though she saved at least two other lives today, somehow killing an individual was tearing her soul into shreds. She wondered why someone should feel so guilty of taking a life when it meant saving lives, even her own.

Jameson anxiously waited to taste her lips, relieve her tension, ease the guilt she was feeling. Tasteless, the first shot burned as it went down, the warmth felt good. Taking a deep breath, she quickly exhaled. Replenishing her glass, she let it mellow over ice as the guilt continued to attack her sanity. Her palate experienced caramel and vanilla the second time around, Jameson went down much smoother, warming her soul even more.

Her apartment looked lonely, and the atmosphere was cold and bleak. Another shot of Jameson would hopefully chase away all of her guilt-ridden thoughts and numb her mind. She downed it; Jameson didn't have much life left but continued to taunt her to finish him. A night of living hell was at the bottom of the Irish Whiskey.

Carla would be all alone except for Jameson, her liquid lover. Taking another sip, she savored it just thinking about life in general and Chris. Learning how to live life rather than letting life's pitfalls rule her every waking moment would take time. Still, Carla knew she would get there, and was more determined than ever to have that kind of life.

Her first kill changed her life forever; she wondered if she could go it alone. Taking Jameson to the bathroom, the bathtub began to fill with hot steaming water. Her hand felt its warmth, adjusting it to her liking, she slipped out of her clothes of despair. Bath oil and liquid soap sent ripples across the smooth watery surface. Removing her Victoria Secret ensemble, she gazed into the mirror. Her reflection showed a tired body needing rejuvenating and loved.

While relaxing in the soft fluffy bubbles, Jameson helped her reflect on just about every moment of her life, the good and the bad. In her mind, thoughts of Chris warmed her soul as the hot water soothed her tense body. She couldn't fathom why one of the best weeks of her life ended up so horribly. The water was now lukewarm, and her hands showed signs of wrinkling. She didn't know how long she was in the bathtub, but her glass was now empty.

Opening the drain, today's guilt and misery swirled

into a world of emptiness. After toweling off, her body looked new and alive. Choosing the pale-yellow pajama bottoms and the white form-fitting blouse that Chris liked so much, she remembered his expression that night in Lewisburg. Her body still wet, the dampness outlined her sensuality, that until now, remained hidden.

With her glass in hand, she walked to the kitchen. Jameson was on life support, his final ounce of life splashed over the ice in her glass. While tasting his flavors, his warmness eased her guilt-ridden soul. Savoring the changing nuances of his last few drops, Jameson was gone; her apartment was still cold and lonely.

Eyes glistening, tears trickled down to the crown of her mouth. While her emotions exploded, the doorbell startled her. Still charged up, she grabbed her Glock, ready to act. Slowly her right eye covered the peephole. After a deep breath and a big sigh, she smiled. Flinging the door open, Chris swaddled her in his arms. Guilt-ridden tension rushed out into the night air as the door closed. Tears of joy replaced the demons of guilt, zapping her soul. Wiping her cheeks dry, he kissed her tenderly and deep, igniting her hormones.

Overwhelmed by emotions, her embrace searched for more of his love. Her firm breasts pressed against his chest, arousing the heat building in his groin. Primal urges teased each other as she led him to her bedroom. Her silky and sexy body next to him was everything he had imagined, and his hormones wanted quenching. Darkness surrounded them as their bodies found the passion and love they had denied themselves all their lives.

Freshly brewed coffee permeated her senses as she stretched and yawned in the bed after consummating their relationship last night. Chris placed a cup of coffee, just how she liked it, on the bedside table. Smiling, she leaned up and kissed him. A lingering passionate, and exploring kiss sent electricity throughout his body, sending his heart racing. After pulling him on top of her, raw passion exploded once more.

An hour later, a new pot of coffee was ready. Chris had breakfast under control while Carla was cooling down in the shower. A refreshing shower invigorated her soul. Wanting to keep the fire going, she appeared in the kitchen wearing only his long-sleeved shirt flaunting her irresistible sexuality.

The bacon was sizzling, as was she. An omelet was ready to be plated, bacon, and toast graced the table. Following a short prayer, the local Saturday morning news filled the room. The recap of the rescue of Judge Ashley Harrington was still the big story. A video of the judge filled the screen praising the courageous efforts of Detective Carla McBride and Bernie Kowalski. The judge called them heroes while Chief Evans praised his detectives.

A rehashing of yesterday's events wasn't something Carla wanted to hear first thing in the morning or at all, she killed a man yesterday, and hated it. Guiltiness crept back in her mind. The television screen went dark, and silence returned. Peace, tranquility, and solitude were what she needed; Chris was what she needed to forget yesterday's life-altering tragedy.

While Chris cleared off the table and put the dishes in the dishwasher, she dressed for the day. She hoped

Bernie's smile could help eliminate the guiltiness crashing her soul. Many times, in her life, she'd been told that time eventually heals even the deepest wounds, she could only hope that Father Time had the right anecdote for her.

CHAPTER 38

Recovering in his private room, Bernie reflected on yesterday; he had never taken a bullet before. One bullet grazed his left thigh, and the other entered just below his left clavicle, serious enough but not life-threatening. He was thankful for that. Carla saved his life, and he was grateful for that; however, knew he could never repay her for that. He believed in living life as though he was dying, coming close to death yesterday was a life-altering event for him. Having time off for medical leave would test his resolve whether he wanted to remain a police detective. With his wife, Lydia, by his side, he knew he was a lucky man for many reasons, and she was at the top of the list.

Even though he was counting his lucky stars and praying a lot, his mind drifted back and forth about yesterday. He couldn't help thinking about how Carla was handling her lowest low, taking a human life. The thought of taking a human life disturbed him, and he couldn't even fathom how he would feel, much less her. As far as he knew, she had to deal with it alone.

Even though Carla called him this morning and said she was doing fine, the inflection in her voice told him differently. He couldn't wait to see her and thank her for saving his life; butterflies floated in his stomach, waiting for her.

Entering the hospital, Carla wondered what to say to Bernie and his wife. They both dodged bullets yesterday, figuratively and literally, she had no idea how this would play out. Seeing him, she hoped her instincts would tell her the right things to say. As the elevator began its trek to the third floor, unexplained emotions tugged at her heartstrings.

Room 307 was a few steps down the busy corridor. Nurses and doctors were scurrying in different directions paying no attention to them. Facing the door, she took a deep breath and knocked. A stunning Caucasian lady with brunette hair greeted her. She had never met his wife before and wasn't sure what she looked like.

"Hi, I'm Carla McBride, is B—"

"Yeah, Bernie is okay. I'm his better half, Lydia." Nodding and expecting to shake hands with her, Lydia opened her arms, welcoming Carla with a big hug. "Thank you for saving his life." It was a short embrace, and a few tears surfaced between them, Carla's fears of how to handle this encounter subsided. "Come in; he's on pins and needles waiting to see you."

Nodding, she and Chris entered. She introduced Chris to Lydia, stating he was her boyfriend. Bernie was sitting up in the bed, waiting for Carla to acknowledge him. Although Bernie was on medication, it didn't keep him from getting angry.

"Carla, close the damn door and quit ignoring me.

I'm the one that got shot, not her. Now, introduce me to, did I hear you say, boyfriend?"

"Yeah, umm, meet my boyfriend, Chris Abbott. He's general manager and golf pro at Avondale Country Club. We've been best friends most of our lives, well, I guess we still are, but it's a different kind of friendship, one we've both, no, I've denied that kind of love until now. I'm pretty sure he's always loved me, so yeah, we're a couple."

"Nice to meet you, Chris. Golf pro, huh, could you teach me to golf?"

Chris nodded, and before thinking, he replied, "Listen, if I can teach Carla, then I can teach you." Chris grunted and rubbed his side; Carla's elbow packed quite a punch. Letting out a big laugh, Bernie coughed because of the pain. Carla's expression quickly wiped Chris's smirky grin away; he knew he misspoke and would pay the price.

"What did you mean by that, so, you're saying I was a difficult student?"

"Uh, no, you were, um, yeah, you were a perfect student, honey."

"Right answer, but you'll still pay for that later." Focusing her attention on Bernie, she asked, "How are you doing, partner?"

"All things considered, I'm doing fine and feeling lucky to be alive. Thank you for saving my life."

"You're welcome, I owe you one as well, you know, for saving my butt as well."

"Yeah, yeah, you're welcome, partner."

Lydia was watching the bantering take place and shook her head back-and-forth. "I should leave and let you guys catch up; I'll be back later with your lunch.

They don't have any Polish sausage here, which is his favorite. So, nice to meet you both, and Carla, please don't take it easy on him, you know what I mean."

Carla nodded, while Bernie grimaced with laughter, "I don't plan to Lydia, you have a great day."

Nodding, Lydia left. Bernie said, "Carla, how are you coping with it all? I know it got pretty dicey in there yesterday, but we got Judge Harrington and our asses out of there alive, and that's all that mattered. You know, I'll be out of commission for a while, and I needed the time off anyway, you know for some R-and-R. So, I guess it all worked out for me in a funny kind of way."

"Bernie, you can be such a real dickhead."

"Yeah, I know." Looking at Chris, Bernie replied, "That's what I like about your woman. I wouldn't have her any other way, so don't change her. And oh, can I call her your woman?"

"Absolutely, and I wouldn't change a thing about her either."

"Well Bernie, I guess we should leave and let you get your beauty rest, you certainly need it, partner."

"Watch it, McBride."

"Bite me, dickhead."

"That's my girl, thanks for visiting me. See you soon."

As they were leaving the hospital, Carla received a call from Chief Evans. They chatted for a few minutes, and the call ended. While walking to her car, her subdued demeanor grabbed her soul. Inside the vehicle, breaking the silence, Chris said, "I'm not trying to pry or anything, but who was that?"

"Chief Evans, he told me the paperwork and my statement of what went down yesterday could wait until

Monday. He told me to have a great weekend and praised my handling of yesterday's difficult and dangerous stand-off. He said I did the right thing."

"Then why the gloomy face and disposition?"

"I don't know, maybe, um, like I'm not important anymore, yesterday was a defining moment in my career. It's like I finally took a life, and the game is over. It's like, you know, an empty feeling."

"Hey, let's talk about something more pleasant like what we will do this weekend."

"Yeah, I guess you are right."

"What do you want to do?"

"I don't know. You pick something."

"How about a walk around Lake Catalpa? It's a sunny day and not that cold out. Then we can get lunch and take in a movie. And tonight, dinner. Let's invite Laura and Walt if you don't mind."

"Sounds great. Come here, lover boy."

She kissed him softly and whispered in his ear. He smiled and nibbled on her ear. On the way to her apartment, she called Laura to invite her and Walt to dinner with them at Pascali's Italian Restaurant.

CHAPTER 39

Returning to desk duty on Monday, Carla didn't quite know how she would handle it, never being in this situation until now. She had to write in detail what happened inside that vacant building last Friday. Everything had to be there, crossing every 't' and dotting every 'i.' That would take up most of the morning. In the afternoon, Internal Affairs would interview her, where she would have to repeat everything she already wrote in her statement of the incident. What a waste of time, she thought.

Bernie, released from the hospital, was being pampered by his wife at home. It was strange not seeing him across from her and the constant bantering between them. She now liked him rather than loathing him. And his antics kept things lively and loose. He was partially responsible for her new outlook on life. Well, not totally, the black rose she received was a life-altering moment, and what went down last Friday, sealed the deal to live life as if she was dying. She didn't have a bucket list per se, but she was ready to try

new things and new experiences. And more importantly, she had someone she truly loved to do them with
now. Chris was her knight in shining armor and much,
much more.

With her statement and reports finished, she went to
see what was in her mailbox. As she approached the
mailbox unit, she couldn't help noticing the white
package glaring back at her. This package had the same
weird demented address label on it, just like the package
that contained the black rose. Of course, she was feeling
some anxiety in her body. Back at her desk, she laid the
package down and looked through the other mail first.
Nothing caught her eye as being important, and she put
them aside.

Observing the white package, she squeezed it. It felt
familiar, angry butterflies nibbled on her stomach.
Preparing for the worse, and taking a deep breath
calming the butterflies down, she opened it, peeking
inside. The butterflies fluttered once more. Different
from the one last week, someone had taken the time to
paint the edges of the black rose with red fingernail
polish resembling blood. Attached to it, a strip of paper
increased her anxiety. She read it to herself twice. Several
slow deep breaths calmed the angry butterflies wanting to
rock her soul.

It read: *"eternal peace shall come to you when it is
least expected, embrace it, and your spirit shall be eternally set free."*

Reading it a few more times, she studied the red-
trimmed black rose wondering what might be next. She
knew the person who placed it in the package wore
gloves, and no fingerprints would be found. Feeling the
rose petals, she knew it was the same as the others in

evidence. Although she knew it would be a waste of time, she took it to forensics for analysis, just the same.

In her dream, the faceless and beastly man wanting to kill her, had a black rose clenched between his teeth, it appeared to be the same as this one. She wondered whether her dream was an omen of impending peril or death, which she had just escaped last Friday. She pondered what this black rose meant. The song lyrics to Tim McGraw's song were dancing in her head to calm her down. She just couldn't get that tune out of her head as it was becoming her anthem and psychological safety net.

Bernie was home recovering, and she needed someone to ease the emotions rocking her soul. Bernie informed her that his wife was driving him crazy, and he welcomed a visit from her. She knew he loved that his wife was pampering him, but it was getting under his skin, and a visit from her would be great.

He lived in an old-established part of town near the university. Older homes on tree-lined streets, some kept very nice while others showed their age and mother nature's abuse. His house was a two-story gray craftsman style home with a classic red door and shutters. It was updated, showing his love and care for the neighborhood.

As Carla pulled in front of his house, Lydia was just coming out to run those errands he created for her. She showed her into the living room where Bernie was on the couch with his legs elevated. While taking advantage of his medical leave, a cold beer sat on the coffee table. Before Lydia left to run her errands, she brought lunch in and set it on the coffee table. Giving him a little peck on the forehead, she told him to call her if he needed anything else while she was out.

Carla smiled at Bernie and said, "So, partner, how's that leg doing?"

"Getting better each day. You know, Polish sausage, kraut, and spicy mustard is the best way to eat it, try it, you'll love it."

"Sure, I'm willing to try anything these days." Just as Bernie described it, Carla savored her first bite. "So, how many days will you be off?"

"The doc says probably about three weeks, damn that means I'll miss class, shit, I'm really disappointed about that."

"Right, dickhead."

"What's going on with the case?"

"I got another black rose today."

"Shit, I'm sorry. Same rose and all?"

"Yeah, but the edges had been painted with red nail polish, I assume resembling blood."

"Um, I wonder what that means, anything else?"

"It had another fortune cookie saying on it. This time it read: 'eternal peace shall come to you when it is least expected, embrace it, and your spirit shall be eternally set free'."

"Looks like you've got a real sicko on your hands, are you okay?"

"Yeah, um, I was prepared for it today and all. At first, I was feeling some anxiety until Tim McGraw's song popped in my head. Thank you for introducing the song to me."

"So, is anything else going on with the case?"

"Well, we have no other leads. I'm convinced that Fisher and Brown are indeed Hewitt and Bowen. They faked their deaths for financial reasons or something far worse. I think they killed Gonzalez, why, I don't know that yet. I believe they are in Oakmont held up somewhere until they make another move. I think they killed Bocconi on their way here as revenge for John. I believe John is orchestrating all of this from his new life. The black roses I'm getting are to shake me up. It's like a psychotic game he's playing with me. I'm not sure why. Maybe he wants something from me."

"Okay, take another bite of the Polish kraut hoagie as I call it, and then continue."

After another big bite, she continued, "Now, what I'm going to tell you must be kept confidential. No one else except Patsy Groves, our sketch artist, knows about this. I believe I've found Gina Dickerson in Lewisburg, West Virginia. It was sheer dumb luck, but I think she is now Alicia Maddox, assistant manager at the General Lewis Inn. That's where Chris took me to get away for some R-and-R."

"So, what good is that?"

"Not sure, but I think it will come in handy in the end. Not sure why at this time. It's just a gut feeling I have."

"Okay, it doesn't sound like you have much at all."

"I'm beginning to think we must make the next move, like trying to flush Fisher and Brown out of hiding. It may be risky, but we're at a standstill, and this case is getting colder."

"Any ideas?"

"I'm going to talk to Walt about it. He helped us in the Gold Fedora case, so I'm sure he is willing to help us."

"How?"

"Ironically, just like the Gold Fedora case. We publish artist renderings of Hank Fisher and Charles

Brown as persons of interest in the Gonzalez murder. That they are the same men as Grayson Hewitt and Parker Bowen that live in Bayside, Texas."

"You know it could backfire, don't you?"

"Yeah, guess that's a risk we may have to take. I better run since I must meet with Internal Affairs in an hour. Thanks for the sausage and kraut hoagie and your time. Get well and see you soon. I'll let myself out."

"Sure, hang in there, partner, we'll get those assholes."

After meeting with Internal Affairs for two hours, they concluded she acted appropriately during the stand-off. Lives were in danger, and she had no choice but to take Adam Prescott down, her kill was clean. Returning to her desk with her service weapon and badge, she finished her reports on Adam Prescott, and never felt so good. Her iPhone dinged. The message on the screen read call me.

Dialing Laura's number, *Your Song* by Elton John, played in her ear. Putting her phone on speaker, she sang along with him until she heard Laura's voice. "Hey, Carla, on Thursday, do you want to accompany me while I take Walt to the airport for his flight to Pensacola, Florida? Then we can stop by the high school track and get some laps in like I did this morning. Then we can have a light breakfast at the coffee shop. His flight is at Six-Twenty AM. What do you say?"

"Seriously, I have class Wednesday evening, and that's a little too early for me, I will pass on it; however, I'd love to have breakfast with you. We can meet at the coffee shop, how's that sound?"

"Sounds great, how about Eight-Thirty AM?"

"Yeah, can't wait. See you then."

CHAPTER 40

lad to return to Oakmont, Daisy loved working at Whisman's and missed the locals, and bantering with them. Wednesday would be her first day back to work after returning from Vermont, her safe haven for the past several weeks. She was also glad to be returning for another reason, one that meant so much to her, a 5K race benefiting Hospice. Her mother died there; breast cancer took her life a year ago.

An avid runner, she promised her mother she would honor her by entering all races supporting those worthy causes. A Hospice event in the spring and a breast cancer awareness race in the fall would fulfill her promise to her mother. Her favorite place to train was the high school track near her apartment. Ever since a female jogger was found dead at Lake Catalpa, she didn't consider that location safe any longer.

Daisy's first day of training was on Monday. The high school track was within walking distance, and she used that time to stretch her legs along the way. When she arrived, two men in their fifties were jogging together, and she thought nothing of it. She felt safe at the high school; it was in a residential area and adequately lighted. Loosening up, she began her jog of eight laps around the track. Another lady with dark hair in a ponytail passed Daisy on her final lap.

Two men, already on the running track when Daisy arrived, were warming up. After two laps and lapping them twice, she thought they were probably out of shape. One more lap to go, Daisy picked up the pace sprinting to the imaginary finish line. With her laps finished, she walked around the track to cool down and assess her workout.

The two men caught up with her, introduced themselves, and they began a casual conversation. A people person, Daisy thought nothing about talking with them; they seemed friendly and harmless. They spoke of races they had entered, and she did the same. Commonality made it easy for her to engage in a comfortable conversation, and not fear for her safety.

New in town, they wanted to find a good neighborhood bar to get a beer and a sandwich. Recommending Whisman's, she gave them the address. Since she would be working the night shift on Wednesday evening, she invited them to stop by for a beer and a sandwich. Thanking her, the two men continued jogging around the track. She walked one more lap while enjoying the fresh air and a beautiful sunrise. Walking home, she thought about how aggressive she was with Frank, aka Spike. She made a vow herself to take it slow with any new men she met.

Daisy's second and third days of training went the same as Monday. The weather had turned milder, and she was glad because it made it easier to breathe and train better. Each morning, the two men she met on Monday were training as well. They talked more and got to know each other a little better. Feeling more comfortable with them, she didn't have any concerns about her safety.

Finished with her eight laps, she walked around the track, thinking about getting back to her routine and her night shift at Whisman's. The two men passed her a few times and started their cooling down regimen. Before she left, she reminded the men to stop by Whisman's tonight, and the first beer would be on the house. While walking toward the school on her way home, the lady she saw on Monday had just arrived to begin her workout.

The day went by quickly for her, and before she knew it, she was getting ready for her first day back to work. She always walked to work since her apartment was close to Whisman's. As she turned the corner, she noticed Whisman's parking lot looked busier than usual; she thought nothing of it since more patrons equaled more tips. Finally, reaching Whisman's, she entered the bar. Surprise, surprise echoed off the walls, and her scream pleased her boss. Looking for him, she found him behind the bar grinning ear-to-ear. It was Gabe that pulled off this surprise party, and she would make him pay when he least expected it.

Hugs and kisses were coming from every direction. Gabe gave her a big bear hug lifting her off the floor. She loved it, and she was glad to be home. The night was all about her welcome home party, and enjoying reminiscing with all her old friends, a matter of fact, everyone in the place was her friend. With a beer in hand, she made her rounds visiting, soaking up all the attention she was receiving. Happy to see everyone, she felt loved and at home.

While visiting with Rufus at the bar, two men sitting in the corner of the building met her gaze and waved. The booth brought back bittersweet memories; it was Spike's favorite booth. Approaching them, she smiled. "So, nice of you to come to my party. Let me get you the beers I promised you." They nodded, she left and returned with their beers. "Here you go, guys. I need to visit some more old friends, so enjoy yourselves and try the fried hot banana peppers, they're the best you'll ever have. See you in the morning."

"We'll be there as usual and try to keep up with you."

Letting out a small laugh, she smiled and said, "Bring it on, boys."

Locals left one by one; she enjoyed their welcome back wishes. Glancing around the bar area, she noticed the booth in the corner was empty; her two jogging mates had called it a night. For the remainder of the evening, she and Gabe reminisced about old times. After feeling tired and exhausted, a good night's rest was just a few blocks away. Arriving home mentally exhausted, she fell fast asleep, her bed felt good. Dreams of the good things in her life flowed from her subconscious world. Home for good, she reveled in that feeling while her body and soul succumbed to a peaceful sleep.

CHAPTER 41

With Chris in her personal life in a much different way, happiness was in control of Carla's psyche, and she was living the good life. Although she and Bernie had always been like oil and water, the moment Chief Evans made them partners; her work demeanor went in a new and positive direction.

On many levels, they were still like oil and water; however, their differences seemed to complement each other in an almost endearing manner. Things were looking up for them, and they had the promise of becoming a formidable team. They had grown close in a short amount of time. Working without him, her drive to Flemingsville was incredibly lonely.

A cold day, the interstate seemed bleak to her. Traffic was light. Typically, a heavy-lead foot was her driving style; however, her life changed on Friday. Time to slow down, smell the roses, live like you're dying philosophy controlled her inner thoughts. Maintaining the speed limit, cars zipped by her heading to, well, she didn't care where anymore. Music filled her space; visions of Chris warmed her soul.

"*Live Like You're Dying*" danced in her head, switching the station, that song filled the car, making her smile. Tim McGraw belted out the thought-provoking lyrics, and she joined him with her best karaoke rendition. Thoughts of Bernie sneaked in her mind, and she missed him. Tim McGraw's voice gave way to Kelly Clarkson and Jason Aldean's big hit, "*Don't You Wanna Stay.*"

Lost in those lyrics, thoughts of Chris rushed in, memories of their passionate union, quickened her pulse. In her mind, she tasted his kiss and smiled. The Flemingsville four-miles-ahead-sign brought her back to reality. Her phone rang, she hit the hands-free button. "Hi, Laura, what's going on?"

Laura's teasing voice brought a smile to her face. "Hey, thought I would give you another chance to join me in the morning for a brisk run, come on, it would do you good."

"No matter how much you beg me, I'm sleeping in tomorrow morning. I need rest more than jogging in the frosty air, you understand, don't you?"

"Yeah, I do. Uh, we still on for breakfast?"

"Of course, see you then."

"Be careful in the morning; love you."

"Remember, I can handle myself. I've got my mace. Love you, too."

Phone off hands-free, her exit was one mile ahead on the right. Taking the exit, it was back to the real world once more. All Things Macabre was just ahead on the left. A brief visit of due diligence was a waste of time. A soft rumble from her stomach said, "feed me," and silently, she answered, "we're almost there." A six-inch Italian BMT smelled great. The rumble in her stomach grew louder, rubbing her belly, she silently said, "it's coming."

Leaving Subway, she pulled into the parking lot where her class was; she wasted no time in finding a seat in the concourse area, her growling stomach continued. Ten minutes until her class started, the growling in her belly subsided, it had met its match, a six-inch Italian BMT conquered her hunger.

One by one, her classmates arrived, she thought it was funny she was calling these strangers classmates, what was happening to her, she thought. Shaking her head back-and-forth, laughing at herself, she gathered her things and entered the lecture hall. Professor Don was a few feet behind her. His presence gave her a strange feeling; she didn't know why, just that he did.

Usually, Carla liked being out of the limelight, but something inside her told her to be different tonight. Instead of sitting in the last row like at Sunday Mass, she found a seat in the middle of the second row, front-and-center, with a perfect view of the podium. Professor Don approached the dimly lit stage placing his materials on the podium looking all professor-like. A glance toward the door, a woman smiled at him. Quickly leaving the podium, he joined her just outside the doorway. A good lip reader, Carla knew their brief interlude had nothing to do with education. Returning with a lust-ridden grin on his face, he stood at the podium gleaming at Carla.

"Good evening class, tonight, I would like to begin by asking Detective McBride to share her recent experience of attempting to diffuse a serious confrontation she encountered last Friday. It was all over the news, so I don't see a problem having her talk about it."

All eyes were on her, and she felt them bearing down on her. Muted mumbling quietly filled the lecture hall. Time to collect her thoughts, being blindsided took her by surprise. Her stare bored holes through Professor Don as silence grabbed everyone.

He had pushed her trigger button. Not acknowledging his request, she intentionally ignored him as Tim McGraw's song danced in her head. Eyes locked on him; his face grew tense because he didn't like not being in control. Loud chatter filled the lecture hall, and a loud noise echoed from the stage as his gavel slammed the podium.

"Quiet class, I guess Detective McBride is still too shook up to tell us what techniques she used in the confrontation, that's too bad, I think we all could learn from her experience."

After several deep breaths, Carla stood up and took control. "Professor Don, do you mind if I come down to the podium to speak to the class? Focusing on me, they will observe more than just my explanation, is that okay?" Already using one technique, she had clearly taken control of the confrontational situation. Surprised by her request, silence filled the room as all eyes were now on him. "Professor, I'm ready when you are."

Feeling the pressure of all eyes on him, he had no choice but to play her game or lose the respect of the class. "Well, that's kind of unusual, but sure, come on down. The podium is all yours, detective."

Approaching the podium, she watched his eyes undress her from the neck down. Disgusted, this was not the time to relinquish control. "Thank you. My partner,

Bernie, who is not here tonight, and I faced a life and death situation last Friday. We had a deranged and distraught suspect suffering from Post-Traumatic-Stress-Disorder or PTSD and was holding a judge hostage in an abandoned building. With no electricity in the building, our flashlights helped put us in a position to diffuse the situation. We used many of the techniques we have discussed over the past couple of weeks. We were trying to put the suspect at ease and diffuse this dangerous situation."

Clearly in control, interruptions she hated. Professor Don asked, "Are you sure, detective, that you did everything you could have?"

A deep relaxing breath, she continued, "Yes, we did. However, after about twenty minutes or so, we knew we were not going to have a positive outcome with this individual. Long story short, my partner and I had no choice but to neutralize the suspect and saved the judge's life. My partner suffered two gunshot wounds in the process but is recovering just fine. In these types of situations, the safety of the person being held hostage is our number one priority. There you have it."

Professor Don using a condescending attitude, fired back, "Detective McBride, when you mean neutralized, you mean killed him, and from news reports, you were the one that fired the fatal shots, correct?"

Although his question touched a nerve because of the guilt she was still feeling, she remained calm, taking a deep breath and replied, "Correct."

Continuing his condescending tone and his attempt of agitating her, he asked, "In retrospect, do you think you did everything you could before killing the suspect?"

"I've replayed it a dozen times in my mind, and I

came to the same conclusion every time. Had we not acted, that judge would be dead, and that wasn't going to happen on our watch. Anything else, professor?"

"No, thank you for sharing that with the class. Oh, I do have one more thing."

Ignoring his condescending attitude, she remained cool as a cucumber and replied, "Okay, what is it?"

"I understand from the news reports; this was your first kill, is that correct?"

At this point, his condescending and agitating voice would have pushed her anger button many times over. He wanted her to become combative; however, she took deep breaths to remain calm and replied in a very confident and professional tone of voice. "Professor Don, yes, that is correct. Unfortunately, as a public safety officer, it comes with the territory. We don't like it or get satisfaction from it. I'm very saddened for Adam Prescott's family and that it had to end that way. In some ways, I feel very guilty. Is there anything else I can answer for you or the class?"

For a moment, an eerie quietness commanded the lecture hall. One by one, her classmates stood to applaud her. Carla had control and diffused his antagonistic demeanor. Clearly embarrassed by her, a loud noise exploded from the podium. "Quiet down class, everyone, please sit down, now!" Returning to her seat, she locked eyes with him. Staring at him, egg on his face looked mighty sweet to her. "I think it is time we begin tonight's agenda; we will start by reviewing the twelve basic steps of managing anger and conflict." After a brief review, he excused the class for their only break of the evening.

As classmates filed out of the hall, muted chatter filled the concourse. Before leaving the lecture hall,

Carla approached Professor Don, explaining to him she must go, police business, she told him. Standing just outside the lecture hall, smiles of admiration greeted her, while applause and cheers filled the concourse.

Inside the lecture hall, Professor Don slammed his gavel on the podium out of anger. Victorious, she smiled as she left the lecture hall. Walking past her classmates, Carla acknowledged their appreciation. A celebration with Jameson awaited her back at her apartment, and she couldn't wait to taste his amber love.

CHAPTER 42

Jameson, full of life, stood tall on her bar, waiting to ease her frustrations. Within minutes, Jameson swished around the clear ice in her glass. Aromas of vanilla and caramel pleased her senses; one sip whetted her palate. Wound up from her victory over Professor Don, she flipped on the television to unwind. Law and Order SVU's opening scene pictured a young girl held hostage and was not what she wanted to see. Switching channels, the USA channel provided the noise she needed. Jameson was warming her soul, savoring its nuances, her thoughts drifted back to Professor Don for a moment.

After replenishing her glass, the television screen faded away. Retreating to her bedroom, Jameson found his familiar place on the nightstand. After undressing, a silky-smooth lingerie Chris would love, clung to her sensual body as her bed welcomed her. After a long sip of Jameson, she said goodnight to him.

Peaceful darkness surrounded her. Her body and mind melted into her subconsciousness. Like most nights, dreams flowed in and out. Pleasant dreams about her childhood made her smile. Visions of she and Chris making passionate love made her embers burn hotter than ever.

However, all her dreams weren't happy ones. Last Friday's hostage situation replayed over and over in her subconscious. Would she do anything different Professor Don asked her, she wouldn't have. The dream was like watching a movie of herself and Bernie trying to diffuse the situation. She observed and listened to the dialogue.

Her subconscious replayed the final scene of the shootout several times. Suddenly, her dreams moved deeper into the darkest recesses of her mind. The red-trimmed black rose surfaced once again. Waking up briefly, she chased it away; she no longer feared it. Jameson set on the nightstand, down and out in one swallow, her anxiety subsided. Her head fell softly on her pillow, and darkness enveloped her once more. Dreams flowed again, and as usual, they started with happy ones. Dinner, the other night with Laura, Walt, and Chris, had been special. Laughter and happiness were all around; a subconscious smile crossed her face.

Her dreams continued, but in a different direction again, one she didn't like and couldn't control. It was like being seated in a movie theatre watching Laura jogging around the high school track. Suddenly out of the pitch-black darkness, a man tackled her. She was screaming and fighting back. Laura was a strong-willed woman and wouldn't give up without a fight.

Then a second man, much shorter, entered the scene; that was too much for Laura to handle. They dragged her behind a set of bleachers. On her stomach, the weight of the man was too much for her to withstand. Her breathing became labored and shallow. Carla wanted to help her, but her body remained frozen in her subconscious world, she was a hopeless bystander in this nightmarish movie of impending death.

Carla watched the taller man wrap a ligature around her neck and twisted it tighter and tighter. Laura was still trying to fight back, but the smaller man was helping restrain her. Soon, Laura stopped breathing, and her body went limp. Carla witnessed Laura's soul leaving her body and looking down upon her lifeless body. Laura's soul watched the taller man turn her over and pull down her jogging tights. He placed a black rose trimmed in red across her naked vulnerability. Attached to the stem of the black rose was a strip of paper. As the two men watched, Carla's subconscious soul walked over to Laura's vacated body, leaning down and reading the message, she had seen it before.

"Noooooooooooooo! Oh, Nooooooooooooooo!"

Sitting up, she hugged her knees, gasping for air. As she shook the cobwebs away, her phone rang, startling her. While glancing at the screen, her pulse raced. She answered and replied, "Male or Female?" It was not the answer she wanted to hear. "What color hair?" A tear fell from the corner of her eye. "Shit, I'm on my way."

The high school field was about fifteen minutes from her apartment. Given the million thoughts racing through her mind, she grabbed the first clothes lying on the floor and put them on. After throwing a baseball cap on her head, she headed straight for the field, not knowing what she would find or who was the victim because Officer Wiesmann had described Laura to a tee. In route to the high school field, Carla dialed Laura's cell. No answer, her voicemail message played. After ending the call,

Carla's pulse exploded as the cabin of her car felt her Irish temper.

When Carla arrived, she noticed Laura's car parked near the track. Her heart was exploding inside her chest as she saw the body about thirty yards away. Sprinting, she needed to either confirm her fears or dispel them. DJ, the coroner, was covering up the body when she finally reached her defining moment. Out of breath, she couldn't bear to look at the body out of fear, but she had no other choice. The outline of the body under the blanket was about the same height as Laura; fear raged in Carla's soul. Looking at DJ, she asked, "What do we have, Officer Wiesmann, said the victim was female."

Reactively, DJ said, "Caucasian, slim and well-toned body. The body is still warm; the time of death was probably at least an hour ago or more."

In a nervous, but erratic tone, she said, "Shit, let's get this over with DJ. Uh, pull the blanket back."

"Okay, I hope you are prepared for this, here you go."

With a look of sheer relief, Carla remorsefully exclaimed, "DJ, that's not her, that's not her. Shit, shit, shit!"

With a surprised look on his face, he said, "What are you saying, do you know this lady?"

With joyous tears of sadness, Carla sniffled and responded, "Wanda Jordan, dammit, Daisy, I'm sorry. I told her it was safe to return home. And now look at what happened to her. Um, that son of a bitch John Dickerson; one day, I will find that asshole and blow his freaking brains to hell. I promise I will, DJ!"

"Dammit, Carla, calm down, and get a hold of yourself."

Taking a couple of deep breaths, she wiped her tears

away. She continued, "Officer Wiesmann said there was something else I needed to see."

"Yeah, there is, let me pull the sheet down further. It doesn't appear she was sexually assaulted, but we'll process her when we do the autopsy."

While trying to hold her emotions in check, she replied, "I guess I should have expected this, because this was in my dream last night. A black rose trimmed in red nail polish with a fortune cookie proverb taped to it. It reads: 'ye who hath received a single black rose shall be granted eternal peace', isn't that right?"

"Shit, that's correct, how did you know that?"

"My nightmare, but in it, the person murdered is a friend of mine."

"What?"

"Nothing DJ, who found Daisy?"

"Officer Wiesmann is interviewing a lady out on the track. I believe her name is Laura Watson."

Without responding, Carla sprinted towards the track where she could see Laura talking with him. When she arrived, Officer Wiesmann was just finishing up interviewing her. She could hear him saying, "I guess that's all, for now, Ms. Watson, if we need any further information, we'll give you a call."

Carla, out of breath and visibly shaken, said, "Laura, thank God, you're okay. I thought it was you."

"Me…Carla, what the hell are you talking about?"

Another hug, Carla grabbed Laura's hand and walked with her to her car. As they walked, Carla agreed to meet her at her office at nine o'clock. As Laura's Mercedes drove out of sight, Carla returned to where Daisy died. DJ informed her that the cause of death was severe strangulation by use of a ligature, and whoever did this left it intentionally. She told him she already knew who did this.

Scanning the parking lot and the school, she said, "DJ, it appears there is a security camera on the back of the school, I'll check and see what it may have recorded."

After checking in with the principal, he directed Carla to the assistant principal, who monitored the security cameras on the school campus. After entering the information, the video played. Grainy and dark, the images were low quality but good enough to show two men attacking Daisy and dragging her behind the bleachers out of sight of the camera. Five minutes later, the two men shielding their faces ran toward the parking lot and out of view.

Switching cameras, the one in the parking lot showed the two men getting in a white Toyota Camry and quickly driving away. Although the video was low quality, it captured a partial view of the license plate, at least she had something to work with now. Given the number of white Toyota Camrys on the road, odds of finding these two men weren't on her side.

CHAPTER 43

D aisy's body, accompanied by the black rose, pushed her queasiness to new heights. Dead bodies had never bothered her that much before; this one was different. She knew Daisy, who had helped her in the Gold Fedora case. She warned her of the possible danger and told her she should seek a safe haven. Carla then informed her it was safe to return home, which got her killed. As guilt invaded her soul again, Carla questioned her decision not to jog with Laura, had she, then Daisy might still be alive.

She didn't understand why Daisy was a target. Since Rocky was dead, Daisy should not have been a threat to John Dickerson; however, she helped with the sketch, which ultimately did Rocky in. The only thing she could surmise was that John Dickerson was a revengeful psychopath eliminating anyone in his way until he gets what he wants.

In a federal witness protection program, John was watching the people that destroyed his political aspirations. That was a problem for Carla and Walt. Al Bocconi tipped off the FBI, and he was now dead. Carla wondered who might be next. Laura was foremost on her mind; in fact, she had great concern for her life. Certain that Laura was the final piece of John's psychotic game, keeping her safe was paramount.

Arriving at Laura's office a few minutes before Nine AM, anxiousness stressed her body as she waited for Laura to greet her. Promptness was a strong suit of Laura's professionalism; however, today was different. Finding a dead body, and frightened by Carla's demeanor at the crime scene, Laura's nerves were shot to hell. Queasiness grew as Carla sat in the lobby, waiting for her. Finally, she heard footsteps coming toward her; she recognized the shoes. A hug greeted Carla; quietly, they walked back to Laura's office.

Solitude surrounded them as Laura sat in her well-appointed burgundy leather chair. Carla sat across from her, and for the first time, realized how beautiful Laura's office was. Laura's whole life was in front of her; a world of happiness waited for her. Nerves were punishing her psyche, while a look of concern painted Carla's face.

"Carla, what's this all about? The look on your face this morning, the look on your face now, tells me you believe I'm in some kind of danger. Please tell me I'm wrong."

Trying to remain calm, Carla replied, "Look, Laura, there's no reason to sugarcoat this situation; I'm not good at that. Last night I had a dream, no, it was a nightmare. In that nightmare, you were the woman found murdered this morning. It was like a movie I was watching, while frozen in time, I was helpless, and I couldn't save you. What happened to Daisy was horrible, and it was all planned. Dammit, I do believe you're in danger."

A stone-cold, pale-white complexion, just like Daisy's lifeless face this morning, overcame Laura, her eyes watered as panic grabbed her soul. A sarcastic laugh interrupted the frightening silence that came over them. "Uh, you're not kidding me, are you?"

"No, I'm not, just call it a female-detective intuition. John Dickerson is behind all of this, I know it, I feel it. The same individuals murdered AJ Gonzalez and Daisy, and I believe you are the next target." Once again, blood drained from Laura's face, and tears trickled down her cheeks, "But, um, why me? Uh, I did nothing to hurt him."

Trying to be as reassuring as possible, she responded, "I believe he is seeking revenge for what Walt and I did that helped destroy his career. That separated him from the two people he cares most for in his life. Doing something to you will give him that revenge because it would hurt us. He probably has an ulterior motive as well, maybe using you as ransom."

"Uh, you're really scaring, uh, me now. What are you going to do about it?"

"Until Walt returns, I'm going to stay with you. I will protect you until we get this all resolved. I'll pick you up from work this evening and take you to work tomorrow. That's not a suggestion, Laura, that's an order you are to follow. What time will you get off tonight?"

"Not sure, I'll be preparing for court tomorrow. Probably around Seven PM, but I will text you when I'm ready to leave."

"Okay, make sure after everyone leaves, you lock all the doors, and don't go outside until I get here. I will not let anything happen to you. Just stay calm and don't do anything stupid."

Nodding, they hugged each other tightly as if this was their final hug, neither wanted to let go. Back at the station, forensics had a poor-quality video to work with but only managed to get a partial plate. Because of the lighting and angle of the still photo, all that forensics could determine was that it was a personalized Tennessee license plate. VOL6 was all they could see. The last number could be a five, eight, or a nine. That was better than nothing, she thought.

Immediately, issuing a BOLO on a white Toyota Camry with Tennessee plates matching those possibilities, she kept her fingers crossed. Searching the Tennessee Motor Vehicle database, it turned up two possibilities. Both were white late-model Toyota Camrys. They added that information to the previous BOLO, and the hunt was on. Bad news came quick, license plate VOL69 was reported stolen from a white Toyota Camry in Knoxville two weeks ago.

While waiting for something good to turn up, Carla visited Whisman's where Daisy was employed. Arriving there, Gabe was checking his cold beer inventory as she stood at the bar. Placing a cocktail napkin in front of her, she flashed her badge.

"Um, I'm not here to drink, sir. I'm Detective McBride, and I have bad news, Daisy was killed this morning at the high school track."

"Oh my gosh, she was such a sweet lady and a hell of a good employee. We had a surprise welcome home party for her last night. Tonight was to be her first shift back. What happened?"

"A lady found her body at the high school track; she had been jogging. Two men attacked her and took her behind the bleachers and strangled her. We are not sure whether a sexual assault occurred or not; an autopsy will determine that."

"Damn. I was glad to see Daisy back, and so were our customers. Do you know why she went away; it was so abrupt and secretive?"

"You remember the murders of Mark and Joanne Alison, then Frank Ramsey, Jr., don't you?"

"Yeah, what did she have to do with that?"

"Daisy had a one-night stand with Frank, and he ended up dead. He and his partner, Rocky, had been here several times, and she helped us produce a sketch of Frank's partner who killed him. I told her she might be in danger and to be diligent. She left until things were solved. Rocky was found dead in Florida. Initially, his death was ruled an accident; however, after further examination, his death was changed to suspicious in nature. We're pretty sure a man named John Dickerson killed him to silence him. John likely had Daisy killed as well, not knowing if Frank told her anything, collateral damage they call it. John Dickerson is playing a sick and psychotic game of revenge." Gabe shook his head back-and-forth and wiped a tear out of his eye. "That's not all of it, but I don't have time to go through everything. She called me last week to see if it was safe to return home. I returned her call, but it went to voicemail. I left her a message saying it was safe because John Dickerson took a deal and was in a federal witness protection program somewhere. Anyway, was there anyone here last night that didn't look like locals? Someone she was friendly with."

"Come to think of it; there were two men here that I had not seen before talking with her. Now, I recall, I received a strange phone call last week asking about her and when she was coming back. Thinking nothing of it at that time, I told him she would be back in town on Sunday and returning to work on Wednesday."

"Did he give you his name?"

"Nah, just said he had been here before and knew her."

"Guess that's not important now, don't beat yourself up about it, I'm the one who told her she could return home. Could this be the two men in here that night?" Showing Gabe her phone, he studied the photo and nodded. "Did she have family around here?" Shaking his head back-and-forth, he swallowed hard, chasing his emotional heartstrings away. She squeezed his hand and left.

CHAPTER 44

The police station was unusually quiet today, making the day even longer for Carla. The hour-hand slowly met the six on the big wall clock. Everyone hated that clock; it was so old school and ancient. Angry butterflies fluttered inside her as her desk phone remained silent, the voicemail button was lifeless. With a stolen Tennessee plate, receiving a tip from the BOLO was next to none, it likely was trashed. Her iPhone screen lit up thirty-minutes later; a text from Laura said she'd be ready in about an hour. Responding to the text, she reminded her to be diligent.

7:05 PM.

Laura remembered she left something in her car that she would need that evening at home. The parking lot looked safe from the back door, and her car was well lit. Out of habit, she unlocked the back door, hit her remote, unlocking her car. Waiting for a moment, she deemed it safe. A few steps to open the driver's side door, reaching inside, she retrieved the items she needed. Suddenly, a steel-hard coldness pressed against her side as warm breaths crossed her neck, skyrocketing her pulse.

As a gun dug harder in her side, she flinched. Whispering in her ear, the abductor said, "Don't scream, don't do anything stupid or you'll die right here. If you want to stay alive, then you will do everything I tell you. One slip up, and Walt or Carla will never see you again, never find your body either."

Shocked and gasping for air, she didn't respond immediately. The steel-hard coldness dug in deeper as the pain burned hotter in her side. Hot breaths against her neck created a nauseous feeling; she swallowed hard, pushing the bile back down.

"I said, you got it?" Unable to speak, she nodded. "Good, now get in behind the wheel. My partner is in the back seat and will kill you if you do anything stupid. I'll be in the passenger seat, and I will tell you where to go. Remember, you do anything stupid, and you die."

Nodding, Laura got in her car. Shaking uncontrollably, she thought about screaming or just running or trying to fight back. While glancing in the back, a gun pointed at her head squashed those ideas. As the other man got in the passenger side, a cold steeliness dug into her side.

"Smart lady, now start the car and take the interstate toward Lexington, stay in the right-hand lane the entire time. Maintain your speed at seventy miles per hour. Take the next exit, turn right, and go one mile. I'll tell you where to stop the car. Do you understand me, pretty lady?"

Vocal cords paralyzed, she nodded. Backing out of the parking lot, she traveled a series of dark alleyways heading for the interstate. Twenty minutes later, she reached the exit and turned right.

7:30 PM.

Carla pulled in front of the building that housed Laura's office. As previously arranged, Laura would wait in the lobby area. Approaching the door, Carla could see in between the blinds covering the door, and Laura was not there. Two minutes later, the lounging area was still empty. Calling Laura's cell phone, it went straight to voicemail.

Knowing Laura parked around back, she drove there. Under her breath, vulgarity spewed, Laura's car was gone. Light from inside the building cast a thin shadow on the ground—more vulgarity. Before Carla entered the building, she called and put a BOLO out on a silver Mercedes with a Kentucky license plate. Although she knew it was likely worthless, she entered with her service weapon drawn. Laura's office door was wide open, her purse and cell phone were on her desk.

Picking up Laura's cell phone, a missed call message glared at her. Knowing it was useless to search the rest of the building, she went to the parking lot looking for security cameras—more vulgarity echoed off the buildings. Inside her car was a lonely place to be, her heart thumped loudly. All hell was breaking loose.

By the time she reached the police station, the State Police had found Laura's car abandoned on a dirt road off of the county road. On the hood was stolen Tennessee license plate VOL69. Left on it, a black rose with a strip of paper attached to it was a bad omen. They canceled the present BOLO. Now it was just for a white Toyota Camry presumably heading north towards Ohio, east towards West Virginia, West towards Louisville, or south towards Tennessee.

Feeling utterly useless, she drove to St. Anthony's Catholic Church. Entering the chapel, she sat down in the first pew on the right. Kneeling, she bowed her head and prayed. After asking God for help, her heartstrings exploded, and whimpering filled the sanctuary. Hearing some commotion from the front of the chapel, she looked up, seeing Father Tim O'Brien walking toward her.

Noticing the fright in her swollen and glistening eyes, he sat beside her. "What brings you here tonight, Detective McBride?"

Between her tears and sobbing, she met his curious gaze. "Father, my best friend, was kidnapped earlier tonight. Uh, I feel utterly helpless, and I don't know what I'm going to do or how I'm going to find her. Uh, I've been asking God for help, but I don't know whether he is listening to me."

Taking her hand in his and speaking softly, he replied, "Oh, my child of God, he is listening to you and watching over your friend. You must have faith in him, and he will send you a sign on how to find her, but you must believe and have faith in him. I will pray with you if you like, is that okay?"

Nodding, she closed her eyes and bowed her head. Once Father Tim had finished the prayer, she opened her eyes and thanked him. He nodded, walked to the front of the chapel, and disappeared through a side door. While remaining in the pew for a few moments more, a special prayer flowed inside her mind. As she left the chapel, cold and blustery winds of uncertainty chilled her soul and spirits like never before. The brisk winds swept away whatever hope she had.

With nowhere else to go, the police station would provide her with the support she needed to get through this crisis. Chris was waiting for her when she came through the door. Even though no one knew they were now an item, she hugged him out of the love she felt for him and his sister. Employees ignored their display of affection.

The first flight out of Pensacola was in the morning, Chris would pick Walt up in Lexington. It would be a long night for everyone. With a new BOLO out, Carla knew she could be anywhere, even right under their noses. Finding her would be a crapshoot or a stroke of luck. She didn't care which one it was; she only cared she would find her before it was too late.

Lots of coffee and conversation, reminiscing about the good times, kept their mind off the worst-case scenario of never seeing Laura again. After a long night, slivers of muted light filtered through the windows blotted with a cold mist of helplessness.

CHAPTER 45

rriving at the Blue Grass Airport in Lexington a few minutes early, Walt anxiously waited for Chris. Laura was his fiancée, his soulmate, his lover, the thought of losing her was horrifying. Spotting Chris's car pull up to the terminal, he grabbed his bag and hurried to his car. Cloudy skies and a light cold rain dampened his already gloomy attitude. Tossing his bags in the back seat, he sat in the passenger front seat. The heat inside the car warmed his body, but not his soul, it remained cold with fearful uncertainty. Chris's expression answered every question Walt wanted to ask, needed to ask. Twenty-five miles of gloominess felt like a hundred miles of heartbreak. Windshield wipers swished away the tears from the heavens while the tears of fear and desperation inside the car were untouched.

Ground zero was Walt's office. The Keurig was working overtime. Hugs and tears gave way to reality to desperation to hope. Remnants of the Gold Fedora case took center stage on the wall as pictures of Hank Fisher and Charles Brown were beside photos of Grayson

Hewitt and Parker Bowen. It was easy to see they were the same. And probably, with the help of John Dickerson, they chose Pseudocide to escape financial ruin or death. Indebted to John on many levels, they became pawns in his psychotic game of revenge.

Chris and Walt were in a state of shock and denial. Carla showed signs of guiltiness; however, her years of experience kicked in, taking control of the situation. Someone had to face the music and exhibit leadership. Chris and Walt nursed coffee while Carla explained her hypotheses. The pictures on the wall seem to track her every move, and she ignored them. Listening to her chronology of John's heinous actions, Chris and Walt found composure and a glimpse of hope.

"I follow all that," Walt responded. "But why kill AJ that didn't even know us?"

"Maybe she was in the wrong place at the wrong time, or Laura was the target, and Frog and Peanuts screwed up, but that's not important at this moment. Then Daisy returned to town and met the same death as AJ, probably collateral damage for identifying Rocky. The black rose became John's signature just as Rocky used the gold fedora ball marker. Laura is the final act of his psychotic game of revenge."

"This may sound morbid, and don't take this wrong, Walt," Chris replied. "But why abduct her rather than kill her?"

Carla said, "He wants us all to suffer. He took the one person that matters to us most. When the FBI stole our case, taking him into custody, that took him away from the two people that mattered most to him, his wife and his son, Landon. He's suffering, and he is making no, wanting us to feel his pain, and we are. He's probably watching and laughing at us. We will hear from him soon, trust me."

"Do you think they kidnapped her and are holding her somewhere, maybe Florida or Texas?" Walt interjected. "Wasn't her car found north of here indicating they either took her north to Ohio or east towards West Virginia?"

"Yeah, that's true," Carla replied. "I believe that was to throw us off; these guys were special forces once. By leaving her car there, it gave them more time to put distance between them and us. We need to find out if Grayson Hewitt and Parker Bowen are back in Texas by calling Alpha and Tango Excursions, and we'll go from there."

"Isn't that risky?"

"Walt, anything we do will be risky, but if we want to find her alive, we will have to take risks and think outside the box. I'm sure they're aware that Walt and Bernie inquired about them. Anyone that calls for them would raise a red flag. They could bolt and never surface again. They've done that before. We could go to the local law enforcement and tell them our story. However, they may take them into custody, then lawyer up, and we still got nothing."

"Carla, either way, we got nothing, and Laura is rotting away somewhere."

"Listen, Walt; I think we have to find out first if they are back and go from there. I'll make the call since Alpha and Tango Excursions already had two calls from males, one from a female might not be as suspicious."

"What are you going to say?"

"Not sure, Walt. I'll wing it, wish me luck."

With her caller ID disabled, Carla put her phone on speaker, and then called the number for Alpha and Tango

Excursions. After two rings, a young Hispanic lady answered, "This is Isabella, thank you for calling Alpha and Tango Excursions, how may I help you?"

"Ah, yes, my name is Tonya Crutcher in Kentucky. I met with Mr. Hewitt and Mr. Bowen about a business deal when they were up here last week, have they returned from their business trip? I have a few questions for them."

"Si, Ms. Crutcher, they returned today."

"May I speak with either one of them?"

"They're not here, they took their private boat, Easy Living II, out in the gulf. Not sure when they will get back."

"That's okay; please tell them I'm ready to make a deal, one they can't refuse. Will you do that, please? I must talk with them as soon as possible."

"Si, Ms. Crutcher, I can do that."

Carla ended the call and looked back and forth at Chris and Walt, and finally broke the silence bouncing around his office. "There you have it guys, now we wait."

"Say they call back," Walt replied. "What kind of deal are you talking about?"

"Once again, guys, I'll just wing it. Maybe I can get them immunity for giving us John Dickerson and where Laura is."

Walt fired back. "That's a stretch, and you know it."

"Yeah, it is, but let's see what happens should they call back. It's late, we all need to get some rest, or we won't be worth a dime tomorrow. Any suggestions?"

"Laura's townhome," answered Walt. "Plenty of room, plenty to drink. Maybe her spirit will be present, you know, send us a message, give us hope."

CHAPTER 46

Laura's townhouse looked different, the walls and the ceiling seemed to collapse on them, smothering them with desperation, then guilt. Just the other day, happiness filled the pictures on the walls, today sadness flowed outwardly.

A portrait of Laura and Walt on the left side of the mantel looked lifeless. Usually, the eyes in the picture followed one's every move; today, the eyes focused on the door willing Laura to walk through it. Walt paced the great room looking at the walls and ceiling, waiting for some feeling or spirit to contact him, worried eyes showed helplessness. Laura's sweater hung over the back of the sofa, and her sensual perfume lingered on the sleeve. For a moment, hope flashed in his mind, making him smile.

On the right side of the mantel, a picture of Carla and Laura dressed up as female rockers from a Pops in the Park event rocked no more. They had fun that night letting loose, she picked it up hoping it would come to life, and that she would feel Laura's spirit. From the picture, a cold chill traveled throughout her body. She knew somewhere in captivity, Laura's voice screamed, hoping someone was listening. After placing the picture back on the mantel, tears trickled down her cheeks. So many memories floated throughout her home, unforgettable times of crying and laughing together. The walls were silent, but the presence of her memories spurred hope of finding her.

Center stage on the mantel, Laura and Chris flank their parents before they died at the hands of a drunk driver. Taking the picture off the fireplace mantel, Chris traced Laura's face hoping to touch her soul and spirit. The glass in the frame felt cold, and a bleakness permeated through it.

In the kitchen, red wine stained the inside of a Silver Oak wine glass, while smeared red lipstick coated the outside rim. Laura's favorite shade of red complimented her dark hair and haunting green eyes, that's why she wore it every day. Walt touched the red lipstick hoping for a sign. Unfortunately, it was dry and lifeless as despair battled his fading hope.

Laura's memories were everywhere; however, they could only soften the pain of her abduction. Like the many celebrations before, the kitchen was the focal point, where everyone ended up, Laura made sure of that when she entertained. Tonight was no different with one exception; Laura was absent. On the counter, a bottle of Jameson, and a bottle of Woodford Reserve stood tall like courageous soldiers ready for battle. Although everyone was tired and weary, Jameson and Woodford Reserve came to life, Jameson for Carla, Woodford for the guys. On the sofa, they sat holding hands, reminiscing, each person telling their favorite story about her. After many drinks, Jameson and the Woodford Reserve were gone, total exhaustion had set in. A moment of prayer gave them hope as muted darkness filled the room.

As rays of hope filtered through the blinds, it chased the night's darkness away. Freshly brewed coffee reached every room of the townhome the next morning. A familiar aroma rekindled memories of Laura, her love of whole bean coffee grounded to perfection always brought joy to her senses. Robust coffee they would need, and not the decaffeinated kind, Laura was a high-energy woman always drinking high-test java.

A gourmet breakfast compliments of Chris warmed their souls; remnants of Laura were everywhere, helping ease the frustration and tension attacking their psyche. Sunday Mass uplifted them, giving them new life and a new attitude needed to save Laura.

An afternoon of boring football dragged on. Their favorite team won; however, Laura's cheers were silent. Pizza for dinner led to an evening of haplessness, no calls from Grayson Hewitt, Parker Bowen, or Isabella. Laura had been missing for almost seventy-two hours, and hope was fading fast.

Carla's iPhone screen lit-up, a ding filled the air. She hoped this was what she was waiting for. Unfortunately, for them, Professor Don sent an email canceling class on Wednesday, personal business to attend to out of town was the reason given. Given the situation, she hadn't planned on attending class anyway, her priority was finding Laura safe, and alive.

Everything still came back to Grayson Hewitt and Parker Bowen. Things were not looking up for anyone. Finding John Dickerson, who orchestrated everything, appeared to be their only hope. There are reasons people were in a witness protection program; they didn't want anyone finding them. Her brief experience with the FBI didn't go well; forget that option, she thought. If she attempted to flush out John Dickerson, there would be many risks involved.

Monday morning, fresh ground coffee snaked throughout the townhome once more. Although sleep was at a premium, Carla, Chris, and Walt were in pretty good spirits. Considering everything in action to find Laura, each of them knew life had to go on as best it could. Agreeing to stay in touch, Walt returned to the newspaper, and Chris had meetings at the country club. At the same time, Carla would continue investigating her disappearance, waiting for a break in the case.

Where was John Dickerson, who was he now, all questions she needed to answer if Laura and Walt would walk down the aisle in April? Dumb luck helped her find who she believes is Gina Dickerson, his wife. Another wild hunch kept bothering her. Ever since she met Professor Don, something about him bothered her. According to FBI Agents Slack and Stewart, John Dickerson wouldn't be that close to Oakmont. Still, then again, they had no clue about his identity and where he actually was. Thus, the chances of him being Professor Don were not good.

Patsy Groves, the police department sketch artist, stopped by Carla's desk, inquiring if anything had come of the sketch, she created from Gina Dickerson's photo. Carla shook her head back-and-forth, and Patsy began walking back to forensics.

"Hey Patsy, I got another job for you."

Turning around, Patsy approached her. Carla handed her a manila file folder. Patsy walked back to her desk and dropped it on her desk. With a cup of fresh coffee, she opened it. A picture with specific criteria challenged her. Opening her software program, she scanned the image and applied Carla's criteria, tweaking it every so often. Satisfied with the result, she grabbed it from the printer, placing it in the folder. The job was not much of a challenge; within ten minutes, she laid it face down on Carla's desk calendar.

After Carla retrieved her mail, she approached her desk; the file folder caught her attention. Picking it up, she opened it when her iPhone screen lit-up. Bug-eyed, she recognized the caller ID. Pulse racing, Alpha and Tango Excursions flashed on the screen. Although she was standing near her desk, she needed privacy. She quickly walked to the nearest interrogation room to take the call. Listening to Isabella, three minutes later, the call ended. She screamed vulgarity, her pulse raced, finding Laura just became much more difficult. Grayson Hewitt and Parker Bowen were dead, execution-style she was told.

Back at her desk, her attention returned to the file folder on her desk. Opening it, she swallowed hard, silently expressing several four-letter words. She pulled out the file on Gina Dickerson that included the sketch that Patsy created. Maybe the information in both file folders would help her find Laura. She pondered how to proceed, with the folders in hand, she walked to the inter-rogation room placing them side by side on the table. After opening them, her wheels turned, her phone rang, interrupting her thoughts. Caller ID unknown it displayed. To answer it or let it go to voicemail were her choices. It kept ringing, and her intuition was to answer the call.

After answering it, heavy breathing blasted her ear. "Hello, is anyone there?" Carla asked. More heavy breathing, more silence. Frustrated, she started to end the call when a muffled voice broke the silence, and heavy breathing continued.

"Who is this, and how did you get this number?"

"That's not important; I have a deal from John Dickerson."

"What kind of deal?"

"Laura Watson for Gina and Landon."

"That's not much of a deal, they are in a witness protection program somewhere, almost impossible to find."

"That's your problem, if you want to see your friend alive again, you must find them. John says you are an excellent detective, so use all the resources you have. You have one week to find them."

"How do I know Laura is even alive?"

"You will just have to trust me on this."

"No, I need proof. You need to trust me as well."

"Okay, you will receive an email within thirty minutes. A photo taken a few days ago will be attached. Use that email to contact me when you find John's wife and son; I'll arrange the trade."

Silenced buzzed in Carla's ear as the file folders flew onto the floor. Disgusted, she screamed vulgarities as her respiration attempted to keep up with her raging pulse. She sat, wondering how she was going to find Gina Dickerson and Landon.

CHAPTER 47

Finding Gina and Landon were almost next to impossible, and with no help from the feds, it was virtually hopeless. Patsy Grove's photo was her only hope. The probability that Alicia Maddox is Gina Dickerson was probably fifty-fifty, not bad odds, she thought. Lewisburg was at least a five-hour drive, and there was no guarantee she was still there. A quick web search found the number; Carla clicked on the call icon; it rang a couple of times, then it was answered.

"Good morning, is Alicia Maddox working today?" She listened and pumped her fist. "Thank you, have a great day."

Her chances of finding Laura increased dramatically; however, time was paramount, confronting her in person was the only option she had. Although she had a week to find Gina and her son, Landon, she knew the week would fly by. Driving was out of the question. Taking a commercial flight was not an option, as well. Private charter or helicopter was her only option requiring the help of Chief Evans and Mayor Lester James.

While Chief Evans and Mayor Lester James were calling in favors, Carla met with Chris and Walt to bring them up to speed on these new developments. Although Walt felt compelled to go, she shot him down right from the get-go. Chris was a better choice since he had already been there, and he wasn't the investigative type, he would be along for support. Thirty minutes later, she received a call from Chief Evans, and her helicopter flight would leave the county airport at One PM for Lewisburg.

Two hours later, after a trip over eastern Kentucky and southern West Virginia, the National Guard helicopter made its descent into the Greenbrier County Airport. Trees glistened like twinkling stars; a fresh dusting of snow lost its grip on the landing pad. Steam spewed out of the exhaust pipes of a Greenbrier County Sheriff's vehicle waiting for them. As the chopper blades slowly eased to a complete stop, the chilling pangs of winter met their hope for optimism.

Anxiousness and uncertainty surged as they sat in the rear seat of the sheriff's car. Already informed on their schedule, the sheriff's deputy proceeded to the General Lewis Inn. Streets and houses looked familiar, Carla and Chris had made great memories during their brief stay in one of the best small towns in America; however, today those memories left a bittersweet taste in their mouths. If Alicia Maddox is Gina Dickerson, they had a chance to save Laura. If not, then the trip had been a waste of precious time.

A circular driveway fronted the historic hotel; its classic white columns looked impressive as the sheriff's car stopped at the wide steps leading up to the extensive patio. Fresh snow covered the ground, while icicles glistened from the roof. Their moment of truth stood just inside a massive set of oak doors. The registration desk set just inside the doors; a familiar man greeted them.

"I remember you both, weren't you here about two weeks ago?"

"Yeah, that's right. Chris and I had a wonderful time; however, we won't need a room this time. Is Alicia Maddox still here?"

"I'm sorry, she left for the day but will be working in the morning. Would you like to leave her a message?"

"No. We must see her today. I can't tell you why, but it's a matter of life and death. Do you know where she lives?"

"That's confidential information."

"Yeah, I know."

Pulling out a fifty-dollar bill, Carla laid it on the counter. Two minutes later, with the address in hand, they pulled out of the circular driveway onto E. Washington Street, heading east. After two blocks, she ordered the deputy to pull over and park. The presence of a sheriff's car in front of Alicia Maddox's house would be a red flag, they couldn't take the chance of spooking her, especially if she was Gina Dickerson.

One block to go, butterflies took off inside her gut. With each step they took, anxiety increased two-fold. The yellow house, nestled in between two pale white houses, seemed to glow. Several steps led up to a small concrete porch, a green door accompanied by green shutters framing the windows, stood between them and hope. A knock on the door, they heard footsteps thundering across the pine hardwood floors. Anticipation, and anxiousness, ran through her body as the door opened. Behind a storm door, a young boy with blonde hair and blue eyes smiled.

"Mommy, some people are here to see you."

Carla said, "Hi, what's your name?"

"Marcus."

"That's a handsome name, Marcus."

The young boy smiled and blushed. His mother quickly appeared.

"Hi, I'm Alicia Maddox. How may I help you?

Still curious about what these people wanted, Marcus said, "Mommy, are they here about daddy?"

"No, Marcus, please go to your room and play while I talk with them."

Frowning, Marcus ran to his room. Alicia responded, "Wait a minute, didn't you stay at the General Lewis Inn within the past two weeks?"

"Yes, we did. Thank you for being so nice to us."

"What are you doing here? How did you know where I lived?"

"That's not important, may we come inside? I have something important to discuss with you." Flashing her badge, she continued, "I'm Detective Carla McBride with the Oakmont Police Department in Kentucky. He's Chris Abbott, my boyfriend."

"What's this about, I don't know anyone in Oakmont or for that matter anyone in Kentucky?"

Adamant about talking with her, Carla said, "Please, Alicia, may we come inside? I'd rather not talk to you out here where people might see us; it's that important. It's about a life and death situation. Please give us a few minutes of your time."

Silent behind the storm door, she contemplated for a minute. The coldness in the air pressed against their faces, chilled their spirit. The glass storm door separated despair from hope. Remnants from Carla's big sigh were swept away by the chilling wind. "Please," mouthed Carla as she rubbed her hands vigorously for warmth. The door opened, pulse raging, Carla heaved a big sigh of relief, and entered. Seated in the living room, Carla took a sheet of paper out of her purse and unfolded it. With her heart thumping hard, she handed it to Alicia. While staring at a woman from her past, Alicia's expression was a delight to Carla. "You know who this woman is, don't you, Mrs. Dickerson?"

After taking a deep breath, Gina sighed, and replied, "I've often wondered whether someone would figure it out. I was doing so well and getting more comfortable each day. Days turned into weeks, a week into a month. I was just starting to live my life again. I guess that's all over now, right?"

Showing empathy, Carla replied, "Not if you don't want it to be. We are here for information, and that's it. Once we leave, your secret is safe with us. Finding you was just dumb luck. Chris brought me here to get away from a very stressful situation. When I first saw you, I thought I recognized the face. It wasn't until I got back to Oakmont that I remembered where. A sketch artist created that. Like I said, dumb luck or maybe fate, we are only here because we desperately need your help."

Somewhat reassured, Alicia nodded as Carla continued, "Your husband is holding his sister, who is my best friend somewhere far from Oakmont. To save her life, I must take you to him. I guess he still loves and misses you." Disdain met Carla's gaze; her pulse raced. "I've got one week, or she will die in captivity. He has orchestrated this sick psychotic game of revenge. All of his Alpha Tango buddies are now dead. Laura Watson needs your help."

Bewilderment crossed Alicia's face, with eyes glistening, she wiped the tears away. "I don't want to see my husband or have anything to do with him ever again. Our marriage was just that, a marriage. I knew he was different, and sometimes he scared the hell out of me. It was all about him. He lived his life; I lived mine. That's why I ended up having an affair with Mark Alison and ended up pregnant. I sent him a picture of his son and me, that's when Mark started blackmailing me."

More tears trickled down her face, sniffles followed. A tissue calmed her emotions; silence stood still. Alicia's openness was hopeful, but at the same time, disturbing. She was adamant and strong-willed. More silence as their eyes connected. Reading Alicia's raw emotions were hard.

"Alicia, I know this is difficult. Do you need to take a break?"

Shaking her head back-and-forth, she continued, "No, it will do me good to finally tell someone the whole story and get it off my chest. When John found out Mark was blackmailing me, he got very mentally and verbally abusive. We argued a lot. I wanted to keep paying Mark, so it wouldn't come out and destroy his political ambitions. That's when he told me to stop the money, or he would take care of it. So, I did, I feared John would get violent."

"Really, how did Mark take that?"

"At first, I guess okay, then one day out of the blue, he called me and threatened me if I didn't continue paying him."

"Threatened you with what?"

"John's dirty little secret." Pupils wide open, Carla nodded. "Her name was Debbie, Debbie Castle. John told me he met her in a bar on a business trip, but I didn't believe him. Then nine months later, Shane was born, a baby girl. Wanting them out of our life, he paid her off. Eventually, she moved to, um, I believe Kentucky or West Virginia where her parent's lived. I thought she was out of our life until Mark threatened to expose John's dirty little secret, which would have been far worse than exposing Marcus."

Dumbfounded, bewilderment, four-letter words all rolled into one painted their faces. Jaw-dropping anticipation sent their hearts thumping. Alicia, remaining silent, watched as Carla and Chris looked at each other in shock-and-awe.

"Yeah, I know, it's a lot to take in."

Carla replied, "Debbie Castle worked at Mark's newspaper, she is dead now, died in a car accident. She was run off the road, hit a tree, died at the scene. Shane was not with her. Nothing ever came of it. Damn, I get it now, John eliminated her like everyone else. Wow, didn't see that coming, how did Mark find out about Shane?"

"I don't know, maybe dumb luck, just like you in finding me. I started paying Mark again. That went on for about two months; somehow, John discovered that. I told him why, he went ballistic, scared me, threatened me. He was out of control, ranting about Mark, that's how I found out Mark was in the army, he was the base photojournalist, went by the name Picman, John never liked him, anyway, John told me he would take care of him."

"Hold on, John and Mark knew each other, didn't see that coming either, go on."

"Yeah, they did. The next thing I heard, Mark is dead. When I got word about what happened to Joanne, I knew he was a sick and psychotic bastard. At that point, as far as I was concerned, our marriage was over, I was ready to get out. The witness protection program, in many ways, freed me from the monster he is."

"I don't know what to say. Will you help us?"

"I will not play his sick game, leave me out. You will have to find another way without me. I'm sorry I feel that way, but for the first time in my life, I'm free from his craziness, mental abuse, bipolaronic episodes, and psychosis. I know he is very dangerous; I want no part of him ever again."

Sympathetic to her feelings and concerns, Carla replied, "I understand how you feel, and maybe you can still help us. Is there any place you know of where he might have Laura? You remember Hank Fisher and Charles Bowen, don't you?" She nodded. "They're dead now, and probably John is responsible for their deaths. Did you all have a beach home or cabin somewhere? Any information would be helpful."

"The federal government seized everything we had when we entered the witness protection program."

"Okay, is there anyone else that John did business with that might have a place somewhere?"

"He had many business associates that probably had homes or cabins, but I wouldn't know them because he kept his business dealings private."

"What about his buddies from the Alpha Tango unit, they were all in your wedding?"

"The only one that he ever talked about was Rocky. I believe Rocky worked a lot for John in his real estate development company. Yeah, that might be it. John said that Rocky had a place in the Pensacola area, but I don't know where it is. I don't know whether he owned it or just rented it. John said that all members of Alpha Tango had keys to it and used it when Rocky wasn't there or working on his other place."

"His other place, where is it?"

"I don't know; John just told me Rocky bought another cottage and was going to flip it. He did a lot of that, and who knows, Rocky and John might have been partners in that as well."

"Is there anything else you can think of, no matter how trite it may seem to you?"

"No, I just want to be left alone and continue to live my life as Alicia Maddox with my son Marcus. As far as I'm concerned, Gina Dickerson is dead, Landon is dead." Alicia stood up, shaking, crying, she continued, "I think it's time for you to leave now and leave us alone so that we may continue our new life."

No words could describe what just took place. All along, Carla was sure that exposing Marcus was the reason John had Mark killed, now she wasn't so sure. However, that part of this twisted puzzle didn't matter at all, finding Laura was the only thing that she cared about. Leaving without what they came for, they still had a small sliver of hope that Laura was at one of Rocky's cottages, it just made sense.

Two hours later, the chopper blades sliced through the frosty air as they landed in Oakmont. The winter chill of darkness dampened their spirits as they pulled into the driveway of Laura's townhome. Just inside the door, Jameson and Woodford Reserve waited to be loved, warming their souls as they brought Walt up to speed on their visit with Gina Dickerson. Enduring another night without Laura challenged their inner strength and faith.

CHAPTER 48

Restless nights were hell, and morning couldn't come soon enough. The gloominess of the early dawn gave way to slivers of sunlight. As the aroma of freshly brewed coffee filled the townhome, it aroused their senses, and they were encouraged and hopeful of finding Laura. Although Father Time was ticking away, life had to go on as normal as possible.

While Chris and Walt found diversion in their work, Carla focused on her notes and interview transcripts in the hustle-bustle of the police station. Black roses, left on AJ and Daisy, had no bearing on Laura's disappearance, while evidence from her previous case, the Gold Fedora, was not helpful as well.

Gina mentioned that every member of Alpha Tango had keys to Rocky's cottage. Unfortunately, all of them were dead, except for John Dickerson. For some reason, Keith Edwards' name popped in her head. That was it, Keith had stated that he and Nicole had vacationed at Rocky's beach cottage several times. Happy butterflies fluttered in her gut as hope and faith found a resurgence.

Calling Keith's direct line at Alcom Industries, it went straight to voicemail. Listening to his greeting changed hope to despair. No need to leave a message, he was out of town until next Monday. His greeting stated if there were any urgent issues, Kimberly would address them. As far as Carla was concerned, her problem was critical, but Kimberly thought otherwise. With the wind knocked out of her sails, a loud crash interrupted the peacefulness in the station. Eyes and sneers smacked her in the face. Hope faded to despair once again.

There was always more than one way to skin a cat, not that she would ever do that; ideas bounced around, one stood out, Nicole Edwards had been to Rocky's cottage. Although Carla didn't have a lot of kind words for Kimberly, niceties pleased her. Keith was alone on his business trip; his wife was at her job teaching the young kids of tomorrow. Unfortunately, hope slid closer to despair, Nicole Edwards was not available. Disdain and sneers were zeroing in on Carla as her vulgarities filled the common area. Carla would have to wait for a return call.

Feeling deflated, the big clock on the wall stood still. Five minutes had elapsed, no call. After ten minutes, sweat dotted Carla's brow. Fifteen minutes, she exploded. Words unbecoming of an officer bounced around, laughter filled the common area, she flipped a flock of birds in their direction. Despair was winning. The caller ID sent her pulse even higher; her moment of truth had arrived. Grabbing the receiver, she listened, a smile crossed her face, hope now had a chance.

"Detective McBride here." Eyes were moving around, head nodding as Nicole greeted her. "I need to ask you a few questions about something your husband told me during my investigation of Wylie Adkins. He told me you, and he had vacationed at Wylie's place before, is that correct?" Carla smiled. "Do you know where it is?" A frown crossed Carla's face. "What do you mean it doesn't have an address?" Disappointment painted her eyes. "I'll be there." Hope was gaining ground again.

Bay Colony Commons was an upscale subdivision built around the city's only public golf course. Entering the development, she took a right. At the end of the cul-de-sac, a traditional brick house loomed. Pulling into the driveway, Carla exhaled before opening her door. A curved walkway led to a red front door. She had never met Nicole Edwards before and wasn't sure what to expect. Maybe homely or a plain Jane; her husband must have had reasons for visually undressing about every woman he's ever met. Nicole, dressed in a pair of skinny jeans and a fitted blouse that accentuated her full chest, was nothing close to what Carla had imagined. Blonde hair, shoulder-length, framed a beautiful smile, her blue eyes spoke friendliness and love. As Carla flashed her badge, she shook her head back-and-forth so slightly. She asked herself, how could her husband do that to her; this lady was hot, even to her. The house was warm and inviting, just like Nicole. Handing Carla, the photo interrupted their casual chit-chat. Nicole and Keith, in bathing attire, stood in front of a small sea-foam green cottage. Broad smiles, sunglasses made their sunburn look brighter. Over the door, a white wooden plaque stood out, One Seabreeze Lane, gave Carla hope.

Picking up Chris, fifteen minutes later, they pulled in front of the Daily Reporter. Walt was pacing just inside the main doors. Stressed-out and tired, his demeanor was worse, fear plastered his face. Silence followed them to his office. The closing of the door echoed down the tiled hallway, startling employees in the break room.

"Carla, please, tell me you have something. I've been racking my brain and pulling my hair out. Do you have anything at all?"

"It's a long shot, but it's all we've got."

"What is it?"

"Gina Dickerson told Chris and me that Wylie had a small beach cottage in Florida."

"Where?"

"Santa Rosa Island near Pensacola. I remember when I interviewed Keith Edwards, he told me that Wylie had a small cottage somewhere in Florida. I called Keith, but he was out of the country on business. I tracked his wife down and met her at her home, where she gave me this picture."

Walt snatched the picture out of her hand. "Okay, so, we have a picture, what do we do with it?"

"Do you remember who Bernie spoke with about Al Bocconi's death?"

"Um, I believe it was Detective Ramirez, yeah, Jimmy Ramirez. I'll have to pull up the story in the Pensacola newspaper and get his contact information."

"Do it, then scan this picture so we can email it to him." Several minutes later, he pressed the send button, an email with the photo was traveling through the internet, anticipation was mounting for a breakthrough. "Put your phone on speaker and call the number, I'll do all the talking." The traditional ringing filled the office, several more rings, pulses racing as they waited. A click, a brief second of silence, stares greeted each other's eyes. A big sighed filled the room as the voice of hope spoke loudly.

"Detective Ramirez."

"Yes."

"I'm Detective McBride with the Oakmont Police Department in Kentucky. Last week, my partner Bernie Kowalski called you about Al Bocconi's death, do you remember talking with him?"

"Yeah, I remember, is this about that?"

"No, it's about a friend of mine that may be in an abandoned cottage on Santa Rosa Island. I know this is way out in leftfield, but I don't have a lot of time to explain the whole story right now. Walt Blevins, the publisher of the Daily Reporter, emailed you a photo of a small cottage on the island where we believe our friend might be."

A moment elapsed, and Detective Ramirez responded, "Okay, I got it. Yeah, I know the place. We've sent squad cars there on numerous occasions because of nuisance complaints. You know those Special Forces' boys can get out of control sometimes, and we would have to settle them down."

"Yeah, well, I firmly believe a friend of mine, Laura Watson, is there. She was abducted several days ago as an act of revenge. Does John Dickerson sound familiar?"

"Yeah, is he involved?"

"I believe so, but I don't have time to explain why. That cottage needs checked out right away, it's a matter of life and death, you must believe me."

"Okay, I'll send someone and call you back when I know something. Then you must tell me the whole story."

CHAPTER 49

Twenty minutes seemed like an hour. Walt's phone was lifeless; the tension was smothering the air in his office. Pacing around the room, beads of panicky sweat dotted his forehead. With Carla's eyes glued to his phone, she willed it to ring. Her pulse was racing, waiting was hell on everyone. Walt's phone flashed; the ringing was deafening. Had their moment of truth arrived? The caller ID read Oakmont Chamber of Commerce; seconds later, his voicemail light lit up.

Desperation was growing; the Keurig hissed as coffee filled Walt's cup, then Carla's, then Chris's mug. Caffeine wasn't what they needed; they needed their prayers answered. Ringing caused Walt to spill his coffee; the caller ID read Escambia Sheriff's Department. Everyone stared at the flashing light while fearful anticipation gripped their soul. Their moment of truth was upon them as Walt pushed the speakerphone button. As a voice resonated, their breathing grew heavier.

"Detective McBride, are you there?"

"Yeah."

"Uh, I have some bad news. Demolition had begun on that house when the deputies arrived. The demolition stopped while the house was searched, and no one was found inside the cottage. Sorry, I wish I had better news to give you."

"Are you sure they went to the right place?"

"Yeah, we've been there plenty of times to quiet those boys down, I'm sorry we couldn't be of more help. If you come up with any other ideas, don't hesitate to contact me."

The call ended, and the annoying dial tone crushed their spirits. Their mood resembled paying their last respects at a gravesite on a cold, damp day. Emptiness, vulnerability, despair, and hate all came crashing down upon them; any hope left died in an instant. Carla cried out, "Dammit, I was sure she was there; it just made sense."

Walt asked, "What's next, any other ideas?"

"Walt, stay calm, we will find her."

"How? Where? When? That's the only thing I want to know."

"I don't know, but something will come to us, I just feel it. We all have to believe that God will help us answer those questions."

Grief and sadness were sabotaging their faith; the walls of silence began to smother any hope left.

Walt said, "It's too damn quiet in here; let's step out on the deck to clear our minds. I know it's a little chilly, but we need something to wake us up and chase the desperation holding us hostage. We need to talk this out before time runs out."

After stepping outside for a few minutes, the bitter cold wasn't helping. Carla shivered and said, "Damn, it's freezing out here, and it's not helping, let's go back inside."

Walt replied, "Just a little while longer, we need to focus. Carla, when you talked to Keith, did he mention another place that Wylie owned?"

"No, just that one."

Numbed and shivering, Chris jumped in, "Carla, that's it. Remember, Gina Dickerson mentioned to us that Wylie had just bought another place to flip. She didn't say where it was, but maybe that's it, but how do we find it, guys?"

Hope gained against despair. Walt exclaimed, "Public records, if Wylie bought one, it would be in real estate transfers or tax records, let's give Detective Ramirez another call."

As warmth met their frigid fear, Walt put his phone on speaker and dialed his number once more. After one ring, he answered.

"Detective Ramirez, Walt Blevins again. We have a hunch."

"Okay, I'm listening."

"Gina Dickerson told Detective McBride that Wylie Adkins had bought another beach cottage to flip. So, if he did, wouldn't it be in the real estate transfers?"

"Uh, yeah, I suppose."

Walt said, "We need you to send someone to go through the real estate transfers to see if Wylie bought another cottage to flip. It is our only hope to find Laura. She is my soulmate, and I can't let her die a slow, lonely death."

"I can't send anyone at this moment, and by the time someone would get there, they would be closed."

Walt responded, "Wouldn't they be available on the

internet, here in Kentucky, all legal advertisements are online."

"Let me see what I can do, I'm not that savvy with computers, but I know someone that is. Let me call you back."

The call ended, and that annoying dial tone abruptly stopped. An eerie quietness surrounded Carla, Chris, and Walt as they waited for a miracle, for God to answer their prayers. Everyone was doing their best to keep their emotions in check, gathering for a group hug, tears swam in their eyes. Time was running out; death and despair were hovering above them, ready to squash them. They weren't sure how long it had been, but Father Time was pissing them off. Caller ID lit up the screen, Walt shook his head back-and-forth.

The tension was running rampant; time slowly ticked away. A glance at the clock on the wall showed it had only been twenty minutes since the last call. Suddenly, his phone rang again. Walt nodded and put in on speaker-phone. Pulses raced as they waited.

"Detective McBride, I'm here with the best tech lady we have. We've been searching for Wylie Adkins in the database, but nothing is coming up, sorry."

Carla said, "Shit. Guys, we need to think outside the box. Any ideas? Detective Ramirez hang with us for a few minutes, okay?"

"We're here, and we want to help you find her."

"Thanks, we will put you on hold." The hold button flashed as they brainstormed. "Any ideas, guys?"

Glancing stares at each other, wide-open mouths were frozen it time. Pacing the floor, Carla and Chris heard a loud smack. Walt hit the hold-call button, and back-ground noise filled the speaker.

Walt said, "Detective Ramirez, try searching for Alphatango, LLC, or some variation of that."

"Give us a minute." Keystrokes could be heard in the speaker; otherwise, the silence was annoying. Even though it had been just a minute or two, it seemed like ten minutes had passed before the silence ended. "Guys, we may have something." Another minute of silence went by before Detective Ramirez spoke up. "This could be it. I've got an address near the other cottage; we will send deputies right away. We will call you back once we know something. Keep your fingers crossed."

Emotional hell was just that, a living hell. Runaway rollercoaster nerves maneuvered the twist and turns of disappointment and fear, while hope looked for a positive outcome. Caffeine was working overtime, pushing anxiety and tension higher and higher. The digital time on the phone screen appeared frozen as frustration smacked the receiver shattering the nail-biting atmosphere trapped in the office.

Two minutes passed, the rollercoaster of emotions sped up—ring, ring, ring. The rollercoaster screeches to a dead stop. They held their breath, the caller ID spelled out a false alarm, illumination painted the voicemail button. Respiration is now fast and furious as the rollercoaster torpedoes forward to depths of limited emotional barriers. Ten minutes of hell elapsed, smothering any chance of hope.

Maybe it was delirium or an omen. Carla appeared to be in a mental trance focusing on transporting the spirit of life through sheer nothingness to save Laura. In her mind, she envisioned Laura, a tattered woman, fighting off evil demons from robbing her soul.

Riding a white stallion, the knight pointed his sword

toward her casting the light of life. Galloping gracefully, Laura is swept up into his firm and courageous arms, defeating death. Chris and Walt noticed Carla was still staring into space; her mind was somewhere else.

"Carla, what is it?" asked Chris.

"I had a vision, maybe a premonition, or maybe I'm hallucinating, I don't know, something tells me we will get your sister back, trust me."

Twenty minutes of rollercoaster hell tested their resolve and faith—ring, ring, ring. Deep breaths tried their best to calm their thumping hearts, their desperate respiration. Walt shook his head back-and-forth.

The voicemail indicator read two messages in waiting. The digital clock on the screen moved forward as the rollercoaster of despair barreled toward the highest arc. When reaching the apex, its descent stopped—ring, ring, ring. Escambia County Sheriff Department lit up the caller ID, the moment of truth had arrived. Breathless, a soft buzz filled the room.

"Detective Ramirez, please tell us you have good news this time." In the background, muted voices filled the room. "Detective Ramirez, did—"

"We found her." Elation broke loose. "She's on her way to Pensacola Medical Center for treatment. She is in relatively good shape, a little bruised and cut from smashing a wood chair through a window, and mildly dehydrated, but all things considered, she should recover just fine. Detective McBride, are you there?"

"Yeah."

"Detective McBride, after she calmed down, she told Deputy Esposito to let you know she was sorry."

"Sorry for what."

"Not sure, but she said she was sorry. I know you all

have been through hell, but when you are up to it, detective, you owe me the whole story."

A dial tone blared from the speaker and was quickly silenced. The news was too much to take, tears of joy flowed from the spigots of their heartstrings. An eerie silence filled Walt's office. Carla melted into the arms of love and tenderness; Chris sobbed, holding her tight. Stunned and lonely, Walt joined their celebration of life, three friends became family as emotions tied their hope and faith as one. No words could express the wind in their sails at this moment. While Chris continued holding Carla, Walt booked the last flight to Pensacola that evening. While Chris took Walt to the Lexington airport, Carla brought Chief Evans up to speed on the rescue of Laura Watson.

At her apartment, Jameson stood willing and able to help mend her soul. A double shot on the rocks made her smile; her lips tasted his calming recipe. Alone with her liquid lover, her emotions finally exploded. Two ounces of Jameson numbed her senses, calmed her anxiety. Forty-five minutes of solitude returned her to reality, and revenge began to build, John Dickerson would pay the price for this cowardly deed.

A familiar knock on the door made her smile. Opening the door, Chris entered with a Reuben from McGruder's. Emotionally drained, but still wired from all the tension of the last three days, Jameson and Woodford Reserve eased their emotional heartstrings.

The darkened room provided peacefulness as their bodies moved in rhythm; their anxiety and stress were set free. Eyes closed; happiness crossed Carla's face while Chris succumbed to the touch of her sensual body next to his.

CHAPTER 50

As the landing gear screeched on the runway in Pensacola, emotional hell lingered in Walt's soul. Lonely streets matched the remnants of emptiness inside the cab as it pulled up to the emergency entrance of the medical center. As the doors opened, patient services loomed straight ahead. His heart in a state of sustained tachycardia kept him on edge as he approached the counter.

On the elevator to the second floor, visions of Laura faded in and out of his soul. Anticipation and concern filled his blue eyes as the elevator doors slowly opened. Her private room was a few steps away, sending his pulse faster and faster.

Emotions welling up in his soul, a partially open door stood between him and his soulmate. After knocking on it gently, a scratchy voice spoke beckoning him inside. Laura's beautiful smile tugged at his heartstrings. A smile crossed his face; a hug chased his fears and tension into oblivion.

Loving happiness exploded in the room. Lips found

each other, and they savored their love as one. Whispers of relief and hope touched their souls. In each other's arms, quiet darkness descended upon them; nurse Jamie McGrew smiled as she silently pulled the door shut.

Through the blinds, the moonlit night cast its glow on his soul. A long night was still holding onto his body. During the night, he allowed Laura to rest peacefully, while he watched over her from a chair beside the bed.

A full night of rejuvenating sleep, Laura's complexion was showing signs of recovering. Rustling in the bed, Laura turned in his direction. Her face felt the warmth of the sun shining through the open blinds. Cracking a little smile, she rubbed her eyes and moistened her lips as Walt caressed her hand.

Squeezing it tightly, he smiled, leaned in, and briefly kissed her weathered lips. "You look much better, honey, how do you feel?" Nodding, she smiled, squeezing his hand harder. "The doctor says you need another night to recover, so I booked the first flight out tomorrow morning. Now, continue to get the rest needed for us to leave in the morning. I'll be calling Chris to let him know what time we will be arriving." She nodded and held his hand even tighter.

Back in Oakmont, the aroma of a fresh pot of coffee made the kitchen come alive. The smell of bacon emanated throughout the apartment, reminding Carla of their last breakfast. With the omelet plated, the toast buttered, orange juice poured, they sat down to nourish their bodies after a night of bonding and relaxation. Given the past few days, Chris offered a small blessing. Halfway through their breakfast, Carla's phone sang a familiar tune, putting it on speaker, the celebration began.

"Hello Walt, how's my girl doing? Let me talk to her?"

"Laura is doing fine and still sleeping. She's been through a lot, and her emotions are still recovering. Her doctor recommended she should stay another night, so I have booked a flight for tomorrow morning, arriving in Lexington around noon. Hey Chris, I assume you will pick us up."

"Of course, how are you doing?"

"Better now that I'm by her side taking care of her."

"Great, call me when she wakes up. I want to talk to her."

"Of course, uh, wait a minute, she's awake now."

Laura, still a little woozy, asked, "Walt, who are you talking with?"

"It's Carla."

Handing his phone to her, she took it and wiped away tears of joy streaming down her cheeks. Laura, in an apologetic tone, said, "I'm so sorry what I've put you through, I'm truly sorry."

"You're safe, and that's all that matters. It's so good to hear your voice. I want you to get your rest, and we will see you tomorrow."

"Yeah, is Chris with you?"

"Of course, here he is."

"Hey sis, so good to hear your voice as well, get your rest, and we'll pick you up at the airport tomorrow, love you."

"Okay, I love you, too. Bye, now."

"Bye, here's Walt."

"Chris, see you tomorrow, she's going to be just fine."

An annoying buzz filled the speaker, Carla quickly

silenced the phone. With breakfast finished, the table cleared, and dishwasher loaded, Carla and Chris retired to the loveseat to finish their coffee. With the television on in the background, they enjoyed the peacefulness surrounding them. Chris, feeling relieved that his sister was finally safe, broke the silence.

"So, I guess this case, um, is finally over now that Laura is safe. We can now get on with our lives."

"Not a chance."

"What do you mean?"

With revenge painted on her face, she replied, "Laura has been through hell. We have been through hell. John Dickerson hasn't been through hell yet, and I'm going to see that he experiences the same hell we did. I'm not sure how I will do that, but I will."

"Shouldn't you just let the FBI take care of him?"

"No way, it will be over when he is sitting in jail. He made it personal. We almost lost Laura. It's game on. Laura will be here tomorrow, and I will be ready to play John's psychotic game on my terms. He thinks he's in control, but he will soon find out you don't screw with Carla Anne McBride and get away with it."

CHAPTER 51

With Laura back in Oakmont, the focus turned to bring John Dickerson to justice. Meeting with Chief Evans, Carla explained her game plan and what help she needed to pull off this sting operation. Replying to the email received a few days ago with Laura's picture, Carla attached a picture of Gina she secretly took while in Lewisburg.

It was time to put her plan into action. In the email, she left a callback number, and that she would only talk with John Dickerson. Within an hour, her phone rang and rang. After four rings, voicemail picked it up. Her voice-mail icon lit up—listening, dead silence. Ring, ring, ring, ring, voicemail picked up his second call, the game had started. Listening, she jotted down a number, John Dickerson's irritated voice brought a smile to her face.

Game on, asshole, she murmured under her breath. While using one of the interrogation rooms, her colleagues were getting ready to trace the call she was about to make. John Dickerson was playing right into her hand. With everyone available, and speakerphone on, she keyed in his number. The ringing stopped. As heavy breathing flowed from the speaker, Carla felt his anxiousness through the phone. A familiar voice filled the room as a digital recorder was ready.

"Detective McBride, what the hell are you waiting on? In the email, you said you found my wife and son and included a picture of her; she looks so different."

"Where is Laura Watson?"

"You tell me where my wife is first, then I'll tell you."

"Doesn't work that way, John. We are playing your sick game on my terms now. If you don't accept my terms, I'll hang up, and you will never know where they are. Oh, and by the way, when I talked to your wife, Landon asked about you."

She had hit John's trigger button. "Okay, okay. We'll play it your way. She's at Wylie Adkins beach cottage on Santa Rosa Island, and the address is 22 Pelican Lane."

"And how do you know that?"

"I had her taken there. Now, where are my wife and son?"

"Remember, we are playing your psychotic game my way. Here's what's going to happen, I'll call the county sheriff there and have them go to that location. Once she is in their custody and safe, then I'll call you back. You'll have to wait it out just like us. It's my way, or I hang up, do you understand?"

A dial tone buzzed from the speaker, and she quickly silenced it. Long enough for a trace, they had enough to get a warrant for his arrest, but she wanted redemption for all the lives he had destroyed. Game on, everything was going to plan. The key to her plan was to make John Dickerson wait and wait and sweat it out, letting anxiety take over his mind, and following her orders precisely, answering all her questions. Carla would use John Dickerson as he used those in his sick and psychotic games.

Although she told John that she would call him back in two hours, she would let him stew until tomorrow morning, which was part of her game plan. Carla needed cooperation from Gina Dickerson to pull off the most crucial part of this sting operation. Knowing that Gina didn't work until tomorrow morning, she would call her then and hope that she would go along with her plan to put John Dickerson away forever. By doing that, Gina and Landon could live their new life without fear wherever they chose.

Several hours later, Carla's phone rang and rang, going to voicemail. The voicemail icon showed one message. Listening, a frantic John Dickerson rambled erratically. Several more calls that evening went straight to voicemail. John Dickerson became more agitated, playing perfectly into her hand. She wanted him down on his knees, begging for forgiveness.

Eventually, the calls stopped, and nightfall arrived. Carla needed a good night's rest to bring the hammer down on John once and for all. Tomorrow would be a day of redemption for Mark and Joanne Alison, for AJ Gonzalez, and Wanda Jordan. John took the lives of every member of the Alpha Tango Special Forces Unit, but she felt no pity or remorse for them. When they did business with John Dickerson, they each sealed their fate.

Chris and Jameson, her liquid lover, was waiting at her apartment. A hug and a passionate kiss greeted her while Jameson eased her tension. Happiness crossed her face; she was entirely at peace about what she intended to do tomorrow.

Getting redemption and revenge was gratifying; however, she would have no regrets on what actions she may take, or what consequences she might suffer in the process. Although she was in complete control of her emotions, she didn't know what tomorrow would bring when she came face to face with him. In kidnapping Laura, John Dickerson made it personal, and all bets were off the table as to what might happen tomorrow.

CHAPTER 52

Game day!

At the registration desk at the General Lewis Inn in Lewisburg, the assistant manager answered the phone. Listening carefully, she placed the call on hold. A quiet buzz annoyed Carla as she continued listening to the historic hotel's marketing message. Finally, a familiar voice filled Carla's ear.

"Alicia, Detective McBride here, please don't hang up. I need your help in putting your husband away for good. He admitted to kidnapping my girlfriend, who is safely back in Oakmont. With your help, we found her; John doesn't know that yet. I told him I found you, but he thinks I will give him that information. Well, that will never happen. If you help us, then you will never hear from me again. And as far as I'm concerned, Alicia Maddox or Gina Dickerson no longer exists. Will you do that?"

"What do you need from me?"

"I'm to call him today, and he thinks I will tell him where you are, well that won't happen. Instead, I want him to think you are at a safe house waiting for him. I must prepare knowing he will likely insist on talking to you, which I know he will. So, I want to record a conversation of you talking with him. I'll tell you what to say; we'll do the rest. Will you help us do that?"

"I'll do anything to put that bastard away forever and keep him away from my son and me; then, I can live my life without fear for once."

Ten minutes later, Carla gave the recordings to the tech gurus, and they were ready to put this diabolical sting operation into action. Dialing John's number, she put it on speaker. Impatiently waiting for her call, he immediately answered it on the first ring.

"Detective McBride, you are wasting my time. Where are my wife and son?"

"Not just yet, I have some questions you need to answer."

"I'm not answering any more questions until I can at least talk to my wife and know where she is."

"Fine, we have Gina, and your son at a safe house in Oakmont, they are secure here. Just a moment while I put her on the line."

A moment goes by to agitate John further. Heavy breathing flowed over the speaker. Finally, Gina's recorded voice played.

"John, how are you doing, honey? I can't wait to see you."

"Honey, I can't wait to see you both. I love you."

"I love you, too."

"Where are you?"

"I'm at a safe house; Detective McBride has the address. How soon can you come to be with us?"

"As soon as I get the address, then I'll leave this deadbeat town forever."

"Great, can't wait to see you, Landon says hi, I love you."

"Tell him daddy's coming, love you, too!"

Carla's plan was working to perfection and ended the recordings. "John, this is Detective McBride again. You know what, skip the questions. I'll email you the directions to the safe house which is guarded by US Marshals. We will reunite you with them and give everyone new identities in a new city."

"Just email the address, bitch."

The call ended, and John waited for the email. With his bags packed, once the email arrived, he would immediately leave Flemingsville for good. His phone dinged, and he smiled as he approached the entrance ramp to the interstate. After traveling for about an hour, the exit was just ahead.

Following Carla's instructions, the white house with a black SUV parked in the driveway came into view. This is the moment he had waited on since being placed in the witness protection program. Pulling into the driveway, government plates on the SUV stood out. Two men on the porch wearing black jackets with US Marshals printed on the back approached his car.

As he exited the vehicle, one of the men greeted him immediately. "John Dickerson, I assume."

"Where is my wife, my son?"

"They're inside. We will need to check you for any weapons before we can let you go in. It's just standard procedure. Remember, they might look a little different because of different hairstyles and other physical changes required by the witness protection program."

"Yeah, I get it."

After thorough body checks with an electronic wand and a pat-down, he was allowed to walk up to the porch. Before opening the door, a US Marshal peeked inside to make sure everyone was ready and in place. John opened the door and entered seeing a lady and a young boy playing cards. With their backs toward him, anticipation ran wild throughout his body. Walking a few steps closer, he called out Gina's name, an unfamiliar voice responded.

An eerie silence blasted the walls of the room; sheer concern crossed his brow. As the lady stood up, turned around, and faced him, searing sensations smothered his face.

"Wait a minute, you are not my wife, and that is not my son sitting there. What the hell is going on?"

An unmistakable voice he hated, emanated from the dimly lit hallway. "This wasn't part of the deal, Detective McBride."

As the hallway illuminated fully, with her service weapon drawn, Carla approached him. "Right, Professor Don. Welcome to Oakmont."

Now, in his face, she pressed her Glock to his forehead. He winced as she pushed it harder; she wanted him to feel its coldness, its finality. While pressing it much harder, her trigger finger twitched ever so slightly. As John taunted her, thoughts of revenge challenged her emotions and sanity.

However, her common sense scolded her for such a display of personal driven thoughts of revenge. Removing her Glock from his forehead, the reddish impression left behind glistened under the cold sweat of fear on his brow. Without warning, a swift knee doubled him over. Grabbing his crotch, he struggled to catch his breath. After Carla stepped away from him, redemption glared at his grimacing expression.

"You know, John, although it would give me great pleasure to put a bullet in your brain, you are just not worth it. You are under arrest for conspiracy in the abduction of Laura Watson. Furthermore, you are charged with conspiracy to commit the murder of Laura Watson and a host of other charges. Officer Wiesmann, read him his rights. Then get him the hell out of here before I change my mind and blow his brains out. By the way, Professor Don, guess I won't see you in class next week, will I? One other question, why kill AJ Gonzalez?"

"Screw you, screw all of you. I will make you pay for this one day, all of you. As for that little hot lesbian nurse, well, it was the unluckiest day of her young life. Frog and Peanuts screwed up mistaking her for your friend Laura Watson. Then, when you discovered I helped them faked their deaths, they had to be neutralized."

Without warning, the wrath of redemption crushed his face. As blood began to saturate his grayish mustache, he wiped the blood away. With retaliation on his mind, he began moving toward Carla; however, Officer Wiesmann quickly jerked him away from feeling the wrath of her Glock again.

"You will pay for that one day. I'm not done with you or your friends; you can count on that."

"Listen, asshole; you'll be in prison for the rest of your life unless someone kills you first, now, get him out of here. Hey, John, one other thing. Where's Sam, is she alive?

"Screw you."

"Get him out of my face before I do something I will regret."

Cuffing John, Officer Wiesmann pushed him through the doorway. Out on the porch, he turned toward Carla, yelling out, "Detective McBride, this game will never be over until I'm back with Gina and Landon, and you are dead. Then it will be 'Game Over' for you...bitch!"

After a night of well-deserved sleep, she looked forward to the rest of the week off to decompress. But first, she needed to complete her statements of the events yesterday. After finishing them, she sat at her workstation, feeling empty and needing some friendly conversation. Looking at Bernie's desk, his friendly smile was absent. After calling him, their conversation ended quickly.

As she pulled into his driveway, waiting for her at the front door, Bernie's ear-to-ear grin lit up her soul. Exiting the car, she approached him, smiling and shaking her head back-and-forth.

"Carla, what took you so long, Lydia is driving me crazy. I can't wait to get back to work in another week or so. Hey, I heard you got that SOB John Dickerson. Very creative police work to sucker him in."

"Ah, it was nothing. Is that Polish sausage and sauerkraut I smell?"

"Yep, knew you would be hungry after what you've been through these past several days. Do you know the name for Polish sausage is kielbasa? I also have your liquid lover waiting for you. Let's go to the kitchen; the table is ready for us."

"How did you know about my liquid lover?"

"Chris called me, said you were taking the rest of the week off and told me about Jameson. Lydia ran a quick errand and picked it up. She's got more errands to run, so we can just relax by ourselves, have a few drinks, and chow down on the kielbasa and sauerkraut. How's that sound?"

Quickly nodding, her face beamed with joy as they entered the kitchen. With her elbows resting on the kitchen table, Jameson enticed her lips, savoring his amber love for a few seconds, she swallowed, enjoying the happiness Jameson brought to her soul.

"Hey, listen, I'm sure you tried to find out about AJ, right?"

"Yeah, he said Laura was supposed to die that morning, said Frog and Peanuts made a mistake."

"Shit, what about Sam, did you ask him about her?"

"Yeah, he told me to screw myself. However, I don't think he knows."

"Why is that?"

"You know, something wasn't right in Sam's apartment, I felt she staged the whole thing, you know, to make everyone think something terrible happened to her."

"How so?"

"Gut feeling, I think she got really scared and bolted to a safe haven. I believe one day we'll see her cheerful face back at McGruder's."

"I hope you're right."

"Enough about that, let's talk about something more pleasant." While nodding, a crooked smile crossed her face. "You know, we just might make a great team one of these days."

Grinning ear-to-ear, he replied, "You know partner, I think we already have."

Without hesitation and smirking, she quickly replied, "Well, I wouldn't go that far, dickhead."

As a mean scowl crossed Bernie's face, an in-you-face-bird flew at Carla's wandering and rolling eyes. Laughing out loud, she shot him 'the look' he had been waiting and wanting to see.

After a soft gruff, he quickly responded, "Now, that's…my…girl!"

After a friendly fist bump across the table, a celebratory toast got things started. While eating in solemn silence, the kielbasa and sauerkraut never tasted better. Jameson warmed her soul like never before as Bernie's gentle smile grabbed her heartstrings.

ACKNOWLEDGMENTS

After the Boyd County Board of Education didn't renew my contract in 1972, my attempts to find another teaching and coaching position didn't pan out. I answered a classified advertisement in the *Herald-Dispatch* for a Circulation District Manager and interviewed for the job.

Tom Myers saw enough in me to hire me; thus, my forty-year newspaper career was born. We worked together for thirteen years until I was promoted to Circulation Director at the *Marietta Times* in Marietta, Ohio. He had faith in me as well as my potential in the newspaper business.

Another person I want to recognize is Charles Sponaugle of the *Herald-Dispatch* circulation department. After a couple of years of working there, I began to look elsewhere for a new job. I didn't feel newspaper circulation was my future. He got wind of it and assured me things would eventually get better, and they did. I'm glad I listened to him and embraced the business.

Audrey Love, whom I worked with at the *Marietta Times* in Marietta, Ohio, is another individual I want to recognize. During some difficult times at the newspaper, she believed in me and told me my best years were ahead of me. I'm not sure how she knew that, but she was right.

A LOOK AT BOOK THREE:
CHASING TRUTH AND REDEMPTION

In the summer of 1997, Penny Miracle, a beautiful, mature teenager, disappeared without a trace. On that day, up-and-coming rookie police officer, Carla McBride, was one of the first officers to arrive on the scene. Bernie Kowalski, who had just achieved detective status, was assigned as the lead investigator.

After numerous interviews, tips, and dead-end leads, the case fell cold and laid dormant for fifteen years—until the police force's forensic psychologist and Penny's childhood best friend, Beth Pendergast, re-opened the case.

Now, Carla, Bernie, and Beth are thrust into action, on the hunt to solve a cold case that's haunted each of them since that fateful day.

Together, can they seek truth and redemption as a team…or will their lives remain forever changed?

AVAILABLE JANUARY 2023

ABOUT THE AUTHOR

Author Nick Lewis lives in Richmond, Kentucky, with his wife, Bonnie. He graduated from Marshall University in the fall of 1970. Upon graduating, he taught school and coached football for one year at Eidson Elementary. He then switched directions and began a forty-year newspaper career. He held circulation and marketing positions at four different newspapers in Ohio, West Virginia, and Kentucky. In 2004, he was appointed publisher of *The Richmond Register* in Richmond, Kentucky. He retired from that position in June 2013 and began his quest to become a full-time author.

In January 2014, Nick created The Detective Carla McBride Chronicles. The first book in the series, *The Gold Fedora*, debuted in October 2019. *The Black Rose, Chasing Truth and Redemption,* and *Quandary* completes the series to date. Book five in the series, *Enigma*, is forthcoming. He has another published novel, *When Eagles Soared*.

When Nick is not writing and revising manuscripts, he enjoys golf, gardening, and creating new adventures with his wife of fifty years. Bonnie plays an essential role in his journey of writing novels. He is an avid Marshall University football fan with three grown children, three grandchildren, and two cats named Zorro and Ziva.